'No man could comprehend women
until he had known the women of
Japan. As I could never have known
even the outlines of love had I not
lived in a little house where I
sometimes drew back the covers of
my bed upon the floor to see there the
slim golden body of the perpetual
woman.'

Also by James A. Michener

THE BRIDGE AT ANDAU
RASCALS IN PARADISE
THE FIRES OF SPRING
HAWAII
THE BRIDGES AT TOKO-RI
RETURN TO PARADISE
CARAVANS
THE SOURCE
IBERIA (in two volumes)
THE DRIFTERS
A MICHENER MISCELLANY
CENTENNIAL
CHESAPEAKE
THE COVENANT
POLAND
SPACE

and published by Corgi Books

James A. Michener

SAYONARA

CORGI BOOKS

SAYONARA

A CORGI BOOK 0 552 08000 4

Originally published in Great Britain by
Martin Secker & Warburg Ltd.

PRINTING HISTORY
Secker & Warburg edition published 1954
Corgi edition published 1957
Corgi edition reissued 1961
Corgi edition reissued 1968
Corgi edition reprinted 1969
Corgi edition reprinted 1970
Corgi edition reissued 1972
Corgi edition reprinted 1975
Corgi edition reprinted 1976
Corgi edition reprinted 1978
Corgi edition reissued 1979
Corgi edition reprinted 1981
Corgi edition reprinted 1983
Corgi edition reprinted 1986

Corgi Books are published by Transworld Publishers Ltd.,
Century House, 61-63 Uxbridge Road, Ealing, London W5 5SA,
in Australia by Transworld Publishers (Aust.) Pty. Ltd.,
26 Harley Crescent, Condell Park, NSW 2200, and in New
Zealand by Transworld Publishers (N.Z.) Ltd., Cnr. Moselle
and Waipareira Avenues, Henderson, Auckland.

Made and printed in Great Britain by
Hunt Barnard Printing Ltd., Aylesbury, Bucks.

SAYONARA

On April 4, 1952, I shot down my sixth and seventh MIGs. It happened up near the Yalu River and when I returned to base at J-10 I was excited. The Air Force doctor took one look at me and said, "Gruver, you've had it."

Boy, they were sweet words. They meant I was through flying for a while. But since I'm a West Point man I felt obligated to appear eager before the flight surgeon who had been called back from civilian life, potbelly and all. So I frowned and said, "Nothing wrong with me, Doc. A bottle of beer'll fix me up."

"That's right," the doc agreed.

He had taken my eagerness seriously and for a minute I felt a little sick inside. I didn't want to fly any more. Not just then. I wanted to appear rough and ready but I also wanted some solid chairborne duty.

But the doc was smart. He laughed and said, "Don't turn pale, Gruver. I was only kidding. I never take this hero stuff seriously."

I relaxed and said, "Thanks. I could use some Korean sleep."

"It's even better than that," Doc said, putting away his stethoscope. "You're going back to Japan!"

From the way he said this you knew he thought Japan was paradise, but I'd been through the place and it never impressed me much. Dirty streets, little paper houses, squat men and fat round women. I had never understood why some Air Force people got so steamed up about Japan.

I said, "If you go for Japan, I suppose it's good news. I'd just as soon rest up right here at J-10."

Doc said, "You mean you never tangled with any of those beautiful Japanese dolls at Tachikawa?"

1

I said, "I'm a four-star general's son. I don't tangle with Japanese dolls, beautiful or not."

Doc looked at me sorrowfully and said, "Chum, you're sicker than I thought."

I hadn't meant to sound stuffy, but when you know your outfit sort of has you ticketed for fast promotion right through to colonel and maybe one-star general by the time you're thirty-five, a lot of the ordinary razzle-dazzle connected with military life doesn't impress you. On the other hand, I had always tried not to act superior to reserve officers just because they were civilians at heart.

I said, "I'll think of you, Doc, when I hit those clean Tokyo sheets and that good Tokyo beer."

He shook his head with a tricky little leer and said, "For you, Chum, it ain't gonna be Tokyo. For you . . . special orders."

Like a warning flash and without my actually thinking the word I blurted, "Kobe?"

"Yep, Chum! You made it."

Instinctively I put my left hand on my hip and felt for my wallet. I said, "About these special orders? Were they from General Webster?"

"Yep, Chum! You're in." He gripped his hands in a tight little ball and winked at me. "Why wouldn't one general look after another general's son?"

I had always known the doc to be a second-class sort of guy and I refused to be drawn into an argument. I played his game and said, "It's what they call the West Point spirit."

"That's what I mean," the doc said. "Kelly has your orders."

"I'll go see Kelly," I said, glad to get away from this know-it-all civilian.

But as I left the medical tent and started down the gravel path to squadron headquarters where Kelly worked, another civilian called me: "Gruver, could I speak with you?"

I turned and saw the chaplain and since he almost

never spoke to anyone except about trouble I stopped short and asked, "Kelly again?"

"Yes," he said almost sorrowfully. "Kelly."

I waited on the gravel path while he picked his way across the brown Korean mud. J-10 was almost all mud. When he joined me I asked, "What's he been up to now, Padre?"

"This time it's serious," he said sorrowfully. He led me to his tent, a beat-up affair with Bibles, crucifixes and the special silver gadgets for conducting Jewish ceremonies.

"Kelly face another court-martial?" I asked.

"Worse. He's appealed to his Congressman."

I'd always been disgusted with enlisted men who write letters to Congressmen. The Air Force had a sensible and just way to handle any problem. Congressmen weren't needed. So I asked, "Why don't you advise the colonel to throw this guy out of the service?"

"Under the new rules . . ."

The new rules! I was always forgetting the new rules. Starting in 1945 a lot of soft-headed do-gooders in Washington had revised the basic rules for military conduct and as a result you now saw enlisted men writing to Congressmen. I had always agreed with my father. Knock such stoops on the head and throw them in jail. Then the do-gooders could really sob.

"So under the new rules, what happens?" I asked.

"So Kelly gets his way. He goes back to Japan."

"Ridiculous," I said. "The Air Force is becoming a kindergarten."

"And when he gets back to Japan, he marries the girl."

This was too much. I sat down in one of the padre's rickety chairs and asked, "You mean that in spite of all you and the colonel have said to this kid he still gets permission to marry the girl?"

"That's right."

"Why doesn't somebody bust him in the head?"

"That's no solution. I want you to talk with him."

"Nothing more I can say."

"Does the boy realize that if he marries this Japanese

girl he can't possibly take her back to America?" the padre asked.

"Sure he knows. I made him sign the paper proving that he knows. He signed and told me what I could do with it."

"You must talk with him once more, Gruver. He's a misguided boy."

"He's a dead-end criminal, Father, and you know it."

"Not a criminal! A tough boy who's had trouble in the Air Force. He's just hot-headed."

"That's not where the heat is, Padre."

He laughed and said, "You're right. That's why we mustn't let him make a fool of himself."

I was tired from flying and said bluntly, "Look, Padre. Kelly belongs to your church. You're the guy who's got to save him."

Chaplain Feeney became very serious and took my hands in his. It was a trick he used when he wanted to make a point and it accounted for much of his success with the squadron. He was never afraid to plead with a man. "You must believe me when I say I'm not trying to save Kelly for my church. I'm trying to save him for himself. If he marries this Japanese girl it can lead only to tragedy. In ordinary times such a marriage would be unwise, but under the new law . . . when he can't even take her with him to America . . . What's to happen, Gruver?"

He spoke so passionately that I had to give in. "All right. What do you want me to do?"

He was embarrassed at what he was about to suggest and hesitated a moment. Then he said, apologetically, "You're engaged to a fine, good-looking American girl. You showed me her picture one night." He smiled as I automatically reached with my left hand for my wallet pocket. "When you're flying and things begin to get rough you pat that picture for good luck, don't you?"

I said I did. It was a gimmick I had picked up when I shifted from propeller planes to jets. Like most pilots, I was scared of the jets at first so whenever it looked like trouble I would pat my wallet for luck, because Eileen Webster had been good news for me ever since that special week-end I met her in San Antonio.

Chaplain Feeney said, "If the opportunity presents itself, show Kelly your girl's picture. Let him remember what a fine American girl looks like."

I said, "I'm not selling anything."

The padre was a smart man. "Who asked you to?" he said. "When he says he's determined to get married tell him you understand. Tell him you've seen some really wonderful Japanese girls."

"Trouble is, Padre, I haven't. They're all so dumpy and round-faced. How can our men—good average guys— how can they marry these yellow girls? In '45 I was fighting the Japs. Now my men are marrying them."

"I've never understood it. Such marriages are doomed and it's my job to prevent them."

"I agree."

"Then you'll speak to Kelly?"

"Wouldn't it be simpler for the colonel just to order him not to get married?" I asked.

Chaplain Feeney laughed. "Some things can't be handled that way. We've investigated the girl Kelly wants to marry. She's not a prostitute. She's not subversive. As a matter of fact, she got a good recommendation from our investigators. Used to work in a library. Kelly has a right to marry her."

The word *marry* caught me strangely and I was swept back four years to a spring week-end in Texas when a gang of us left Randolph Field for a big time in San Antonio. We were walking down some stone steps to an open-air theater by the river that runs through the middle of San Antonio, when suddenly I saw this beautiful girl coming up. I did a double take and cried, "Aren't you General Webster's daughter?" And she gave me a dazzling smile and said she was and I stood right there staring at her and asking, "Why didn't you look like this when you lived across from me in Fort Bragg?" and she said she'd looked like this but I had been too busy going away to the Point to notice. I tried to recall but couldn't even remember her clearly from those days so I said, "You must have been a long-legged kid of eleven when we were at Fort Bragg." Then she said something which stopped me cold. She ignored the other Air Force men standing beside me and said, "I'm still a long-legged kid." And she was right and eighteen days later we sort of made up our minds to get married. But Eileen's mother and Korea took care of that.

So I brought myself back to Korea and told Chaplain Feeney, "I'll do what I can."

"Thanks, Gruver." As I started to go he asked, "Mind if I speak to the colonel about you?"

"What for?"

"You're as tense as a watch spring, son. I'm going to tell the old man you ought to be grounded."

I laughed and said, "The doc beat you to it. I'm on my way to Japan."

"Wonderful," he said. "Tokyo?"

"No, Kobe. My girl's father is general down there."

"That's fortunate."

"It has its drawbacks."

"I mean Kelly is going to Kobe, too. You can keep an eye on him."

I was disgusted. "You mean you're flying him back to where the girl is?"

"His Congressman insists on it."

I started to say what I thought of Congressmen who butt into military affairs like this but the padre said, "You might save the boy."

I thought of mean, sawed-off Joe Kelly and said as I left, "Nothing could save that bum."

It was a curious day in Korea. Our air base at J-10 wasn't what you'd call warm, but there was a shot of spring in the air and the ground was beginning to thaw and even Korea felt pretty much the way any part of the world feels in spring. I took a couple of good deep lungfuls of air and walked down headquarters street, a dismal drag even with spring nibbling at its edges, and I said to myself, "Skip Kelly. Let him take care of himself."

I headed for my bunk, where there would be some beer and a poker game, but then I realized that Kelly had the hot dope on my orders, so I went into the squadron tent where I found this mutt sitting behind a handpainted sign big enough for a general: AIRMAN KELLY.

He was a runty kid in his teens. I was twenty-eight and everybody younger than that seemed immature, but Kelly really was. He'd never been to school but had a quick animal intelligence and a sort of gutter know-how. He'd come up through a tough section of Chicago and had sandy hair and an up-with-your-dukes Irish face. He was against the world and against all officers in particular. He had the weird record of having been promoted to corporal four times—and busted back each time. He was bitter and always in trouble and the last man in our outfit you would expect to get involved seriously with any girl.

He shoved my orders at me and said, "Pays to have friends."

I had been responsible for one of Kelly's court-martials, but he had astonished me on the second by requesting me as his counsel. He respected no one, but he did like men who flew the jets. When he jammed the papers at

7

me I was going to haul him up again, but he grinned and said, "Hear you bagged two more today."

"Boom, boom."

"How was it up there, Ace?"

"Never gets easier."

"You know what's in your orders?" he asked in a snide way that a gangster might use in asking about a pay-off.

"Kobe," I said, picking them up.

"Yeah, but I mean how you happened to get them?"

"I've never discussed things like orders with enlisted men," I said, turning for the door.

Kelly was different. He said, "What I mean is, did you know about General Webster writin' to the colonel?"

It was infuriating. I wanted to bust this little twerp in the face but he kept me on the hook. I hesitated and said, "They're friends."

"Sure, but these letters were about you."

"Me?"

"Yeah, General Webster started all his orders, 'Of course I don't intend to intrude on your handlin' of the squadron but . . .' He always got the *but* in."

"But what?"

"But he would sure like to have Major Lloyd Gruver come right the hell down to Kobe."

I stuffed the papers into my pocket and said, "I didn't ask for orders like that."

Kelly laughed in an ugly way and said, "You ain't heard nothin' yet, Ace." He seemed to despise me for being an officer yet to tolerate me because I was a working pilot. He said, "General Webster's had you assigned to the Interservice Aviation Board, which means you sit on your parachute all day long and do nothin'." Then he grinned and added, "But oh them nights."

"What nights?"

Kelly poked his blunt little head in one direction then the other and asked, "Ace, can you keep a secret?"

I had always been careful never to discuss military secrets with anyone and I said, "I'd rather not hear about it."

Kelly threw me a nasty salute and said, "This ain't Air Force secret. It's Ace Gruver secret."

"What do you mean?"

"Why do you suppose you're gettin' orders to Kobe? And a cushy job? And a priority flight?"

I sensed that I was getting in too deep with Kelly and changed the subject. "Chaplain tells me you're heading for Kobe, too."

"Yep."

"I hear your Congressman arranged it."

"Yep. Chaplain said no. Colonel said no. You said no. But the Congressman said yes."

I let him know by my manner that I was disgusted with such procedures and asked with some irony, "And I hear you're getting married."

"Yep."

His insolence killed any intention I might have had to help Chaplain Feeney by arguing with this low-grade character. I signed the receipt for my orders and headed for the door. But Kelly stopped me short by saying, "I hear you're gettin' married too."

"What do you mean?" I asked.

"The general's daughter is arrivin' in Kobe. Tomorrow."

Kelly stared up at me with a nasty grin and when I asked if this was true he said, "Yep. General Webster arranges it so you can marry his daughter. My Congressman arranges it for me. Generals for the officers. Congressmen for the peasants."

Kelly and I looked at each other in one of those odd moments when you seem to see life in absolutely clear cold light. You see another human being without uniform, without degrees, without past or future. There he is, with his own problems and ambitions that are miles apart from yours but which at the same time are part of yours. The Secretary of War once told me that my father's great success in the Army sprang from his ability to see each man he had to work with dangling in free space, suspended by a string leading to the hand of God. I could respect Kelly.

He was trying to get my goat and he was an evil little twerp, but I could respect him.

I took out my wallet and asked, "Have I ever shown you a picture of the general's daughter?" I think Kelly must have been looking at me in that same cold clear light for he leaned forward like a human being and said no.

But I got mixed up—I'd never before bagged two MIGs in one day—and the picture I grabbed was not my prize shot but one of Eileen and her mother. Kelly studied the picture and asked, "Is the battle-axe your mother-in-law?"

I recovered the picture and said, "This is the one I meant to show you."

Kelly whistled and said, "Wow! She sure fills a bathing suit."

I said, "She intended to."

Kelly said, "She's a dish. Even for a general's daughter, she's a dish."

I said, "It's pretty exciting to think of a girl like that waiting for you in Kobe. Thanks for the good news, Kelly."

He said, "You ever seen Katsumi?"

"Where's Katsumi?" I asked.

"The girl I'm marryin'."

"I'm sorry. I don't know Japanese names."

"Think nothin' of it," he said brashly.

He produced a small P.X. picture of his girl. I was embarrassed because this Katsumi was certainly no Madame Butterfly. She had a big round face, prominent cheeks and what looked like oil-black hair. If you'd never been in Japan you'd probably have taken her for an Indian or an Eskimo maybe. But if you've ever seen Tokyo you'd recognize Katsumi at once. She was one of the millions of girls who could never be pretty, who did all the heavy work and who dressed as if the only clothes in Japan were made from old flour sacks.

I had to say something and by the grace of God I remembered about her working in a library. I said, "She sure looks intelligent."

Kelly said, "She's a lot brighter than me."

I was about to leave when I recalled my promise to the padre. I asked, "Aren't you taking a big risk?"

"Risks don't scare me any more," Kelly said defiantly.

"I mean about not being able to take her home?"

"That's what don't scare me," he said.

"How old are you, Kelly?"

"Nineteen."

"You're only a kid. Why don't you think this over?"

"I have. The Army and the Air Force and the State Department have ganged up to keep me from gettin' married. Only makes me more determined."

"What do you mean, ganged up?" I don't like people who feel sorry for themselves.

"When my Kobe skipper saw I was really gettin' serious about Katsumi he gave me the bum's rush to Korea. Then the doubledomes in Washington set a deadline. 'If you marry a Jap girl after then,' they said, 'we won't let you bring her back Stateside.' So I drew a court-martial for demandin' that I be sent back to Japan to marry the girl before the new law. I never made it. And now each week Father Feeney hands me a pamphlet provin' how stupid I am even to be thinkin' about such a thing."

He ripped open a drawer and slammed down some mimeographed sheets widely used in our area to bring young kids to their senses. The one on top was titled, "But Will Your Family Accept Her?" Kelly grabbed it in his hairy hand, crumpled it up and pitched it into the basket.

"They've tried everything to stop us, but do you know what I'm gonna do, Ace?"

"Something stupid, I'm sure."

"That's right. I'm stupid enough to be in love. It happens that I love this girl. And if I have to give up my American citizenship to marry her, that's O.K. with me." He was trembling mad and put his girl's picture back in his desk.

I was outraged to think that any American man would dare to talk like that. Give up his citizenship! I wanted to grab the young idiot and knock some sense into him, tell him that anyone who even thought of surrendering his

American citizenship for a Japanese girl ought . . . He turned his back on me and started on some paper work, as if to dismiss me.

I don't take that from anyone. I got sore. I reached out, grabbed him by the shirt and spun him around. "Who in hell do you think you are?" I cried.

To my amazement he cocked his fist and threatened me. "I'll let you have it, Ace."

For one brief moment I wanted to mix with this squirt and pin his ears back, but I realized that would be murder. I could have massacred him any day in the week. So I dropped my hand and said, pretty well shaken up, "You get to be a hophead with these damn jet planes."

Kelly was completely at ease. He laughed and said, "We could use some more men like you."

I said, "Excuse me, Joe. But you sounded crazy when you said you'd give up your citizenship—for a girl."

"I am crazy," he said. "I'm in love—crazy."

I felt a little dizzy and said, "Let's go over to my bunk and split a beer."

"Wonderful!" he cried, slamming his desk shut. As we walked through the late afternoon sunshine with the hint of spring warmth about us he said, "You know, Ace, back there I wasn't afraid to sock you. Because I know that if I did you'd knock my block off fair and square and you wouldn't yell for a cheap court-martial."

"Oh, brother! How wrong can you be? I just finished arguing with the chaplain that you ought to be court-martialed for having written to your Congressman."

"I mean, you wouldn't turn me in over a personal grudge."

I thought a minute and said, "I guess you're right."

"That's what I mean," he said.

We went into my bunk and promoted a fifth of Suntory. I said to Joe, "The Japs must make this out of farmer's socks." But Joe took a murderous gulp and cried approvingly, "Wow, that's man's stuff."

It was obvious that he wanted to talk with someone. He asked, "You really do think I'm nuts, don't you? The guys

at the mess hall do too. That is . . ." He paused, looked
at me carefully and said, "That is, some of them do. But
you know a strange thing, Ace? In the bunks at night you
never hear one man who married a Japanese wife complain. You hear a lot of other guys complain about their
women. But not the ones who got hitched in Japan."

This seemed so unlikely that I took a long pull at the
bottle and asked, "How come?"

"Sounds old-fashioned, Ace, but it must be love. If a
white man with good Air Force pay goes ahead and
marries a yellow girl, it must be love."

"That's ridiculous!" I felt the old yearning coming back
to knock some sense into this kid but he was dragging on
the bottle again, so I said, "I'm in love. Half the men
around here I know love some girl back in the States.
What's so special about loving a Japanese girl?"

He said, "You ever been in the bunks at night? Men
with wives back in the States talk about Junior's braces
and country-club dances and what kind of car their wife
bought. But the men with Japanese wives tell you one
thing only. What wonderful wives they have. They're in
love. It's that simple."

This flustered me because he might have been talking
about my own family. My father was a four-star general
with a tremendous reputation as a result of what he accomplished in Guadalcanal and the Philippines, and my
mother had written a couple of stories that had appeared
in the *Atlantic Monthly*. They were excellent people, they
were exciting people, but they had never been in love. In
his bunk at night I think my father must have talked about
my braces and the kind of car my mother drove. I'm sure
he never talked about love.

I said, "There's a better explanation. The guys with
Japanese wives are younger. They don't have kids to talk
about."

Joe thought that one over, took another swig, and said,
"You could be right, Ace. But I ain't takin' no chance.
Because when I see Katsumi I see a dame who could fill
my heart for the rest of my life." He looked down the tent

as if pondering his next comment, then went ahead and made it. "Tell me, Ace, do you feel that way about your girl?"

He had me again because I was a professional soldier. My future was all cut out and I knew that I would never find any one girl whose presence filled my heart forever and ever. Among the young officers in my gang love wasn't like that. You looked the field over and found a good-looking solid citizen who could stomach you for the rest of your life and if she came from a military family, like Eileen, so much the better. I couldn't explain to Kelly that Eileen would be the finest wife an Air Force officer could have and yet not be the way he was describing.

I said, "You come see me in ten years and you'll see a happy citizen!"

Joe took a final slug and cried, "I believe you, Ace. Boy, Ace, you're one in a million. Ace, you're one officer in a million I could talk to." He shook my hand clumsily and banged his way out into the dusty company street. Then he looked back and cried, "Boy, Ace! We got it made! We're gonna get married!" and he staggered off to the mess hall.

MRS. WEBSTER: "I don't mean the Japanese are inferior, but I do mean we ought to remember who won the war."

On Monday Pvt. Kelly and I flew over to Japan on the same plane and as I watched him strap himself into his bucket seat with real joy at the idea of getting home to his girl I thought how different our two journeys were. He was heading for dumpy, round Katsumi and a future that no one could guess, while I was heading for the big surprise that General Webster had arranged for me: a safe desk job, marriage to his beautiful daughter Eileen, and before too many years a promotion surely to colonel and maybe to general.

I didn't talk with Kelly on the trip over because there were some colonels aboard and it seemed wiser for me to sit up front with them and exchange ideas about the Russian pilots we were meeting over Korea. But when we reached Japan the medics came aboard to disinfect the plane, and while I was standing in the aisle Kelly whispered, "Ace, you're the only friend I know here, and you bein' with the squadron . . ." I thought he was going to touch me for some cash and I prepared to hand him a fin, but he said, "I was wonderin' if you'd be my best man. Saturday?"

The colonels started moving out and I couldn't stand there arguing. My whole inclination—everything I had ever been taught, all I had experienced—led me to say no, but I blurted out, "O.K."

"Thanks," he said, and as he trudged across the field, bowlegged and with a gangster slouch, I thought that this square-headed, sandy-haired kid was not the kind you read about in books when they describe the great lovers. Somehow you didn't think of Pvt. Joe Kelly fighting through the walls of flame to win the princess. You thought of him as the tough kid at the filling station who

15

whistles through his teeth at bobby soxers going past in
jalopies. But he was off to marry an Asiatic girl in a
strange land and I had to admit that he had guts.

I was watching him when General Webster called my
name and when I looked his way there stood Mrs. Webster, too. I shouted, "Surprise! When did you get here?"

Mrs. Webster was a handsome woman—the kind who
appear in ads wearing tailored suits and white hair and
telling the young bride why one cleaner is better than the
other—and it was widely understood in Army circles that
Mark Webster owed most of his success to this brilliant
and energetic woman. I once heard my father say, when
some of his classmates from '22 were visiting, "Mark Webster at the Point was an inevitable colonel. Absolutely impossible for him to go further. But a first-class wife came
along and made him a general." There was no scorn in
his voice when he said this—and no envy.

When Mrs. Webster saw me she hurried forward to
kiss me on the cheek. I had to make believe I didn't know
where Eileen was so I asked, "What's the news from
Eileen?"

The conspirators looked at each other archly. "She's still
at work in the oil company," Mrs. Webster said. "But she
finds Tulsa dull without you around."

"Boy, did I find Korea dull without her!"

General Webster said, "I hope you didn't mind my
dragging you away from the Russians."

"Frankly, sir, I approved. I was getting a bit jittery."

"Well, we'll drive you in to Kobe and let you see what
the setup is. You're on the Interservice Aviation Board,
you know, but you don't start work for a week."

"I'll get some sleep," I said, and the Websters snickered
to themselves.

He led me to a black Cadillac with one bright red
star on the license plate. He had always been something
of a dandy, ten pounds underweight, extra-sharp uniforms and a smart headquarters company to make him
look good. He was what enlisted men call chicken because he demanded all the military courtesies, straight

caps, shined shoes. He himself moved with an exaggerated stride and cultivated a straight-from-the-heart look. Having known my own father well and having discovered in him a real general who cut right through the nonsense to the hard core of every problem, leaving glossy shoes and snappy salutes to others, I often suspected that Mark Webster was merely playing at being a general. Once I remarked on this to my father, who grew very angry. He said, "Look, Know-it-all! The Army needs many different kinds of generals. Mark Webster can do a dozen things I can't do." Then he scowled and said, "Not that I would want to do them. But don't underestimate the men who keep the organization running." About three days later we were dining in a restaurant that featured a lot of swank and father said, "I always admire headwaiters who appear unflustered yet keep the organization running." I put my hand over my mouth and mumbled, "That's what you said the other day about General Webster." He looked up sharply, considered for a moment and said, "I guess that's what I meant—if I said it."

But on this ride in from the airport General Webster was way off stride. He wasn't his urbane self at all. In fact, he was downright uncomfortable, but it wasn't until we neared the center of Kobe that I found out what was eating him. Mrs. Webster was riding herd again.

We were passing a corner at which half a dozen enlisted men—we had orders not to call them G.I.'s any more —were loafing. They were in Kobe for Rest and Recuperation from the front in Korea. Like most soldiers, they were recuperating with streetwalkers. Five chunky Japanese girls were standing with them and as we drove by, one of the soldiers slapped a girl on the bottom. She squealed.

"That's what I mean," Mrs. Webster said.

"Kobe's a recreation center," the general said grimly. "I can't change it."

"It's disgraceful."

"I know it is," the general snorted.

"Furthermore, it degrades the military uniform."

"There seem to be no rules against it," General Webster mumbled, leaning back in a disgruntled slouch.

Mrs. Webster, seeing she could get no further with the general, asked me, "What do you think about it, Lloyd?"

"Don't try to make me argue against a general," I pleaded.

General Webster sat up. "Seriously, Gruver, what do you younger officers think?"

I had just started to say, "I've never understood how any self-respecting officer can go with a Japanese girl" when I stopped sharp. For straight ahead of our Cadillac was a tall Marine lieutenant coming out of a nylon-underwear shop accompanied by the first beautiful Japanese girl I had ever seen. She was slim and black haired and her eyes didn't slant. And she laughed. But this extraordinarily beautiful girl laughed and tucked her parcel of nylon underwear beneath her left arm. Then, like any American wife at a busy corner, she grasped her Marine's hand warmly and smiled up at him.

"It's a disgrace," the general snorted.

Mrs. Webster leaned forward to watch the Marine and his girl. "Why, he's a handsome young man," she gasped. "Probably from a very good family. What's he doing with a Japanese girl?"

I had a smart-aleck reply to that question but stifled it and then caught the general's eye and saw clearly that he had thought of the same reply and had killed his, too, for the same reason that I had killed mine. Mrs. Webster looked at us and asked, "Is it true, Mark, that some of our young men have actually married such girls?"

"About 10,000 of them," he replied gruffly.

"I simply can't believe it! Yellow girls as mothers of an American home! Even the poor fellows who married French girls last time . . . Remember those awful Farringdons at Camp Polk?"

General Webster asked, "Any of your outfit married to Japanese girls?"

I said, "I spent all afternoon last Friday arguing with

a kid nineteen who's determined to marry one of them."

"How deplorable!" Mrs. Webster sighed. She spoke with real compassion, and it was apparent that she honestly felt sorry for any nineteen-year-old boy who, far from home, had got himself mixed up with a Japanese girl.

At that moment a fat Army major, obviously a civilian, came ambling down the street, window-shopping as he might have done in San Francisco, and on his arm, window-shopping too, was a Japanese girl. Some fellow officers wandered by and the fat major stopped them to introduce his girl just as if she had been a girl he was dating at home. The girl chatted with the other officers for a moment and then led her major on down the street.

"You must do something about such behavior," Mrs. Webster said grimly. "At least on the officer level."

Our Cadillac stopped at Camp Kobe and General Webster bounded out of the car and said, "I have one disagreeable job to do. Nancy, you go on back to the club. Lloyd and I'll meet you there soon."

Mrs. Webster smiled at me archly and said, "They're having a special luncheon for us today. I might almost say an extraordinary one."

The general showed me a davenport in his outer office —paneled in Japanese pine and very handsome—and told his aide, "All right, I'll see him now." A colonel with highly polished boots disappeared into an inner room and said crisply, "General Webster will see you now."

Through the door came sawed-off Airman Kelly. Playing the Air Force game, he never acknowledged he knew me but stared straight ahead, following the spruced-up colonel, but as he disappeared through the door leading to General Webster's inner office, he shrugged his shoulders.

I studied the maps in the general's waiting room and browsed through his copy of the *Infantry Journal*, but my reading was disrupted by the general shouting, "Why in hell do you want to marry her, anyway?"

Then I heard the colonel argue more persuasively, "But, Private Kelly, if you do marry her you can't take her back to the States."

Kelly's response was muffled but judging from what happened next the kid must have said, "I don't want to go back to the States," because the general shouted, "By God, I'll send you back whether you want to go or not. Colonel, send this young whippersnapper home. Tonight!"

That was when I first heard Kelly's voice. He said, "I won't go."

The general exploded. "You won't go!"

Kelly said, "That's right, because Congressman Shimmark has arranged it for me to get married."

I have found that no matter where you are in the military—Army, Air Force, Navy, it doesn't matter—things quiet down when somebody mentions Congress. I remember hearing about the time my father was stuck in the Philippines without supplies. It was during the battle when he got his fourth star and MacArthur could drop dead and Nimitz was a bum and he would bust Roosevelt in the nose. But a five-foot-four-inch Congressman appeared and Father became as smooth as butter. Because he knew that Congressmen run the military. They approve the budget.

So General Webster retreated before the name of Congressman Shimmark. "All right," he blustered, "go ahead and ruin your life. I've done my duty. I've tried to stop you." Then he apparently turned to the colonel, for he snapped, "Arrange the young fool's wedding. Next we'll be running a nursery."

The colonel was grim-lipped as he led Kelly back into the waiting room. "Who do you think you are," he muttered savagely, "speaking to a general that way?"

Kelly said with great finality, "I ain't takin' no more pushin' around. I'm gettin' married."

The colonel showed him to the door and said, "You'll regret it as long as you live."

Kelly looked at the colonel and laughed. Then he saw

me and shrugged his shoulders again. "Saturday," he said through the corner of his mouth.

When he had gone the general appeared. He was red in the face and mumbling. "By God, in the old days we'd have thrown an insolent moron like that into the stockade. Now it's the new Army, and every young pup writes to his Congressman. Damn, I wish all Congressmen would drop dead." Quickly he looked about the room to see if anyone had heard this remark.

The colonel tried to make a joke and said, "You can't stop men from marrying women!"

The general looked at him as if he had gone off his rocker and growled, "But you can keep officers of the United States Army from making utter fools of themselves in public. And by God I will."

Then he saw me and, taking me by the arm, said, "Lloyd, I certainly do wish the imbeciles I have under me were sensible like you. But then you've been reared in a tradition of service to the nation. You understand what a uniform means." He looked for his Cadillac, which hadn't yet returned, and called for a Buick instead. As soon as we got inside he said, "Speaking of Eileen, let's eat."

"I wasn't speaking of Eileen." I laughed.

"I was," he said. "Because . . . I mean . . . it's inconceivable that these officers you see parading Japanese girls could ever have known clean, decent American girls like Eileen. . . ."

He turned abruptly and his voice sputtered like a volcano gasping for air. Across the street stood the fat major and his window-shopping Japanese girl. They were looking at dresses, holding hands in the spring sunshine. The general leaned forward and asked his driver, "Isn't that Major Bartlett?"

"Yes, sir."

"A shoe salesman in civilian life," the general snorted. "What can you expect?"

The driver corrected him. "Major Bartlett's the one who owns the chain of filling stations, sir."

General Webster relaxed, "God, what an army!" he sighed.

We drove up to the de luxe Japanese hotel which housed the officers club and I could sense the general becoming excited at the prospect of surprising me with Eileen. As a matter of fact, I got pretty steamed up myself because I hadn't seen Eileen for more than a year. Nervously I slapped my wallet for good luck and started up the marble steps.

A Japanese bellhop greeted the general. A Japanese bell captain handed him some papers. A Japanese elevator operator took us briskly up to the general's suite and a Japanese chambermaid hurried down the hall ahead of us. A Japanese butler opened the door for us, grinning happily, and a Japanese housemaid bowed almost to the floor, honoring the general.

I stood at attention, waiting for the tall library doors to open, and I remember saying to myself, "Now look, squarehead, you've got to act surprised." But I didn't need the coaching, for Eileen appeared unexpectedly from the hallway and she was twice as lovely as I had remembered. "Wow!" I cried, hurrying to her, and I noticed that she was more what you might call curved, more lovely when she smiled.

She hurried to meet me and we kissed and I said, "Wow! what a wonderful way to bring a man back from Korea!" and she said, "I wanted to cable you the minute the Army said I could come, but Mother said, 'We'll surprise him.' "

Mrs. Webster interrupted, "We didn't want to take your mind off your flying," she said.

Eileen asked, "Was it pretty rough this time?"

"They've got the first team playing."

I held her two hands tightly and stepped back to study her. "Hair fixed differently, eh? Oh, that beautiful blonde hair when everyone out here has black. And your dress . . . It seems to go in and out a lot—nice."

"It's meant to go in and out." Eileen laughed. "I go in and out."

General Webster coughed and I said, "You're much prettier than any photograph you sent me—except maybe that special one in the bathing suit. Boy, did that one go in and out!"

Eileen said, "That one was all out. I weighed eight pounds more that summer!"

General Webster said, "Do you suppose we could go down and eat?"

But Mrs. Webster was enjoying the romantic scene she had arranged and said, "First we'll drink to the young lovers." She produced a set of shimmering wine glasses and explained, "From the P.X. The little Japanese sales-clerk said they were made right here in Kobe."

General Webster poured the sherry and declaimed dramatically, "To the lovers!" Then he looked at his wife and complained, "What an ugly phrase! Aren't lovers French people who live in an attic and never get married?"

"No!" Eileen cried. "Lovers are people in an English movie who live in a grass cottage and the vicar's wife condemns them."

"Very unpleasant word, anyway." He poured fresh sherry and said, "To Major Lloyd Gruver and Eileen Webster, United States Air Force. That sounds a damned sight more American and a damned sight more healthy."

Mrs. Webster laughed. "You're right, Mark, but *lovers* has another perfectly good meaning too. Average American people whatever their ages who love each other—even when they've been married twenty-six years." She went over and kissed the general warmly.

My own father and mother had never gotten along together too well and from about ten on I realized that no matter what great advancements my father received and no matter how ordinary Mark Webster's career turned out, my parents envied the Websters because Mark and Nancy were in love while my father and mother were not. Sometimes Father would betray his contempt for Mark Webster's willingness to be pushed around by his wife, and my mother, who came from a famous Ger-

man family in Lancaster, Pennsylvania, usually stayed
there with her circle of friends and spoke sadly of Nancy
Webster, "chasing about the world like a camp follower."

At this moment in Kobe, when the senior Websters
were kissing, I shared my parents' feelings and for the
first time I realized with a certain degree of shock that
when I married their daughter Eileen I would more likely
resemble my father than become a second Mark Webster.
There would always be some restraint upon me; yet
standing there before Eileen and seeing her so radiantly
lovely I concluded that I was deeply in love—in my way
and my father's way, and I thought in that hesitating
moment that my partial love, as you might term it, could
lead to the creation of a solid family like Father's, to
my promotion in the Air Force like his promotion in the
Army, and to a substantial position in society like the
one my mother enjoyed in Lancaster. I said to myself,
"This is a soldier's way of loving."

But I think Mrs. Webster, who knew my parents well,
must have sensed my thoughts, for she cried, over her
husband's shoulder, "Kiss the girl, Lloyd."

I did and the general begged, "Now can we eat?"

We went down to the dining room, where the Japanese
headwaiter had arranged a pretty dazzling table with
flowers and a church carved out of ice. Three Japanese
waiters held our chairs and a three-piece Japanese orchestra hammered out a jive version of "Here Comes the
Bride." The officers at nearby tables rose and applauded,
but the luncheon was spoiled because right next to our
table sat the Marine lieutenant with his beautiful Japanese girl, while next to the orchestra were the fat major
and his window-shopping girl.

Mrs. Webster fidgeted with her napkin and said, "If I
knew it wouldn't humiliate you I'd leave. Who won the
war, anyway?"

Eileen grasped her mother's arm and whispered,
"They're fine girls. Please don't create a scene." Mrs.
Webster subsided and started to splash her spoon in her
cup but soon stopped.

"I simply have no appetite," she said firmly.

The luncheon was a calamity and as soon as he could decently do so General Webster dragged me back to his office where he shouted at his aide, "Go out and haul in Major Bartlett." Then he called his secretary and dictated a sharp note: "Effective immediately no Japanese nationals shall participate in any functions of the Kobe Officers Club, including specifically but not exclusively eating in the Club dining room."

"Post it conspicuously!" he said, and as the secretary started to leave the general boomed out, "Be especially sure there's one in every elevator."

When Major Bartlett appeared the general really ate him out. The fat major, one of those particularly exasperating civilians who won't take military life seriously, didn't even bother to snap to attention.

"Your behavior is a disgrace."

"I understand."

"You can't understand, or you wouldn't go lollygagging down a public street holding hands with a Japanese girl."

"I understand."

"Damn it all, these people were our enemies a short time ago."

"Not mine. I fought in Germany."

"Well, your country's. You ought to respect your nation's responsibilities."

"I understand," the major droned in an unusually offensive way.

"You understand that you're not to bring that girl into the Club again?"

"I understand."

This infuriated the general, who said sharply, "And you're not to be seen on the public streets with her."

The major looked at me, raised his eyebrows and said, "I understand."

This was too much for the general. He said sharply, "Major Bartlett, I've been ordered to send a levy to Korea. You'd better go along."

"Certainly."

Now I'd had enough. I cried, "Certainly, *sir*. You know there's such a charge as insolence through manner."

"Certainly, sir," the fat man said to me, nodding slightly.

"Stay out of this, Gruver," the general commanded. "Bartlett, the levy moves out tomorrow."

"Certainly, sir!" he said with the greatest military precision, throwing us each an extra-snappy salute.

When he had left the general said, "The perpetual civilian. Well, there's no use court-martialing a man like that. Maybe Korea'll knock some sense into him."

"I wish you'd let me handle him," I said.

"You'll learn that the Army gains more in the long run by taking civilian nonsense. But, by God, you don't have to take it at meals."

That evening when we returned to the Club and entered the elevator, the general noted with satisfaction that his memorandum had been posted, but when he read to the bottom of the typed sheet he turned a bright purple, for someone had scrawled in pencil, "Signed, Mrs. Mark Webster."

"Who did that?" the general shouted.

The Japanese girl who ran the elevator could not read English and had no idea of what the general was enraged about. He pointed at the penciled signature and demanded, "Who do this?"

"Me no see," she whispered, cowering in the corner.

In her confusion the elevator stormed past the general's floor and by the time the frightened little girl could get it back under control, General Webster had ripped down the announcement. Then he dragged the girl into his suite and rang furiously for the hotel manager, who established the fact that Major Bartlett had ridden in the elevator that afternoon. But it was impossible to prove anything and by mealtime every officer in the hotel knew about the incident, for civilian officers are like schoolboys —always giggling with delight when something embarrasses the headmaster.

Dinner that evening was a chilly affair. Eileen and I

sat in silence and absorbed the hateful stares of the officers who normally brought Japanese girls in to dinner.
Major Bartlett appeared, bowed my way and sat right
where the general would have to see him, chatting
happily with some cronies and telling dirty stories. But
the principal target of the icy stares that night was Mrs.
Webster, who didn't seem to mind at all. She had been
through many Army crises with her husband—some, like
this, which she had precipitated—and she had never
wilted under criticism. My father did not approve of her
meddling in Army life but once said, "If you ever get into
trouble, Lloyd, be like Nancy Webster. Stick your chin
out and take it."

Now she brazenly pointed at a table where three American schoolteachers were dining with some civilian men
employed by the Army to run the gasoline-supply system.
In a voice just loud enough to be heard by eavesdroppers
she said, "Isn't it charming to see those pretty American
girls at that table?"

Somebody had to say something, so I offered, "After
you've been in Korea, it's wonderful to see an American
girl."

I realized immediately that this sounded pretty awful,
and I was sure of it when Major Bartlett suddenly picked
up his spoon and started polishing it like mad. I glared
at him but he simply looked at the spoon, breathed on
it the way you do when you're polishing apples and
polished some more.

Any trouble between me and the fat major was averted
by the appearance of the young Marine lieutenant and his
lovely Japanese girl. He had apparently not seen the
notice, for he headed toward a vacant table and everyone
in the room looked up to see what would happen.

The headwaiter pounced on the couple, explained the
situation to the girl in rifle-hot Japanese and the obviously
well-bred girl turned away in an agony of embarrassment.
The Marine wouldn't take this. Calmly he grabbed his
beautiful girl by the hand and led her against her will
to the table. The headwaiter was furious. He hissed in-

structions at the girl and he had the bad luck to use
some words which the Marine understood, for the American let go the chair he was holding for the girl, hauled
his fist back and launched a haymaker.

Another Marine anticipated this and deftly caught his
friend's hand. Then he explained the new rule and joshed
the troublemaker into leaving, but the first Marine now
realized that General Webster and his party were in the
room. He was aghast. Quickly he shooed the slim Japanese girl out the door and came over to our table and
said briskly, "I'm extremely sorry, sir. I thought they
were kidding me."

"It's all right," the general laughed.

"I'm extremely sorry, Mrs. Webster."

She was most gracious and the general felt good. He
said, "Lieutenant Bailey, may I introduce Major Gruver.
He joins your board next week."

The Marine said, "We've heard about you. Seven
MIGs?"

I winked and he said, "We could use you." He bowed
and left and the general said, "Somehow or other you've
got to respect the Marines. They're publicity hounds but
they know what discipline means."

Mrs. Webster said, "It's not that I dislike Japanese.
Goodness, they're wonderful people. So clever and all
that. Even in the short time I've been here they've shown
me unusual courtesies. But a conquering army must re-
tain its dignity."

"I agree," the general said, "but those yokels in Washington say we've got to woo them now. Nancy, you ought
to read the directives I get!"

"I approve one hundred per cent!" Mrs. Webster insisted. "Japan is now a free country. We must woo them
to our side but we must also remember our position.
And be firm." Ignoring the fat major, she proceeded to
eat her dinner with relish.

On Friday Mrs. Webster gave striking proof that she really did like the Japanese—if they kept their place. She and Eileen called for me about noon and drove me a short distance out into the country in the black Cadillac. Mrs. Webster said, "I have a real treat for you, Lloyd. We're going to Takarazuka."

"Where?" I asked.

"Takarazuka," she repeated slowly.

"What's that?"

"For one thing it's a village with a delightful zoo. But it's also something especially Japanese."

"For instance?"

"You'll be amazed!"

In a few minutes we entered the Japanese village of Takarazuka. At the head of an extremely narrow lane we got out and walked into a kind of fairyland. For it was now mid-April and the path ahead of us was lined with cherry trees and I had never seen such trees before. The blossoms were extraordinarily profuse, a kind of grayish, sandy purple, rich and delicate. Laden branches dipped down over us and the blue sky of spring showed through. The walk was filled with people hurrying beneath the blossoms to some destination I couldn't see. There were women in kimonos, young girls in bobbysocks, old men in black, babies in bright clothes and half a dozen brilliantly beautiful girls in a kind of green dress that swirled about their ankles as they walked.

"Who are they?" I gasped.

"Those are the Takarazuka girls," Mrs. Webster explained.

"What's that mean?"

"The most famous collection of girls in Japan."

29

"What do they do?"

"That's the big surprise."

But I wasn't to find out for some time because she led us down the flowered lane past scores of little shops that sold mementoes of the village, past old trees that offered shade and past minute restaurants at whose doors women stood offering cheap food. We were in the heart of Japan and Mrs. Webster was enjoying herself as much as any Japanese.

We had gone only a short distance when a thin young man in black joined us and bowed very low, drawing breath in through his teeth. "Many, many pardons," he said. "I was waiting for you at the main office." He took us to the zoo, where there were beautiful lakes and flower beds and charming benches on which you could sit beneath the cherry blossoms and watch children play.

The young man asked in good English, "Are you the pilot who shot down seven MIGs?" He was impressed and said, "I used to be a flier. Now I work here."

"What is this place?" I asked in a low whisper.

"You don't know?"

"Never heard of it."

Mrs. Webster saw us talking and cried, "Oh, Lloyd! Don't spoil the fun!"

"I hate mysteries," I said.

"All right, we'll go."

She and the thin young man took us out of the zoo and up to an enormous building which looked like an armory in Kansas City. It was a theater. We went to our special seats in the very first row and there we faced one of the largest stages in the world on which was enacted the most amazing performance I had ever seen.

I can't say I understood the play. It was called, the young man said, *Sarutobi Sasuke*, meaning *Little Monkey Sasuke*, and Sasuke is a boy's name. It dealt with some children who accidentally conjure up a wizard who helps them save a castle from the enemy. Who the enemy was or what the castle I never understood because at Takarazuka it wasn't the story that counted. It was the over-whelming effect of size.

The play started at one and ran till six. It had thirty-four different scenes, each the biggest and most lavish you could imagine. I never saw a Ziegfeld show, but Mrs. Webster said that any Takarazuka scene outdid the best Ziegfeld ever put on. There was music, there was dancing, there were songs. In fact, there was everything. In this one show there were two gorillas, a jeep, two live pigs, a wizard, three different trios singing three different kinds of songs, a ballet, a football game, a live goat, a motion-picture sequence showing the wizard at work, a passage from an opera and a cave whose trees moved about. But most of all there were girls.

There were more than a hundred girls on stage, and they were all real dazzlers. I thought to myself, "And you were the guy who said he'd never seen a good-looking Japanese girl! Wow!" But at the same time there was something ridiculous about this excess of beauty, for there were no men actors. The most striking girls played men's roles, and I whispered to Eileen, "This show could use a few Clark Gables."

Mrs. Webster heard me and laughed. "In Tokyo there's another theater which has no women. There men play all the parts."

"Doesn't sound sensible," I said.

"It's Japanese," she explained.

I soon tired of the show—one enormous set after another and beautiful girls making believe they were men. I said I was willing to leave whenever the others had had enough. Eileen said, "I'm ready," and as we walked up the darkened aisle I began to appreciate the enormous size of this theater. It must have seated more than 3,000 people. I asked our guide, "Is it always filled this way?" for there wasn't a vacant seat. He sucked his breath in proudly and said, "Every day in the year. Twice on Satur-day and Sunday." I didn't tell him so, but I figured there must be something in a Takarazuka show no Ameri-

can could understand because I was bored by this one
and so were Eileen and her mother. But the Japanese
loved it. They sat on the edges of their seats, their round
faces transfixed with intense pleasure.

We started to return to our car but the guide stopped
us and said, "The Supervisor has invited you to attend
a special rehearsal of our next month's show."

"Have you two companies?" Eileen asked, a bit be-
dazzled by the 115 girls she had just seen.

"We have four," the guide said proudly. "One plays
here, one in Tokyo, one tours, and one is in rehearsal."

He led us to a huge empty stage where some young
girls in green skirts were walking through an intricate
dance, while a man at the piano hammered out a tune
that sounded like Schubert. In another empty room another man played a song that sounded like Gershwin for
a trio of young girls, also in green skirts. "They wear the
Takarazuka costume," the guide explained.

Then suddenly he came to attention and the girls at
the piano stopped singing. Everyone looked at the door
where an elderly man with a white beard stood for a
moment, discovered Mrs. Webster and hastened toward
her, bowing very low and saying, "Mrs. General Webster!
It is a superb honor." He waved his hand deprecatingly
and said, "Rehearsal only."

As he turned he disclosed behind him a most lovely
slender actress in a plaid skirt, brown vest, and cocky
green tam o'shanter set saucily over one eye. I did a sort
of double take and whispered to Eileen, "That's the girl
who was with the Marine lieutenant." Eileen studied her
and said, "Of course it is."

The Supervisor saw us staring at the remarkable girl
and said, "Mrs. General Webster and honored guests,
may I present Fumiko-san, one of our finest actresses?"
Although I am certain the girl recognized us, she did not
betray that fact but stepped sedately forward and bowed
low before Mrs. Webster. When she reached me I held
out my hand, but she started to bow again, whereupon
I withdrew my hand and saw that she was looking up at

me with immense gratitude for my not having recognized
her in front of the Supervisor. Eileen saw this too and had
the presence of mind to say, "We did not see you on
stage, did we?" The girl replied in a soft voice, "I not
play this week. I . . . Moon . . . Troupe."

Hastily the guide explained, "The four troupes each
have a name. Moon, Star, Snow and Flower. You would
say that Miss Fumiko is one of the best stars of the Moon
Troupe." I was about to say that I had already seen Miss
Fumiko when a distinct glance from her begged me to
remain silent.

With extraordinary grace Miss Fumiko walked over to
a piano, but I didn't hear her sing, for just as she began
we left for the flower path leading back to our Cadillac.
As we walked beneath the swaying cherry blossoms I
noticed that each of the shops we had seen earlier had on
display large glossy photographs of the principal Takarazuka actresses. As we passed slowly along, the pictures
of the beautiful girls, half of them dressed as men, had a
mesmerizing effect, but while I was studying them Eileen
discovered one of the real phenomena of Japan. "Oh,
look!" she cried.

The play *Sarutobi Sasuke* had ended and from the
dressing-room doors the Takarazuka girls were entering
the flower walk. The youngest were dressed in formal
green skirts and about them pressed an adoring crush
of people trying to touch them, trying to lay hands on
the green skirts or press a letter or a gift upon the actresses. When a particularly famous girl appeared the
crowd would utter a little cry and fall back and the actress would move on in a kind of courtly grandeur.

The Takarazuka girls passed along the flower walk,
their green skirts swaying softly beneath the cherry blossoms and I could hear a sigh go up from the crowd as the
girls turned the corner, entered upon a bridge and crossed
the river to the other side, where I was told they lived
like nuns in a secluded dormitory. When they were gone
the crowd at the dressing-room doors looked about idly
as if now there was nothing to do, and for the first time

I realized that every person in the milling mob was a young girl. There were no Stage-door Johnnies. They were all Stage-door Jills.

Mrs. Webster said, "The young girls of Japan idolize these actresses."

Eileen said, "No wonder! The actresses are so beautiful."

"And the girls outside are so ugly," Mrs. Webster said. "Have you ever seen so many round, red faces? Such dumpy little creatures?"

"I don't know," Eileen said. "America has its share. When I was thirteen I would stare in the mirror and pray God that I might grow up to look like Myrna Loy."

"Ah, but you were never a square-beamed little urchin! Lloyd, this child was always beautiful." Then she played her trump card. "I'm having dinner with the Supervisor— that sweet old man with the beard. He's very important. You two drive along home."

And she looked at me with that perfectly frank stare as if to say, "You're twenty-eight, Lloyd. You should have married Eileen four years ago. Grow up." And she was, as always, 100 per cent right. Even though she herself had prevented the marriage that first year—she hadn't been aware of the fact—and even though I could use the Korean war as an added excuse, I had never been able to explain to myself honestly why Eileen and I were not married. We had fallen completely in love, she had risked a lot of public trouble by riding a bus down to a remote Texas air base for a crazy week with me, but we both knew that whenever the big moment of actually getting married approached, I shied away. With jet airplanes I was comfortable. With women I wasn't. I guess that watching Mrs. Webster and my mother had made me gun-shy.

One night I heard one of our medical doctors talking in a bar. He'd been a big shot in civilian life and he was saying, "We find that if a man comes from a broken home he's apt not to marry early. It's as if he had to be introduced to love. If he doesn't meet love in his own family he could, conceivably, go through an entire life without ever meeting it. Of course," he had added, "at any time almost any girl could provide the introduction if she wanted to take the trouble. But spoiled men who don't marry before they're forty—the men who have never been introduced to love—are hardly worth any girl's trouble. So we can say that some men actually do pass through an entire lifetime without ever meeting so simple a thing as love. No one bothered to introduce them." I often recalled the doctor's words but I was satisfied I wasn't like that, not in all respects. True, my parents had failed to introduce me either to their own love or to the idea of having a home with some girl's love as the central pillar. I think that explains why I was twenty-eight and vaguely in love with Eileen and unmarried. And I think Mrs. Webster knew it and now she was pushing us together.

"I'll see you in the hotel," she cried and left us, towering a good four inches over the little Japanese man who was leading her back to the Supervisor.

I had been hoping for a chance to talk with Eileen alone and as soon as Mrs. Webster left I pulled her into a corner of the Cadillac and gave her a big kiss. She said, "All the way out on the plane I dreamed of meeting you in a romantic spot like this." She pointed out of the car to where we were passing little rice fields pressed close to the road and tiny houses set back among the trees. There was a sweet heaviness of spring in the air and as we watched the little workmen of Japan trudging along the footpaths at dusk we felt very much a part of this strange country.

Eileen whispered, "I didn't want to leave America. The idea of . . ." she hesitated, then added, "getting married in a foreign land didn't appeal. But now . . ."

I pretended not to have heard her remark about marriage and said, "I was proud of you today."

"About what?"

"That girl."

"The actress?"

"Yes. You knew she was the one your father threw out of the dining room. But you didn't embarrass her."

"Why should I? She came to the Club as a guest and she seemed a very pleasant girl."

"But your mother . . ."

"Mother's all right. She just has to feel that she's running everything."

I asked, "Would she be frightfully sore if we didn't show up at the Club dinner?"

"She knows we're courting."

"What a quaint word for a Vassar girl!"

"I'm not always a Vassar girl. Don't let the tag fool you. Pardner, I been a-livin' in Tulsa, where folks go a-courtin'."

"Let's court."

"What had you in mind?"

"A Japanese night club."

She thought a moment, then smiled and said, "Let's court!"

The driver reluctantly dropped us at a corner and even more reluctantly indicated how we could go halfway up an alley and find the Fuji Nights, which turned out to be a tiny room specializing in beer and fried fish. A geisha girl, her face white with cornstarch, came and sat with us and showed us how to order. Soon four other white-faced geishas came up to admire Eileen's blonde hair. One who could speak English placed a strand of Eileen's against her own jet black hair and sighed, "How beautifur!"

Eileen said, "Isn't it fascinating, the way they can't say *l*."

I asked the geisha, "How do you say *lovely lady*?"

She laughed and said, "You tease."

"Please!" I begged.

She put her slim fingers under Eileen's chin and said, "You have one ruvrey radie."

Eileen clapped her hands and said, "Your kimono is lovely, too." The girls talked for a while and then the radio was turned on and we danced. The geisha who could speak English said to Eileen, "May I dance with your officer? Very important we know American dancing." Eileen said, "Sure," and for the first time in my life I danced with a foreign girl.

It was pretty dull. The geisha had something sticky on her hair and so much cloth about her middle that I couldn't hold onto her anywhere. She had apparently run into this problem before, for she took my hand and slipped it securely under a particularly huge bundle of cloth and in that way we danced. I asked her why geishas wore so many clothes and she said shyly, "I not real geisha. I only après-guerre geisha." I thought she had used a Japanese phrase and asked her what it meant. "Après-guerre," she said. "Maybe French. After-the-war geisha." I still didn't catch on and asked if that were some special kind. In real embarrassment she looked away and said, "In here we only make-believe geisha. (She pronounced it *onry make-berieve.*) To be real geisha need many year study. Many kimonos. We poor girls. We buy one kimono, make believe for Americans. We got to make money."

When she led me back to the table two of the other make-believe geishas started talking in a real jabber and finally one of them ran to the back. It was amusing to see her move, for such girls walk extremely pin-toed, which gives them a peculiar sing-song motion. In a moment she appeared with a Japanese newspaper and there, about the size of an American penny, was my picture. This excited the five geishas and they made me stand up so they could inspect my uniform. One held up seven fingers and I nodded, whereupon the girls gasped and the first geisha said to Eileen, "You must be very proud."

"I am," Eileen said, and later that night, as we drove home she kissed me warmly and whispered, "I like courtin' with you."

I remember that I thought to myself: "This is it, squarehead. Either you get this woman problem settled now or quit for good." So I took the plunge and said,

"Where I come from, Podner, courtin' means marryin'. When?"

Eileen smiled gently, as if something very right had happened, and said, "I want to get married . . . if . . ."

I had dived in and the water wasn't as frightening as I had expected so I struck out and said something pretty polished for me, "I've been flying where seconds mean hours of ordinary time. I don't want to wait a single day."

She laughed nervously and said, "Can't a girl be jittery over her first proposal?"

I was eager to play the determined lover—I was beginning to like the role—and said, "You've known all along I could live with no wife but you."

It was then that I first saw she actually was perplexed. She was honestly in doubt. She fumbled a moment and said, "It's difficult for me to explain, but several times here in Japan I've wondered whether you would ever make a better husband than your father."

"What do you mean?" I gasped.

"You know. Everybody knows your father lives for one thing. The Army."

"Is that bad?"

She ignored my question and said, "I've had a weak and terrible feeling, Lloyd, that the day would come when you would think of me as your father thinks of your mother."

Suddenly the water I had dived into was bitter cold and I asked, "You think there's something wrong with my father?"

"Frankly, I do," she replied. "The way he's content to leave your mother walled up within a circle of a few close friends, there in Lancaster, while he plunges off to the wars. That isn't good enough for me."

I said, "We'd better get our feet on the ground and get some things organized."

She accepted my suggestion. She opened the car door and stepped into the street. "Good idea," she said.

We dismissed the chauffeur and wandered aimlessly along the streets of Kobe until we reached the waterfront where the great Inland Sea of Japan has from the most ancient times provided an anchorage for roving ships and their rich cargoes. Eileen studied one of the dark vessels and said, "I came to Japan because I wanted our marriage to start right. I'm younger than you are, Lloyd, but I'm just as smart. And I think I'm just as brave. I want to be with you . . . in all kinds of weather."

"I don't get what you're talking about," I pleaded.

"About us. No, I'll be honest. About you."

"What's about me?"

"I've never told you this, Lloyd, but nine months ago I visited your mother. I was driving through Pennsylvania and stopped off. I was appalled at the loneliness in which she lives . . . in which she's always lived."

I felt weak. I knew what Eileen was saying was true but nevertheless I protested. "Mother wants to live that way."

"Nonsense! No woman wants to live any way but body and soul with the man she loves. Your mother may be a fine sport about the way she has to live, since she has no other choice . . . Lloyd, tell me this. That time I followed you down to the air base in West Texas . . . Why were you so scared?"

"I was worried about you."

"What about me?"

"Well . . ."

"You mean . . . my reputation?"

"Well, yes."

"Rubbish, Lloyd! The reason you were scared stiff was that you discovered you had on your hands a girl who would insist upon sharing your full life. Well, you were right. You could never tuck me away in a corner of Lancaster."

I felt blood rising into my throat and said dizzily, "I think I'd better take you back to the hotel."

There was an ugly moment of silence—which I now know I should have broken with a rousing kiss—and when I did nothing Eileen said dully, "I guess you're right. Which way is the officers club?" We walked in gloomy silence for a few minutes. Then she said, "Lloyd, dear. Don't get little-boy sorehead about this. It's of absolutely fundamental importance. Please think about it."

"About what?" I shouted.

"Don't lose your temper. About the fact that half a marriage isn't good enough for either you or me. I've got to have a man who loves me with his whole heart. Go ahead and become the greatest general in Air Force history. But love me too."

"Damn it, I do love you," I protested as the lights of the hotel appeared around the corner.

"Sure you do, in a cold, partial little way. Let's think about this for a few days."

Suddenly I was fighting to get married and I said, "I thought you came to Japan for a wedding."

"I did, but I've got to marry a complete man. Not just the shreds that are left over after he's led the important part of his life somewhere else."

I was infuriated, not because of what she had said, but because she had seen so clearly the kind of man my father and mother had made me. Rationally my father had decided it would be good for him to marry a general's daughter who had a ready-made family life in Lancaster. She wouldn't be an encumbrance and she might prove to be a help. Now I was reasoning the same way. Marry Eileen because she was from a military family and would understand Air Force ropes without a lot of civilian argument. She was beautiful and, as she had proved tonight, plenty smart and courageous. She would be a catch for any man and I wanted her, but she was right when she said that I did not come to her with a whole heart. I knew what she was talking about, for I knew that I had never loved her in the absorbing way that sawed-off Joe Kelly loved his Japanese girl.

But this was the big point: I wanted to learn. In my heart I knew that my parents' way wasn't good enough and I wanted Eileen to help me find something better.

So I took her in my arms and gave her what we called "The Unconditional Surrender," a kiss so long she had to beat on my arms for air. When I put her down she laughed that wonderful golden grin of hers and said softly, "For the first time I have the feeling we'll work this thing out." Then she kissed me in the ear and whispered, "You act a lot better than you talk." And I do believe everything would have turned out all right if it hadn't been for what happened the very next morning.

Before I got out of bed Private Joe Kelly called me and said, "Well, Ace, this is Saturday!"

"What about it?" I asked drowsily.

"Ace, I'm gettin' married!"

I couldn't focus for a minute. Then I said, "Well, congratulations."

"Ace," the little gangster shouted. "Don't you remember? You're gonna be my best man."

I started to say, "Gee, Kelly, I have an appointment . . ." but he was on my team. Wreck that he was, he belonged to my squadron. So I said, "I'll break the appointment, Kelly. Where's the big event take place?"

I walked down to the grubby building in which our consul had his offices and was amazed to find four G.I.-Japanese couples waiting to be married. Any man under such circumstances instinctively looks at the girls to see if there are any he would take for his wife, and believe me there was none I would care for. Katsumi, Joe's girl, looked exactly like her picture: big round face, high cheeks, thick black hair and small eyes. When she smiled during the introductions I saw that like most Japanese girls she had in front a big gold tooth.

"We're gettin' that changed," Joe said with some embarrassment.

Katsumi was uncertain whether she should offer to shake my hand or not, so when I extended mine she collapsed in agonizing giggles and popped her left fist over her mouth. Her knuckles were bright red from chapping, and as I studied these girls I wondered why it was that our G.I.'s—even though we'd been ordered not to use that word, it crept in—always seemed to marry the

42

ugliest girls and never the pretty ones we saw at Takarazuka.

It was a dismal morning. Since Joe's marriage was third in line I watched with mounting disgust the spectacle of American soldiers marrying whatever girls they had been able to pick up. I was ashamed at having been drawn into this sordid spectacle and was looking down at my fingernails when a bright voice called, "Are you Major Ace Gruver?" I looked up and breathed relief, for it was an American girl. She was oversize, but I was glad to know there were some American girls still alive.

She whispered, "I'm a secretary here."

"Interesting job, I bet."

She shook her head. "One marriage after another."

"Don't they know they can't take the girls home?"

"Sure they know. But what I wanted to see you about is that I have a kid brother who is crazy about airplanes. He told me if I ever meet a real jet pilot, to get his ottograft. I want your ottograft!"

She led me into her inner office where she gave me a sheet of paper to sign then added another. "Maybe the kid'll be able to sell this one at a fancy price—like a baseball glove."

"What I don't get," I said, "is why the Government allows these marriages in the first place."

"The Government is smart. Public pressure back home insists the men be permitted to marry, so the Government does permit it, then washes its hands of the whole affair." She showed me a form which each G.I. had to sign, on top of all the others, and it was about the frankest and most brutal I had ever seen. Kelly, for example, acknowledged that he was outside the law, waived his legal rights, said he would look after the girl on his own account and stated in writing that the Air Force was in no way responsible for his wife. At the bottom he swore that he was in right mind and that he had signed before witnesses.

"But these guys go right on?"

"Day after day."

"Why?"

"That's not a fair question to ask me," she said some-what sharply.

"You work here."

"All right!" she said. "Would you call me pretty? No, nobody would call me pretty. I'm a plain Jane who couldn't get married in America so I came out here where there were plenty of men." She laughed at herself in a delightful, horsy sort of way and said bitterly, "They stamp us 'Stateside rejects'! Sure, there were lots of men when I got here. But the damned Japanese girls had them all."

"I still don't get it."

"Like a soldier told me," she explained. "He kept say-ing, 'You American girls wouldn't understand.'"

"Understand what?" I asked.

"The men all say these Japanese girls do something for them."

"Like sex?"

"Not sex. I'm not bitter any more so I don't charge it up to sex. Didn't you notice?"

She showed me a wedding ring and said, "The man I finally got had been in love with a Japanese girl for two years. Said frankly he knew I'd never be half the wife she would have been."

"Then why did he marry you?"

"Said I'd fit in better in Denver."

She went to her purse and pulled out a wrinkled photo-graph. "My rival!" she said in obvious amazement. Before looking at the picture I could guess that the girl probably looked a lot like Katsumi. Red face, round features. The American secretary stared at the picture and said, "To me she looks absolutely ugly. I stole this picture when my husband burned the others. I keep it as a reminder that I must be a good wife."

"Where's the girl now?"

"She committed suicide." She placed the damaged photograph back among her junk and assured me, "It all happened before I met Gus. I had nothing to do with the suicide."

The door opened and the consul hurried through. "We'll be ready for the next one in a couple of minutes," he said. "You the witness, Major? Go on in."

The girl led me into the office from which he had come. It was bleak with a writing table, a Bible, a portrait of President Truman and a coat rack. "This is where the foul deed takes place." She laughed. "I'm always one of the witnesses and it's beginning to tear me apart because every G.I. who comes into this room has the same look in his face that my husband gets when he speaks of his Japanese girl." She hammered the table and cried, "Damn them all! They all have the same secret."

"What?"

"They make their men feel important. I try to build my husband up—as a wife should. But with me it's a game. With these ugly little round-faced girls it isn't a game. It's life."

The door opened and Katsumi came in, followed by Joe Kelly. They expected to see the consul ready to marry them and Joe shrugged his shoulders at me and asked, "They figure out some new way to louse me up?"

The secretary asked, "How long they been messing around with you, soldier?"

"Please, lady! Not soldier! Air Force."

The secretary said, "If the body's warm it's a soldier."

The consul came in and started arranging papers. He was a young man with balding hair, a strained look and very big feet. His hands were awkward with the papers and he was irritated when he saw Katsumi. "You must wait outside," he said sharply.

Obediently, Katsumi left. Joe started after her but the consul told him to stay, so Joe said to me, "Ace, don't leave her alone at a time like this."

I went and sat with the little girl while we heard Joe shout at the consul, "Yes, damn it all, I've read the papers. Yes, I understand I'm forfeitin' all rights. Yes. Yes. Let's get the thing movin'."

"I'm only asking you as the law demands," the consul said.

"And I'm only tellin' you that Congressman Shimmark told me I could go ahead and get married."

I hadn't known it before, but apparently State Department men are just as scared of Congressmen as generals are, because right away the door opened and the consul said brusquely, "Come in, Miss."

He lined the couple up before the desk, had them sign still some more papers, then conducted a brief ceremony. He was mad at Pvt. Kelly, dismayed by Katsumi and fed up with the whole affair. It was an ugly ceremony performed with grudging spirit and I was ashamed at having been witness to it.

But as I looked up from my embarrassment. I happened to see Kelly's face as he bent down to kiss Katsumi and in that instant the ugliness in the room vanished and I had to bite my lip. The horsy American secretary wrote something in a book and wiped her eyes, while the consul said to Kelly, "You understand that you have surrendered numerous rights in this matter?"

Kelly couldn't take any more. He looked at the consul and his nose twitched. "You son . . ." he began and I knew that the consul was about to get the full Kelly treatment, which is about as profane as anyone can get. But Katsumi, already the wife, quietly took her husband's hand and said, "We go now, Joe."

Joe collapsed like a ruptured balloon. He looked at me and said, "It's hell to be married. Take it from me, Ace." Then he asked, "Ain't you gonna kiss the bride?"

I was unprepared for this and must have betrayed some shock for I could see Joe cringe with bitter humiliation when he realized that I had absolutely no desire to kiss that big mouth with the bright gold tooth. I, in turn, wanted to drop through the floor for having insulted a member of my own squadron at such a time. Mine was the last in a long line of insults administered by his nation, his commanding officers, his consul and even his religion. In my defense it had never occurred to me that anyone would actually want to kiss a yellow-skinned Japanese girl. You fought the Japs on Guadalcanal. You organized their country for them in Kobe. You defended them in Korea. But it had never crossed my mind that you kissed them.

I took Katsumi's big face in my hands and said, "The secretary told me Japanese girls make wonderful wives. You be a good wife to Joe." Then I kissed her. It was repugnant, but at the same time I felt that I had in some trivial way helped one of my men marry the girl he loved.

"Good luck, kids," I said.

"Thanks, Ace," Joe replied.

When they left the consul said, "Such marriages are dreadful mistakes. We do our best to prevent them."

"Do you succeed—very often?"

"You'd be surprised. We make the paper work so cumbersome a good many of the young hotheads lose steam. Actually we've helped forestall some inevitable tragedies."

"You didn't have much success with Joe."

"We see everything here. Fights, tears. But if a boy's had the gumption to write his Congressman we know he's determined to go ahead. Now all Joe has to do is get his Congressman to pass a special bill and he'll get Mrs. Joe into the States. Frankly, between you and me, I hope he succeeds. But it's my job to paint a gloomy picture."

The secretary stepped out of the room to call the next couple and the consul whispered, "Take that girl you just saw, my secretary. She's married to a G.I. with whom I had some luck. He was going to marry an extremely ordinary Japanese girl, but our paper work and delays brought him to his senses."

"What did you say to him?" I asked.

"As I remember, he was from Denver and I simply asked, 'If you take this girl back to Denver will she fit in?'"

"What happened to the girl?"

"You saw her. She works here. My secretary."

"I meant—what happened to the Japanese girl?" I wanted to hear his explanation.

Before he could reply the secretary brought the fourth couple into the office and the consul droned, "You understand what you've signed?"

The young man, a sailor, stood on one foot then the other and replied with studied patience, "Yes, sir. Yes, sir."

The girl was just as ugly at Katsumi and I started to leave, but the consul called me back and said to the sailor, "How would you like to have Ace Gruver be your witness?"

"You Ace Gruver?" the boy asked.

"That's right."

"I'd be proud," the boy said. He turned to his girl and spoke to her in rapid Japanese, using his hands to indicate airplanes in combat. The girl looked at me, giggled furiously and clapped her hand over her gold-crowned teeth.

It was this same well-meaning consul who got me into my big trouble, for when he turned in his weekly report on G.I. marriages to General Webster he must have mentioned his surprise at seeing me as Joe's witness. At any rate the general called me into his office and stormed, "I'm astounded that you should lend yourself to such a thing—especially since you know Mrs. Webster's and my objection to fraternization."

"This wasn't fraternization, sir. It was marriage," I said.

"To a Japanese," he stormed, spitting the words out.

"The kid's from my outfit in Korea, sir."

"All the more reason you should have tried to save him from such folly."

"I did try, sir."

"Carstairs tells me you even kissed the girl!"

"I did. He asked me to."

"Who, Carstairs?"

"No, Kelly."

The general was outraged. He banged out of his chair

and stood looking at a map. Finally he exploded. "I'm damned if I can understand how a man like you, brought up the best traditions of the service, can outrage military propriety in this way. Such marriages are sordid, disgraceful things. We have to tolerate them because Washington says so, but we don't have to polish our buttons and go down to kiss the bride!"

"I . . ."

"Nauseating. The whole thing's nauseating, but it's especially sickening to have a member of your own staff —you might say your own immediate family . . ."

The bawling out I got from the general was nothing compared to the one I took from his wife. She was sweet as butter during dinner but after the general and Eileen had left on prearranged signals she said bluntly, "Do I understand, Lloyd, that you actually encouraged a Japanese marriage this morning?"

"One of the men from my outfit."

"But you surely didn't attend—not officially?"

"He asked me to help him out."

"And you went to the consulate, before other Japanese who might know you . . ."

"Look, Mrs. Webster, it was a guy from our outfit."

"It wasn't just a guy, Lloyd. It was humiliation to the service and a direct slap in General Webster's face."

"I didn't approve of it, Mrs. Webster. I argued against it for days."

"But your very presence signified approval. In this dining room right now half the officers are laughing at me."

So that was it. She wasn't really concerned about the welfare of the service nor the standing of her husband. She was angry that something which she had started— non-fraternization—should have backfired and brought ridicule upon her. She was especially angry that the instrument of this ridicule should have been, in General Webster's words, a member of her own family.

I asked, "How could I have refused to attend the wedding . . ."

"Don't call it a wedding! It was a mean little surreptitious ceremony on the most sordid level. It was permitted only because some lily-livered idiots in Washington have no courage to face facts."

"I agree with you, Mrs. Webster."

She didn't want agreement. She wanted to knock me into shape, once and for all. When I saw her closing in on me, trying to make me apologize for what I had done in good faith, I sensed pretty clearly that she saw herself fighting her daughter's marriage battle. Years before she had taken on young Mark Webster in just such a fight and she had been victorious and the entire Army knew she had won and from that time forth she had molded and marched Mark Webster into a one-star generalship that he could never have attained by himself. Now she was going to teach her daughter how to march me into four or five stars.

She frowned and said, "If you expect to make a name for yourself in service, Lloyd, you can't offend the proprieties. You can't insult generals."

I got mad and said, "I've made a pretty good name for myself so far. Shooting down MIGs, not worrying about social life."

She gasped and put her hand to her mouth as if she had been slapped. With profound rage she cried, "You're an insolent little upstart." Immediately she was ashamed of herself and tried to recover by saying something half-way sensible but fury was upon her and she stormed ahead, "You're like your insufferable father." I knew that Mark Webster was afraid of my father—he was deathly afraid of anyone who had more stars than he—and I was surprised that Mrs. Webster should have launched an assault on someone who might be in a position to affect her husband's career, but she was trembling mad and didn't care what she said. She added, "You ought to be careful you don't grow up to be a second Harry Gruver."

She sounded exactly like her daughter and I recalled with a sense of shock that almost every time I had seen Eileen's picture in the society columns of towns where she had lived, she was invariably with her mother. They were like sisters, shoulder to shoulder against the world.

My father had commented on this once and had said he knew there were two kinds of Army marriages, his where the wife stayed home and Mark Webster's where the wife tagged along. He told me he would honestly have preferred the latter, but he observed that it usually did hard things to the wife. "She's always on the move and her children are always on the move. So the women folk band together in tough little cliques. I can honestly say I never feared the Japanese or the Germans but I do fear such cliques of Army women."

I heard Mrs. Webster saying bitterly, "I should think Eileen would be ashamed and disgusted."

I didn't say anything. I didn't even say that I was sure she would see to it that Eileen became disgusted. Instead I looked at her very carefully and when I saw her clean, handsome, hard face with not a wrinkle out of place I thought of Joe Kelly's Japanese girl whom I had kissed that morning, and all at once I caught a glimmering of what the American secretary must have meant when she said, "These damned Japanese girls have a secret." I had an intimation of their secret: they loved somebody—just simply loved him. They weren't going to make him a four-star general or they weren't going to humiliate him over some trivial affair for which he had already apologized. They just got hold of a man and they loved him.

I had now seen two American marriages at close hand: my parents' where people got along together in a respectful truce, and the Websters' where there was an early surrender followed by a peace treaty without vengeance. But I had never witnessed a marriage where two people loved each other on an equal basis where the man ran his job on the outside and the woman ran her job at home and where these responsibilities were not permitted to interfere with the fundamental love that existed when such things as outside jobs and inside housekeeping were forgotten.

Mrs. Webster said acidly, "Eileen asked me to tell you she'd be at the hairdresser's."

I thanked her, held her chair as she rose and showed her to the elevator. I think she knew that she had presented a dismal picture during our talk, for she said, "I do hope you won't embarrass the general again." I promised her that I wouldn't irritate the general and refrained from pointing out that we had been talking about something quite different: my irritating her.

I went down to a lower floor of the hotel where there was a hairdresser for the American girls who worked with our Army in Japan, and there I saw Eileen coming out more brilliant and lovely than I had ever seen her before. She had what *Life* magazine once called the well-scrubbed look and was absolutely adorable with the fresh bright charm that only American girls ever seem to have. I was disgusted with myself for having quarreled with her the night before and suggested that we sit in a corner of the elegant lounge, where a Japanese boy in bright blue bar-boy's uniform served us drinks.

I said, "If you looked so adorable all the time no one would ever be able to fight with you."

"We weren't fighting last night," she teased.

"I'm glad," I said, "because I've got to keep in the good graces of at least one of the Websters."

She frowned and asked, "Mum give you a bad time at lunch?"

"Very bad," I said.

"Mother's a special case, Lloyd. The Army's her whole life. She watches over Father like a mother hen and she's been very good for him. Therefore he's got to trust her and if she says she doesn't like to see American officers with Japanese girls . . . Frankly, I don't think Father approves of all the orders he's had to issue because traditionally the Army is pretty adult about men and women getting together—any women. But he's learned that in the long run Mother is usually right."

"Is she?"

"Yes."

"Now it's my turn to be scared."

"What do you mean?"

"You're afraid I'll be like my father. I'm really scared you'll be like your mother."

"What's so bad with that?" she asked.

"I can't stand being pushed around."

Eileen lifted her glass and made circles on the marble table. She said slowly, "I don't think I'd be bossy the way Mother is because you're much stronger than Father ever was. But mostly I wouldn't hurt you because I love you so much."

That was what I wanted to hear and I said, "I'm twenty-eight now and I've been going around with too many airplanes. What I want now is a wife and family." She sneaked in a kiss and I said, "Whenever I've thought about a family it's with someone like you—a girl with an Army background like my own. . . ."

She became gently irritated and protested, "That's just what I mean. Why do you say, 'a girl like me'? I'm not a type. I'm me. Damn it all, Lloyd, haven't you ever wanted to just grab me and haul me away to a shack somewhere?"

Now it was my turn to get on edge and I said, "When you're an officer you meet endless problems of enlisted men who just grabbed something and hauled it away. It doesn't appeal to me."

She said, "Lloyd, a man has to surrender himself sometimes. You're not so important you have to defend yourself like a fort."

From the manner in which Eileen spoke I could tell that she was just as tense as I was and it occurred to me that if I married Eileen we would always be a little bit afraid of each other, a little bit on edge always to be ahead of the other person. Mrs. Webster, frankly, had scared the devil out of me and now I could see the same marital tendencies in her daughter. I could see her organizing my life for me solely on the grounds that she loved me, but the definition of what was love would always be her definition; and I thought of Joe Kelly and the girl he had found. Their fight was with the outside world—the Army and State Department and General Webster—but with themselves they were at peace.

Now Eileen had me scared exactly the way her mother had a little while before. I've learned to admit it when I'm scared because it takes courage to know when you ought to be afraid. I remember when I was fighting three Russians up at the Yalu. I didn't see my wingman get shot down, but all of a sudden I thought the world had gotten awful quiet and I got scared as the devil. I started to run like hell and just as the MIGs were closing in for the kill four of our planes turned up in the distance. I didn't care how bad I looked because I was scared. Point is, if I hadn't been frightened silly I wouldn't have started running and my four rescuers would never have reached me in time.

I said, "What you said last night turned up a lot of new ideas."

"You make it sound very unpleasant."

"Didn't you intend it that way? Your mother sure intends it when she gives a man hell."

She got out of her chair and said, "I don't think you want to take me to the dance tonight."

I didn't want to answer this so I said, "Some of the things you said last night made sense. We ought to think things out."

"That's fine with me. I suppose you want to do your thinking—tonight—alone?"

I said, "O.K. by me," and she started walking across the lounge. It was late in the afternoon and the place was empty, so I ran after her and said, "Eileen, what are we fighting about?"

And she replied, "The next fifty years," and she looked so cold and so much like her mother that I turned and walked away and caught a ride out to Itami air field, where I astonished everybody by reporting for duty two days early.

You could say that Itami is right in the heart of Japan, for it st nds in the triangle formed by the three great cities of the south: Kobe, Osaka and Kyoto. Actually the three are one big city, for you can travel all the way from Kobe to Osaka without ever being in the country but for some reason they've been kept apart: Osaka criss-crossed with hundreds of canals, Kobe with its big docks, and Kyoto with endless museums and temples. From Itami you can get to any of these places in a few minutes, so that a man stationed there has right at his elbow all aspects of Japanese life, if he were interested.

As soon as I got to Itami that Saturday night I felt better. I was home. Planes, neat air strips, men I knew. My work there was a dead cinch. General Webster had arranged it as a kind of present to his daughter, so I could be with her. The board I was on met a couple of times a week but the three senior members did all the work and had a bunch of us pilots in from Korea for consultation, if needed.

One of these was Lt. Bailey, the Marine who had brought the Japanese actress into the Kobe Officers Club that day. He was a real hot-shot jet man, and since we agreed on most problems the older officers were quite satisfied if we missed meetings because they never liked what we had to say. So Mike Bailey and I really had things squared away and at the end of the first week he said, "We ought to see something of Japan. I finagled it so you can move into the Marine hotel. Proved it was necessary for our consultations. And I promoted a Chevrolet." He loaded my gear into it and we set out for his quarters.

"We live six miles from the air base," he explained.

55

"Extra advantage is that we're not hooked into the Itami phones. They don't bother us much, Son, I got us really fixed up."

He drove so fast that it seemed only a couple of minutes before we came to an interesting town with narrow streets and hundreds of people wandering about. We inched our way down an alley and up a small hill to a big rambling four-story hotel.

"Marine Barracks," he said proudly. "Look at that Jap kid come to attention." A bellhop tossed Mike a snappy salute and whispered, "Seven o'clock, Makino's." Mike gave the kid 100 yen and said to me, "Finest people in the world, the Japanese."

I said, "I thought you told me you fought them at Tarawa."

"Who bears a grudge?" He told the boy to show me the room vacated by the Air Force major who had preceded me on the Board and when I got there I found I had an excellent view of the town. Below me was a wide and rocky river which cut the place in half. Up our side of the river came a railroad from Osaka but right below us it cut across to the other side and stopped at the edge of a beautiful park. There were some very large buildings facing me and, as I watched, huge crowds of people left them and started hiking toward the train.

But as I studied these people pressing toward the station I saw another crowd gathering at the rear of the buildings and into this crowd plunged a dozen young girls, arm in arm, each wearing a long green skirt that swished about her ankles.

"Hey, Bailey!" I cried. "What's this town called?"

"Takarazuka," he yelled.

"These girls in green . . ."

Mike rushed into my room and looked across the river. He grabbed me by the arm and shouted, "My God! We're missing the show."

He shoved me out the door and down the steps onto a narrow street along which we hurried to a large and handsome stone bridge bearing the sign in English, MUKO

RIVER. CARE PEDESTRIANS. With a long finger Mike pointed across the bridge and said with drooling relish, "Here they come, the pedestrians."

Then I saw them, the Takarazuka girls coming home to their dormitory after the day's performance. First came the beginning students whose job it was to crowd the back of the stage in big numbers. They were the fifteen- and sixteen-year-olds, and they walked proudly in their long green skirts and cork zori. Already they considered themselves to be Takarazuka girls. Bailey nudged me as they passed and asked, "Ever see more beautiful kids in your life?"

I had already seen these dazzling children at the rehearsal and I knew they were beautiful but as I watched them disappear into the evening twilight they seemed to drift away from me with extraordinary grace. They walked in a curious way, one foot set carefully before the other so that their long green skirts swayed noiselessly above the dusty streets. They had now passed so far from me that they were becoming haunting ghosts when Mike nudged me and said, "Watch this one! Imagine General Webster tossing her out of the Officers Club that day."

I looked across the bridge and there came the exquisite girl I had met during my visit to Takarazuka. She was accompanied by two other actresses and they formed such a gracious trio that townspeople who were attending the procession drew back against the sides of the bridge to watch them go by. As they approached us, Mike's girl kept her dark eyes straight ahead.

I asked Bailey, "Aren't you going to say hello?"

"In public?" he cried. "A Takarazuka girl! You must be nuts."

The three girls were now abreast of us and Bailey's girl, without actually turning her head, gave him ever so slight a nod, which Bailey pretended not to have seen. Then, like green shadows over some field at the end of day, the girls passed down the narrow street.

Now came a lively burst of fifteen or more, all chattering happily among themselves, all making believe they were unaware of the crowds who watched them. They were young, they were pretty, they were graceful. They wore little makeup, spoke in soft voices and kept their eyes straight ahead when the American Marines on the bridge stared at them. They were true Takarazuka girls, probably the most curious and lovely group of women in the world, and as I watched them pass in the strangely warm April twilight I was captivated by the poetic swaying of their long green skirts and the lithe, hidden movements of their beautiful bodies as they passed into darkness.

At last the principal actresses appeared, the ones famous throughout Japan, tall, stately girls whose distinguished and memorable faces advertised all kinds of products in the magazines. They moved with special authority and were besieged by mobs of young girls seeking autographs. Among these actresses I noticed several who took men's roles on stage and who now dressed like men in public. That is, they wore slacks and sweaters and berets, yet in doing so they managed to look enticingly feminine. They were subjected to special crowding and sometimes grown women would press in upon them demanding a signature across the face of a photograph purchased that day.

The formal procession of the Takarazuka goddesses was ended, but on the far end of the bridge appeared one last girl in a soft white stole, gray kimono and rippling green skirt. She had been delayed and was hurrying to overtake her friends. Her green zori tapped out a gentle rhythm as she hastened pin-toed toward us, her body leaning forward in unstated urgency. Her face was flushed and extraordinarily beautiful. She seemed more like a country girl than the others, less sophisticated in her precious green uniform and when she passed she looked at me in surprise and smiled. I saw that her face was unusually animated and that her teeth were dazzling white and even. I never saw this girl again; I never even discovered her name. She may have been only a beginner of no consequence, but as I watched her soft disappear-

ance into the spring night I felt as if I had been brushed
across the eyes by some terrible essence of beauty, something of whose existence I had never before been aware.
I desired to run after that strange, lovely girl but she was
gone forever.

Mike Bailey tugged at my arm and said, "Well, let's get
down to the restaurant."

"What restaurant?" I asked.

"Makino's," he said, and he led me through a jungle
of thin and winding streets and I felt that I had never
before really seen a Japanese town: the crowded life,
the tiny shops, the paper doors with small lights shining
through, the people in all kinds of costumes from spec-
tacular kimonos to drab business suits, the varying faces,
the multitudes of children, and the police boxes on the
corner. At times I felt like a whale swimming upstream
against a flood of minnows for I towered over the people
and no matter how far or how fast we walked the same
number of Japanese seemed to press in upon us.

We came at last to an extremely narrow alley and
ducked into a restaurant doorway hung with red and
white streamers that brushed our faces as we passed. Inside were many Japanese crowded at small tables eating
fish, which I have never liked. A Japanese woman greeted
us with three low bows, a little maid fell to her knees and
took our shoes and two powdered make-believe geishas
showed us up a flight of narrow stairs.

We entered onto a top floor where three couples sat
quietly at small tables. I keep using the words *little* and
tiny because it's a pretty powerful experience for a fellow
six-foot-two to travel in Japan. For one thing, you're
always ducking your head to keep from bashing your
brains in on door jambs and everything you see seems to
have been constructed for midgets.

In a corner, imprisoned by a quarter-circle of a rounded
table, stood a fine-looking chunky Japanese man of sixty,
watching over a charcoal stove on which bubbled a large
deep pan of fat, into which he tossed chunks of fish, swish-
ing them around with long metal chopsticks. This was

Makino-san. The après-guerre geishas told us that we
were to sit on the floor at the quarter-circle table that cut
Makino off from the rest of the room.

Mike said, "This is the best tempura restaurant in
Japan."

"What's tempura?" I asked.

"Look." He pointed to a menu painted on the wall in
Japanese and English. Makino-san had twenty-nine
varieties of fish from lobster to eel, including squid, octopus, shrimp, sardines and the excellent Japanese fish, tai.
He also served about the same number of vegetables,
especially ginko nuts, Japanese beans and shallots.

"This is living, son," Bailey cried, putting his arm about
one of the make-believe geishas, who laughed and called
him "Mike-san." The other geisha started to arrange my
dishes for the meal but Mike said, "All right, girls, beat it."
They nodded obediently and went downstairs. I must
have looked disappointed, for he said, "It's silly to keep
geishas at your table when you have a girl joining you."

"I didn't know a girl was eating with us."

"Didn't you see Fumiko-san say she'd be here?"

"The girl on the bridge?"

"Yeah. Fumiko-san. She gave me the high sign as she
passed on the Bitchi-bashi."

"What's this Bitchi-bashi?"

"*Bashi's* Japanese for bridge. We call the one where
the girls pass the Bitchi-bashi because there is so much
lovely stuff there and you can't touch the merchandise."

"Look, Mike," I said. "I don't get this special approach.
You know the girl. Why don't you just go up and ask her
for a date?"

Bailey's jaw fell and he said, "A Takarazuka girl isn't allowed to have dates."

"Why not?"

"Well, in the old days theaters had a lousy reputation in
Japan, so the railroad decided to keep Takarazuka what
you might call impeccable."

"What railroad?" I asked.

"This whole resort grew up as a place for excursion

trains from Osaka and Kyoto and Kobe. Started with a hot springs, then a zoo and finally some genius thought up these girl shows."

"You mean a railroad still runs this?"

"Sure. They don't make a nickel on the town or the theater, but they do a fabulous business on the railroad. Everybody comes out to see the show. Fifty lavish scenes, a hundred beautiful girls—gorgeous, gorgeous, gorgeous."

"And none of those girls has dates?"

"Immediate dismissal. The railroad combs Japan for these kids, spends a lot of dough training them. They've got to behave."

I considered this for a moment and asked, "But if the girls can't have dates, how come you're dating one of them?"

"Like I told President Truman, 'Harry, you was wrong when you sold the Marines short.'" He started to jab me with his long finger when he stopped suddenly, scrambled to his feet and hurried to the door. "Fumiko!" he cried with real emotion.

The delicate actress seemed entirely changed from when we had seen her shortly before on the Bitchi-bashi. Now she wore a kimono and hurried toward Mike in little running pin-toed steps that made her exquisitely charming. Her kimono was a powdery blue and at her neck at least five undergarments showed, each folded meticulously upon the next so as to form a handsome frame for her golden face. Her hair was not fixed in the antique Japanese manner but hung nearly to her shoulder, thus forming the rest of the frame for her slender and expressive face. She wore white tabi socks, white cork zori instead of shoes and an enormous sash tied in a flowing knot in back. When I rose and extended my hand she barely touched it with her own, which seemed impossibly gentle, and I was amazed at how graceful she seemed, how young.

Mike Bailey had passed the point of amazement. He was drooling and arranged her cushions and plates as if he were a French headwaiter. Then he pinched her ivory-colored cheek and said, "It's murder trying to see you, baby." She laughed at this and her voice was high and tinkling like that of a child playing with dolls.

When she sat with us the tiny restaurant seemed to thrust back its walls, our talk grew more expansive and Makino, tucked away in his corner, started to fry the fish. Mike said generously. "This American is Ace Gruver, Seven MIGs." He showed her how jets fight and when she started to admire me perhaps a little too much he tried to change the subject, but she said, "I meet Gruver-san already."

Mike did a double take and Fumiko-san laughed again. "How you like me in *Swing Butterfly?*" she asked him.

"You were wonderful!" he cried. "But I'll bet if you'd put that show on while MacArthur was here he'd have thrown you all in jail."

I asked why and Fumiko said—I can't explain how she talked or exactly what she did with English and Japanese gestures, but she made me understand—"*Swing Butterfly* make fun of American sailors who falling in love with Japanese girls. But Butterfly not commit hara-kiri." Here she grabbed a butter knife and performed the ritual. "If you like laugh, if you not too proud, you enjoy *Swing Butterfly,* I think."

"Did you like it?" I asked Mike.

"Anything this babe's in, I like," he drooled.

"What's she play?"

"I geisha," Fumiko explained. "I fight off whole shipload American sailors."

With a deft twist of her shoulders she demonstrated how she played the role and Makino and two men in the restaurant roared and suddenly I didn't like being in that little upstairs room. I didn't appreciate having a fat cook laugh at Americans. I didn't like being hidden away in a corner with a Japanese girl, no matter how pretty, who ridiculed our men. In fact, I didn't like anything I'd seen happening in Japan since General MacArthur left and I didn't want to be a part of it. I found to my surprise that I was pretty much on the side of Mrs. Webster. After all, who did win the war, anyway? I said to Mike, "You probably want to be alone. I'll blow."

He got very excited and cried, "Hey, you can't, Ace."

I stumbled awkwardly to my feet but he pulled me back down. "Ace," he said. "If any Takarazuka snoopers broke in here and caught Fumiko alone with me. Much trouble."

"What good do I do?" I grumbled.

"You are in the way," Mike admitted, "but it would be a lot easier on Fumiko if it looked like an innocent dinner for three, wouldn't it, lady?" I turned to see if Fumiko agreed and saw to my astonishment that she had turned pale and was trembling.

For at the entrance to the room stood three Takarazuka girls, tall and shatteringly beautiful. Two of them wore the Takarazuka green-skirted costume but the girl in the middle did not. She wore gray slacks, a blue-gray sweater, white shirt and tie and slate-gray cap. She was obviously disgusted at catching Fumiko-san seated with two Americans.

In three decisive steps she stood over us and spoke harshly to Fumiko-san who scrambled away in disgrace. I remember looking up at the strong face of this intruder. She was extraordinarily beautiful, yet strangely cold. I felt curiously insulted by her and cried, "Are you the boss of this outfit?" but she spoke no English and snapped at me in Japanese. Then brusquely she turned away and led Fumiko-san to a table where the four actresses ignored us.

I started to get up but Makino, the cook, grabbed my arm and translated, "She not angry. Only she say very dangerous Fumiko-san walk with Americans."

"She wasn't walking," I cried. "She was sitting here."

"Please!" Makino protested. "I not speak good. Trouble too much."

Now Mike started to join the Takarazuka girls but Makino pleaded with him, "Soon you leave Japan, Mike-san. I got to stay. Please, no trouble." He whisked away the dishes from which Fumiko-san had been eating and

Mike and I sat glumly staring at our mess of tempura. It galled me to be sitting on the floor, Japanese style, while the Takarazuka girls, by whom we had been rebuked, sat at a table, American style. I said, "Let's get out of here," but before we could leave, the leader of the girls—the one in slacks—came over, looked me gently in the eye and spoke softly.

Makino translated, "She have no English. She most sorry but Fumiko-san young girl from famous family in Japan. Suppose she get fired Takarazuka, everybody lose face."

The lovely actress looked at me beseechingly and said, in Makino's interpretation, "Very difficult to be Takarazuka girl. We got to protect one another."

She smiled at me, bowed graciously and returned to her table. I felt lots better but now Mike began to boil. "What in hell am I?" he demanded. "A man or a mouse?" He pushed Makino's restraining hand away, strode over to the table, reached down, grabbed Fumiko-san by the chin and kissed her until she had to struggle for breath. Then he bowed politely to the girl in slacks and said, "I'm mighty sorry, too. But us boys also have to protect one another."

Then we left, but at the door we looked back to see the four Takarazuka girls sitting primly on the chairs, staring at their plates.

When we got back to the barracks Mike and, "I don't blame the girls. They're under strict rules. If they get caught with an American soldier they're fired. But that snippy babe in slacks sort of got my goat."

I asked, "Why do you bother with them, if you can't date them?"

He put down his towel and looked at me in amazement. "Since when does a man have to have reasons for chasing a pretty girl?"

"But you can't even talk with her!"

"Son!" Mike cried. "Didn't you read when you was young? Didn't you stumble upon them there fairy tales?

Where the prince fights his way through the wall of fire?
The more rules they put up against you the more fun it is."

"But she's a Japanese girl."

"Drop the adjective, son. She's a girl."

"When you kissed her . . . It looked as if you could
really go for her."

"Son, when I come to any country I want to do three
things. Eat the food of that country, in this case sukiyaki
which is horrible. Drink the liquor which is also horrible.
And make love to the girls, which in the case of Fumiko-
san would be delirious."

"Even though there's no chance?"

"I hate to be stuffy about this, son, but you Air Force
men wouldn't understand. When you're a Marine there's
always a chance."

"Even with those girls?"

"Son, when I was in New Zealand in the last war, waiting to hit Tarawa, there was a pretty barmaid in town and
all the boys tried to make her. I didn't bother because
there was also a very wealthy and famous gal who lived
on a hill and you'll find as you grow older and wiser in the
ways of the world that they're the gals to go for. Because
they got everything: power, position, the mad acclaim of
the world . . ." He dragged his hand back through his
hair. "But there's one thing they ain't got—l'amour."

I started to ask why he was so sure they were lacking
l'amour but he interrupted me and said, "Same with the
Takarazuka girls. They got fame, wealth, their name in
the bright lights . . ." He started to sob and concluded,
"But it's all like ashes because they ain't got l'amour. And
you watch, son! Takarazuka girls ain't none different from
that there gal in old New Zealand. And I'm the guy who
can bring l'amour into even the drabbest life."

We went down to the shower room and while Mike was
yammering away I had the stifling premonition that I
ought to get out of Japan. When we returned to the hall
Mike headed for his own room but I said, "Come on in
a second," and we talked for a long time. I said, "I had the

strangest feeling just now. I wanted to get out of Japan. I was scared, I think." I started to tell him about my bad luck with Eileen and he interrupted.

"Don't tell me! The general's wife started to throw her hooks into you. I sized her up when she tossed a girl like Fumiko-san out of her third-rate club . . ." He shook my hand warmly and said, "Son, when you escaped Mrs. General Webster, you escaped horrors worse than death."

"But I didn't want to escape," I said. "I wanted to marry Eileen and have a wife I could be proud of and a home somewhere and a good life in the Air Force. Everything was arranged and I liked it all."

"So now what?"

"I had the craziest feeling, Mike, that I was back in St. Leonard's."

"Where's that?"

"Prep school. I went to St. Leonard's. I was all set to take the exams for West Point, but there was a teacher there who loved English literature and he got me a part in the school play. It was by a Hungarian called Molnar, and all of a sudden I didn't want to go to West Point. I didn't want any part of it and my mother, who's written a couple of damned fine stories for the *Atlantic*, came to school and said, 'We've always expected you would go to the Point, like your father and his father.' I said, 'Suddenly I feel as if I'd had a vision of a completely different world.' At that she started to cry and talked pretty incoherently, but what I got was that if you ever once experienced that vision don't let anything stop you. She wouldn't come right out and say I shouldn't go to the Point, because her own father went there and became a pretty famous general. But I could see that that's what she meant.

"For the next two weeks I went through hell. Everybody at the school was just swell. They didn't rave at me and say I was ruining my life if I gave up the appointment to West Point, and the English teacher wouldn't say that if I did go to the Point I was selling out. But then Father flew up from Texas and he was like a breath of sea air in a Kansas drought."

"He put you straight, eh?"

"No. Father never rants."

"He's a general isn't he? Then he rants."

"You Marines get the wrong idea sometimes. Just because a couple of generals fouled up Koje-do, you take it for granted all Army generals are horses' necks."

"Right animal, wrong anatomy."

"If you ever meet my father you'll meet the man who justifies having generals. He looked at me that day and said, 'If you don't want to go to the Point, Lloyd, don't. Unhappiest men I know are those who've been forced into something they have no inner aptitude for.'"

"That was a noble start," Mike said, "but what did he use for the clincher?"

"What do you mean?"

"How did he apply the screws? How did he force you to go to the Point?"

"He didn't. We just talked and he flew back to Texas and I went on to the Point. And up to this very night I've never once been sorry. But tonight that old sick feeling came over me and I had the distinct impression that maybe I didn't want to stay in the Air Force and buck for a star. Maybe I didn't want to marry Eileen and mess around with her silly old man and cantankerous mother." I put my hand against my forehead and said, "Maybe I felt my whole world crumbling under me."

Mike grew serious and said, "Boy, do I know! I watched my old man go through the depression. I watched a world really crumble. That's why I don't put much stock in the permanent security of worlds—of any kind. But what hit you? You don't just decide a thing like that for the hell of it."

"Well . . . I'm almost ashamed to tell you what hit me."

Mike had a very quick mind and he said loudly, "Fumiko-san! You took a good look at Fumiko-san close up.

Well, son, she'd put anyone off his rocker—anyone, that is, but an old hand at l'amour like me."

I laughed and said, "I wish it were so simple. I could duel you for Fumiko-san in F-86's at 40,000 feet. But the other day I was best man at a marriage between a G.I. and a Japanese girl. Boy, she was no Fumiko-san, but she impressed me powerfully. Like a chunk of earth in the middle of a cheese soufflé. And tonight, seeing that other part of Japan I wondered . . ." Suddenly I clammed up and couldn't say it.

"You wondered what?" Mike asked. "You certainly don't want to snatch the enlisted man's wife."

"This sounds silly but I flew down here ready to marry Eileen. When she and I started to hesitate about that, I started to wonder about everything else—even about staying in the Air Force. I know it's ridiculous but that G.I. and his dumpy Japanese girl . . ."

Mike stared at me in slack-jawed horror and asked in a hushed voice, "You mean you're ponderin' life?" He mussed his hair down over his eyes and sobbed, "Oh, what does it all mean—the eternal struggle—sex—the New York Yankees!"

"All right, louse it up. But suddenly I felt as if I were in a world of swirling darkness where the only reality was this earth—this earth of Japan."

"My God!" Mike cried, clutching his head. "A new Sigmund Freud!"

I had to laugh, and while Mike phoned down for some cold beer I asked, "Don't you ever get crazy ideas like that?"

"A million of 'em. They never hurt anybody."

"But to have an idea like that suddenly bust open your whole world . . . I thought I was back in prep school again."

"I think it's easy to explain," Mike said after his second bottle of beer, which gave him added authority. "You've been fighting like crazy up in Korea and you get this big idea about comin' down to Japan and getting married . . ."

"She didn't even tell me she was coming to Japan."

"Don't let details mess up my theory. Then when you see the battle-axe her mother is . . ."

"She's not really a battle-axe."

"Who threw me out of the Club with Fumiko-san?" The question awakened all of Mike's animosities and launched him into a tirade against generals' wives and he never did finish his explanation.

But next night we were at the Bitchi-bashi watching the stately procession of Takarazuka girls as they approached us through the evening dusk to vanish into the deep shadows. I was deeply moved by the passage of these quiet figures and they appeared to me as members of a military group dedicated to their rituals and promotions the way I was tied to mine. They lived and acted with a sense of their military responsibility while I was conditioned by the rules of my army. They were not free and I was not free, for I believe that no man who flies a plane against the enemy or steers a ship into enemy waters is a free man. He is bound by certain convictions and restraints that other men never know.

I was pondering this when Fumiko-san came by. She was accompanied by the actress in men's clothes who had reprimanded us the night before and when the bobby soxers on the Bitchi-bashi saw this tall girl they made a wild dash to surround her and demand autographs. The actress coolly shoved them away but other little girls took their places.

I said to Mike, "She must be somebody."

He asked a Japanese girl who the actress was and the girl broke into horribly confused giggles. She did, however, summon another girl—she couldn't have been more than fourteen—who spoke English and this child said, "She—is—Hana-ogi-san. Number one girl!"

I repeated the name and some children near me, giggling furiously, began to chant "Hana-ogi-san!" and the beautiful actress stopped for a moment on the bridge and looked our way. Mike bowed very low and blew a kiss off his thumb to Fumiko-san but both actresses ignored him and resumed their way into the night shadows.

I had to miss the Monday night procession at the Bitchi-bashi because General Webster sent a message ordering me in to Kobe to report on how my work was going. I know what he really wanted was to ask me why I hadn't been around the Club. No doubt Mrs. Webster had commanded him to find out and I wondered what I would tell him. It was difficult for me to explain even to myself.

It had something to do with the fun of living with a gang of men that you can never explain. The relaxation, the freedom of running down the hall in your shorts, the common interests in a common problem. I remember how my father used to glow when he came in from a six-day exercise with his foot troops. I was a kid then but there was something enormously real and rugged about my father on those occasions. True, he was a fine man about the house—I think a good many other families, mothers and kids alike, would have been glad to have a father like mine—but there were times when he insisted upon living in a man's world and I think that much of his resolute determination to follow the camp fires rather than the bridge parties had been deeply ingrained in me. I had always liked aviation meetings like the ones at Itami. I liked evenings in Bachelor Officers' Quarters. I liked going with Mike to the little fish restaurant. And I liked getting a gang together on the spur of the moment, racing through the dark Japanese night and winding up at some American movie in Osaka or Kyoto. Most of all I enjoyed working at the air strip when somebody I knew in Korea boomed in with the latest hot scoop.

For example, one day a big Swede who flew an Air Force C-47 as a taxicab from one Korean air base to the next arrived in Itami and we had a long night of laughing about some of our experiences in that dismal country. I especially remembered the time he was ferrying a bunch of us into Seoul on a rainy day. The cloud cover was broken and there were only about five holes through which you could descend to the island in the middle of the river where the air strip was. We got tied up behind a Marine pilot who had never flown into Seoul before and he was being extra cautious. He missed the first hole through the clouds, he missed the second and damned if he didn't miss the third. The Swede piloting our plane began to get irritated and he shouted to the tower, "For Christ sake, tell junior to land that kite." When we landed the Marine was waiting for us and demanded to know who had called him junior. We looked among us to see who was tallest and a six-foot-four Air Force man stepped forward and said, "I called you junior. You were screwing up the procession." The Marine looked up at the big man and said, "I'm new around here. I was looking for the island." The real big man said, "I'm glad you found it cause we damned near ran out of gas." I started to laugh and for a minute it looked like a fight and all the rest of the time we were in Korea whenever we saw a Marine plane some wise guy would yell, "There goes junior." I told Mike Bailey about this but he didn't think it funny. Living with these pilots again I honestly did not want to go into Kobe and sit around a fancy officers club and try to explain to Mrs. Webster why I wasn't courting her daughter.

But that's what I had to do. In his office the general asked me a lot of trivial questions he couldn't possibly have been interested in and then led me down to the Cadillac. At dinner I looked for Eileen but he said she was in Kyoto visiting a museum and wouldn't be able to join us. I looked at Mrs. Webster eating her shrimp cocktail and lost my appetite.

It was a chilly meal and after dessert the general excused himself to do some paper work and I observed silently, "If my father ever becomes Chief-of-Staff I'll warn him not to put Mark Webster in charge of intelligence, because he sure telegraphs his hand."

Mrs. Webster didn't bother to telegraph hers. When we got to her apartment she asked bluntly, "What's wrong between you and Eileen?"

"I'm sure she must have told you."

"Lloyd, don't be evasive. You haven't seen her in more than a week."

It was obvious that this was one time when I'd better stick to the truth. I said, "We had a quarrel. She told me . . ."

"A quarrel? Whatever about?"

I gulped and said, "She's afraid I'm too much like my father." Mrs. Webster started at my honesty but made no move to stop me so I finished. "And I think she's—too bossy." There was something in the inflection of this sentence that betrayed clearly the fact that I thought Eileen was too damned much like her mother. But Mrs. Webster never batted an eye.

So I added, "And then I've been working."

"Ridiculous," she snapped. "Mark found you this job because there wasn't any work attached to it."

"If that's why I got it . . ." I began with standard dignity.

". . . you'd sooner be back in Korea?" she concluded.

"Yes."

"Lloyd, don't be silly. It's obvious to everyone in Kobe that you are an extremely brave young man whom General Webster brought back to Japan so that you could be with Eileen. There's nothing dishonest about that—if you plan to get married."

"We planned that for a long time—sort of."

"How do people get married—sort of?" She was sitting on an expensive lounge purchased in Paris and she leaned forward, repeating the offensive words: "Sort of?"

"I mean there's nothing definite. Has Eileen said there was anything definite?"

"Of course she hasn't. She hasn't talked with me about this but I can see how humiliating it is for her. The whole hotel . . ."

I knew Eileen pretty well and I was sure she didn't

give a hoot what the hotel thought. But Mrs. Webster did because if we didn't get married it would make her look ridiculous. I said, "We wonder if we're the right people for each other."

"At this stage? Why, you've known Eileen for years. Same backgrounds. I don't see . . ."

"But that's what Eileen said when she started this fight . . ."

"A fight! Lloyd, this is just a lovers' quarrel and it has no more significance than that."

"Maybe it didn't at the start but Eileen's questions and some of the thinking I've done made me wonder if perhaps my whole idea of life isn't wrong."

Now I had struck something serious and Mrs. Webster accepted it so. She spoke very deliberately and at the same time fidgeted nervously with a lace handkerchief. She said, "If an Army man ever questions the big idea of military service he's lost. Believe me, Lloyd, I've seen it many times and it's the worst thing that can happen to you. From your baby days you were cut out for the service. You've never known anything else."

I could have contradicted her and said that for two weeks—a long time ago—I had imagined another way of life but that would have raised too many questions which I couldn't have answered. It was one thing to confide such a secret to an easy-going mind like Mike Bailey's. It was quite different to give the idea away to Mrs. Webster. In three questions she'd have you undressed and you'd stand there naked to the world, just as stupid and silly as you were back at St. Leonard's.

I said, "Wouldn't it be better all around if your husband sent me back to my outfit?"

"In Korea?"

"Yes. That would settle my doubts."

To my surprise, she agreed. "It does seem better now. But it would be wrong for two reasons. It would make Eileen seem ridiculous. Couldn't hold her man. And it would be the cowardly thing for you to do."

"Eileen doesn't need me," I said.

"You're absolutely right, Lloyd. She's asked to parties every night. But not by Army men. By civilians in Army suits. Suppose she falls in love with one of these civilians? She'll settle down as a druggist's wife in Chicago and that's not for Eileen, believe me."

I found Mrs. Webster a lot too tough for an airman twenty-eight years old to handle. I said, "I'll drop in and say good night to the general."

But this woman kept hold of you like a steel trap. She said, "And there's a third reason why going back to Korea would be wrong. Because you would be running away from your fundamental problem."

I wanted to shout, "What I want to run away from is you. I'm running away from your daughter because she's so much like you." But a man can shoot down Russians and still be afraid to shoot down his commanding officer's wife. I said, "I'll call Eileen tomorrow."

She said, "Good. I know Eileen and I know she wants to marry you. Don't let lovers' quarrels keep you apart. That would be foolish." She tucked the handkerchief into her sleeve and added with powerful emphasis, "And don't let a temporary uncertainty tease you into thinking you've made a mistake on your whole life. You're an Army man, Lloyd. You were bred to it."

I found General Webster in a workroom lined with books. He indicated them with a wide sweep of his hand and said, "The colonel who had this suite three years ago got these books together. Practically any subject you might be interested in."

I said, "I suppose you know what Mrs. Webster and I were talking about. I think it would be better all around if you sent me back to Korea."

The general drummed his fingers and said, "Better, maybe, but it would be so damned obvious. That's what's wrong with military life. Every move can be so easily interpreted by the enemy. But damn it all, Lloyd, what's wrong between you and Eileen?"

"Nothing's wrong, sir. It's just that we both feel uncertain about our getting along—ultimately."

"Very sensible." He poured me a stiff drink and said, "You're not much of a man unless you're scared silly by the prospect of marriage. Take me. Night before my wedding your father had to get me blind drunk to keep me from sending a Western Union messenger to my wife's house. . . . Father was Colonel Keller—got into that serious scrape with the Persian Ambassador. They called it Persia then."

He related in his rambling way the case histories of half a dozen military marriages and of how all the men at some time before the wedding or after had wanted to funk out on the deal. "But in the long run," he assured me, "marriage is the best thing for any man. It was the making of me. And j'your father ever tell you about his classic wedding? He was engaged to your mother, Lieutenant-General Himmelwright's daughter, and two days before the wedding he fell in love with another girl. Just about went mad from indecision. But suppose he had gone off his rocker and said he wasn't cut out to be a general. By God, twenty years later America might of lost Guadalcanal."

He poured us a couple of more drinks and said, "Look at it this way, Lloyd. What the hell were you put in this world for? Be one of those washed-up old fuddies with no home of his own, sitting in a club somewhere yakkity-yakking about China?"

I guess the whiskey made me brave, for I said, "Ask Eileen if she'll have dinner with me tomorrow."

"Good boy!" the general cried, whamming me on the back. "I ordered my wife not to speak to you on such a subject. Humiliating to Eileen and all that. But Nancy said there came a time in every girl's love life . . . Isn't that a horrible word?"

"I'll call Eileen about twelve," I said.

General Webster tossed off an extra one and said, "I feel ten years younger. If you have children, Lloyd, have boys."

As I went down in the elevator I saw a new sign which read, "Officers of this command will not appear on the streets of Kobe walking with girls of the indigenous personnel. This order also applies to officers when on the streets of Osaka and Kyoto. Signed, Mark Webster, Commanding." I thought, "Oh, boy! The general's wife is really determined to clean up all Japan," and then I got to laughing because here the American Army was forbidding its men to be seen with Japanese girls, while the Takarazuka army was forbidding its girls to be seen with American men.

I was still chuckling when the elevator doors opened and I heard my name. It was Pvt. Joe Kelly, wearing a service revolver as big as a cannon. He yelled, "At last the Air Force gave me a break. Transferred me to the Joint Message Center. I got the best job in Osaka." He waited for an officer to sign a receipt for important mail, then joined me. His Ford was at the curb.

"Where can I drop you?" he asked, unstrapping his artillery.

"Look, I work at Itami."

"So what's the difference to me. The Army pays for the gasoline."

"And I live at Takarazuka."

"I'll go that way."

We piled in and he reported on how things were going with him and Katsumi. "We found a nice house. . . . Say, Ace! It's early. Why not drive into Osaka and visit with us?"

He was so energetic and I was so interested in him in the way I had explained to Mike that I agreed. He barreled the Ford along the Kobe-Osaka road and I tried to observe exactly what this ancient and historic Japanese road was like. I saw the little paper-windowed houses stretching mile after mile, with never a sign of countryside. I saw the open-front stores that did business all night and the thousands of people moving along the road in the twilight and of how a single lamp lit in any of the houses seemed to light up the whole section of road near it.

But pretty soon I stopped thinking about Japan and asked, "How fast you driving, Joe?"

"Sixty-eight," he reported.

"Don't the M.P.'s ever pinch you for flying so low?"

"They all know me."

"I'll bet they do."

"First thing I did was invite 'em over to the house and Katsumi fed 'em special grub." He waited till a prowl car came along. Then he leaned way out and shouted some Japanese insults at the M.P. and everybody roared and Joe said, "Great bunch."

As we entered Osaka he bore to the south until we came to a road which dropped down beside one of the numerous canals. Soon it petered out and four Japanese kids assumed guard over the Ford while we hiked up a narrow alley down which two men trudged with wicker baskets of enormous size. As they passed each house light from the paper doors shone on them for a moment creating an impression of deep warmth.

At the far end of the alley stood an inconspicuous one-storied shack made of wood long since weatherstained to a blackish gray. The porch was outlined by concrete blocks which confined the center of packed earth. The roof was of orange tile, laid in Chinese fashion with a slight swoop upward at each end. In the States we would not have called this a house at all. With its sliding paper doors it would have been a shed, and cows or farm tools would have been kept there, but when Joe slid his doors back, there was Katsumi in a kimono, cooking the evening meal. Promptly she took my shoes and offered me a cup of bitter green tea and said in lovely, stilted English, "It is fine to see you among us tonight."

"She's been takin' English lessons," Joe said proudly, "and I study a little Japanese." He rattled off a few phrases and Katsumi beamed at him as if he had written an encyclopedia.

"It's nice here, Ace," Joe said expansively. "Two rooms, the canal down there, a good job and good food. Ace, I'm livin'. For the first time in my life I feel like a human bein'."

He showed me where to put my shoes and how to prop myself up with pillows as we sat on the tatami mats. He said, "I grew up in an orphanage but I was sort of adopted by a family. They found me disappointin' and deserted me—not that I blame 'em, I was a stinker—so I went back to the orphanage and then to reform school. I tried to enlist in the Army for the last war but they trapped me into tellin' my real age and I wound up in Chicago and then the Air Force. Now I'm a family man." He looked at Katsumi with glowing approval and asked, "Notice the big change, Ace?"

"I like the kimono," I said, for Katsumi was one of those ordinary Japanese girls who in flowing kimonos become almost attractive.

"It ain't the kimono, Ace. Watch her smile!" In Japanese he commanded his wife to smile but when she did so I still didn't catch on, so Joe cried, "The tooth, Ace! The tooth!" Then I saw. The big gold tooth had been removed and in its place some Army dentist had fitted a trim porcelain crown. Katsumi really did look attractive in kimono and tooth.

"It's a reformation," I said.

"It's a miracle," Joe sighed. "And she don't giggle no more, do you, Babe?" He dragged Katsumi toward him and kissed her on the cheek. "Because I told her that if she ever giggled again and stuffed her fist in her mouth I'd break her arm off at the wrist." He gave Katsumi a solid wallop on the bottom and she giggled like mad, stuffing her hand into her mouth.

"Sometimes she forgets, Ace, but this is livin'."

He explained to his wife that I bunked at Takarazuka and she spoke in rapid Japanese which he interpreted for me: "A hell of a fine idea, Ace. We're goin' to Takarazuka tomorrow to see the new show. Join us."

"I'd like to, but I have a dinner date in Kobe."

"So what! Show's over by six and I'll race you right in to Kobe, no stops." He pulled an imaginary cord and made like a train whistle. "It's a deal, Ace, because with Katsumi you'll really enjoy it. She knows all the actresses and can tell you what's goin' on."

He gave Katsumi a command in Japanese and she went to a chest where she kept her prized possessions, appearing shortly with a magazine in bright covers. It started at the back, the way Jap books do, and she showed me the photograph of a dazzling stage set. I asked what the magazine was.

"Fan magazine for the Takarazuka shows," Joe explained. "She subscribes to three of them." He shuffled a pile of colorful magazines and I could tell from the devoted way in which Katsumi put them back in order that she had once been one of the enchanted girls who stood each night by the bridge to watch the great stars pass. Now she had become the typical housewife who still treasured autographs of the leading actresses.

"I suppose she belongs to a fan club," I joked.

"Don't kid!" He spoke in Japanese again and Katsumi returned to the chest from which she handed me a stack of photographs. Apparently they went far back in time to when Katsumi had been a child. I asked, "Does she have the pictures of the girls who were in last month's show?"

Katsumi immediately shuffled through the pictures and assembled the entire cast of principals and explained what each did. She even sang two of the songs and I asked, "Does she know all the shows as well as this one?"

Joe patted her arm affectionately and said, "She never misses one. Hasn't for years."

"Then it's a date for tomorrow. But you promise to get me back to Kobe for dinner."

He didn't have to because when I called Eileen next day she played hard-to-get and told me abruptly. "I'm having dinner with a Marine." I said, "That's too bad, how about Friday?" and she said Friday was booked too, so I said, "Boy, I'm playing in tough luck. I'll call you later." But neither of us would have bet much money on when that later would be.

Actually, when I went to the theater that afternoon I was rather relieved. It seemed to me that Eileen and I were pretty well washed up and I didn't have to worry any more about Mrs. Webster. I said to Joe, "I'm sort of steamed up to see this show," but I was hardly prepared for what Takarazuka did to *Madame Butterfly*. At any moment they might run in a scene unconnected with anything that had gone before or would come after. There were old Japanese dances to please the classical fans, jitterbugging to represent 1890 America, wrestling, microphones, a dance hall sequence, mutiny aboard an American ship, twenty stupid Japanese cops and a fire.

But running through this burlesque of a great opera there was one solid thread: ridicule of American military men. I have to admit that Mike Bailey's girl, Fumiko-san, was terrific as a ravishing geisha holding the American fleet at bay. Her fine long face and expressive movements made her hilarious when wrestling with a drunk G.I. on leave in Tokyo. There was nothing really offensive with her pantomime but you felt that all the Japanese in the audience were egging her on because they had had a bellyful of Americans.

But the star's performance was quite different. The girl in slacks who had reprimanded us in the restaurant played this part and her Lieutenant Pinkerton was blatantly ridiculous. He was arrogant, ignorant and ill-mannered. Yet at the same time the actress herself seemed more essentially feminine than any of the other girls on stage and it was this that made her version of Pinkerton so devastating. She was all Japanese women making fun of all American men.

One act of such petty nonsense was enough for me. I

80

didn't think I was stuffy, but I couldn't tolerate people making cheap fun of men in uniform, and when the people doing the burlesque were Japanese I drew the line. When the Act I curtain fell I got up to go, but Katsumi put her hand on mine and said, "No, no! Now is the best!"

From a side entrance the star appeared dressed in old-style samurai costume, pursued by two villains. They attacked her, and in the highly ritualistic dance which followed I for the first time fell under the spell of Japanese art.

I cannot tell you what there was about this dance that captivated me. It might have been the haunting music, for now the Western instruments like violins and oboes were silent and in their place were three horribly weird sounds: the hammering of a slack-headed drum, the clicking of wooden blocks thumped together, and the piercing wail of an Asiatic flute. Or it might have been the dazzling curtain before which she danced, a vast gold-and-blue-and-red affair with eight gigantic embroidered irises standing in solemn Oriental perfection. But mostly it was this remarkable woman I had seen in the restaurant, this Hana-ogi. She wore no shoes, only white tabi drawn tightly about her feet and it was principally her feet that impressed me. She used them as a very great athlete might and slowly I became aware that I was watching one of the greatest dancers in the world. Silently, in the Japanese manner, she wove back and forth between her assailants. Instead of a sword she used the traditional symbol, her right hand held vividly upright, and as I watched this hand it traced a wonderful pattern against the gold curtain. I had never before seen a dancer like this, one who could fill an entire stage with her authority.

The scene came to a frenzied close with Hana-ogi stamping an unforgettable rhythm and weaving that bright hand through the darkness. The crowd burst into applause and I whispered to Kelly, "Tell Katsumi I'd like to meet that girl."

To my surprise Kelly said, "That's easy. Katsumi knows

'em all." But when he spoke to his wife she became grave and Joe reported, "Katsumi says that your particular girl wouldn't speak to an American."

"Why not?"

"We hung her brother as a war criminal. Killed her father with our bombs."

I sat back in my seat and, strange as it may seem, felt exactly the same kind of relief I did when I heard that Eileen couldn't have dinner with me. I had the distinct sensation that I was back in St. Leonard's engulfed in important decisions that I simply couldn't make. At that moment I desperately wanted to be in a jet plane rousting about up around the Yalu. Up there I felt safe and here in Japan I felt dreadfully loused up. As if I were coming back to earth from another world I looked at Joe and thought, "Jesus! What am I doing? Lloyd Gruver, West Point '44, propositioning an enlisted man to arrange a date with a Japanese girl!" I said to Joe, "Let's get some air."

Joe said, "Why not? We'll blow and Katsumi can come home by train."

Right there I could have avoided all that followed, but I cried, "No! I didn't mean that. I want to see the rest." Then I asked, "How does Katsumi happen to know an actress like that?"

Joe laughed and grabbed his wife's handbag, rummaging through it till he found half a dozen pictures. They were all of the dancer, showing her in some of her famous roles. She was a Spanish bullfighter, Venetian gondolier, a Broadway playboy and a Japanese samurai. She was always the man and she always looked devastatingly feminine.

Joe explained, "Katsumi organized a fan club. Osaka girls who idolized Hana-ogi."

"What's her last name?"

Joe asked Katsumi and said, "Just Hana-ogi. It's a stage name. My wife is crazy about her. Until Katsumi married me she was a real moron. Used to stand in the rain to see her goddess."

"But why?"

"Look, Ace. Suppose you were fat and dumpy and had to work like a slave all day. Then there's this tall, slim, beautiful girl who's famous all over the country and makes a lot of dough. One actress like Hana-ogi proves what a girl can become. If you ever break into our house you steal the pots and pans but don't steal these photographs. Katsumi worships them."

Katsumi understood our conversation but said nothing. Quietly she recovered the photographs, restored them to some preferred order and replaced them in her bag. Then she explained in broken English the story of Act II, which she read from one of the magazines which Takarazuka mailed out to its faithful patrons. It contained a large picture section, which I leafed through. I saw some sixty excellent photographs of the Takarazuka girls off stage. They were knitting, or skiing, or promenading, or going to a symphony concert, or strolling. Gradually I began to notice a curious pattern. Always the girls were in pairs or larger groups. Never were they alone and never with men. The photographs portrayed a rich and successful and celibate world and I recalled Mike's insistence that a wise man always looks for love in that kind of world, because, as Mike so eloquently pointed out, such women have everything but l'amour. I felt this especially when I saw the three photographs of Mike's Fumiko-san. She was perhaps the most striking of the Takarazuka girls, for she wore her clothes with dazzling effect and her pictures were additionally interesting to me because in each of her photographs she was standing with Hana-ogi, the star of today's performance, and Hana-ogi invariably wore men's clothing—yet it was Hana-ogi who looked the more feminine and desirable.

Act II was an amazing experience, for Hana-ogi proved that she was much more than a mere dancer. She had a fine clear singing voice, striking power for dramatic scenes and a wanton comic sense. I leaned across Katsumi and asked, "Joe! Do you think this girl could get by in

New York?" He whispered back, "I never been to New
York."

But Katsumi heard my question and she realized even
before I did that I was determined to meet Hana-ogi that
day, so in the darkness she touched my hand and said,
"After, we go on flower walk. I speak you to Hana-ogi-
san."

When the final curtain fell on *Butterfly* I started to
leave but again Katsumi whispered, "No, Ace-san. Now
everybody so beautiful." Quickly the curtain opened and
there was the entire cast of 120 standing in glorious
kimonos, singing a farewell song. A runway reached out
into the audience and the stars came down and posed
right above us. Our seats were such that Hana-ogi stood
very near me and for the first time I saw her in woman's
clothes. She was adorable. True, she was also proud and
combative, nervously excited at the end of an extremely
long performance. But above all else she was adorable
in her triumphant moment. Her kimono, I remember, was
green and white.

Katsumi now led me through the crowd and we came
to the flower walk and the tiny little gate through which
the Takarazuka girls passed on their way to the Bitchi-
bashi. A large crowd had assembled to applaud them as
they appeared and dozens of round-faced little girls
pressed tight against the gate, hoping to touch the great
actresses, and as I looked at the girls it seemed incredible
that any of these pudgy figures might one day grow up to
replace Fumiko-san or Hana-ogi.

Now the lesser Takarazuka girls appeared, then
Fumiko-san and the dancers in green skirts and leather
zori. At last the leading actresses came through the gate as
the crowd pressed in upon them and above the clamoring
heads I saw cool Hana-ogi. We looked at each other cau-
tiously, as if testing to see if either had been offended,
then slowly she moved toward me through the great press
of people and I think my mouth fell open slightly, for on
this day, fresh from triumph, she was a glorious woman.

Katsumi broke the spell by catching Hana-ogi's hands

and gabbling away in Japanese. Finally she said to me, "Hana-ogi-san hope you like her play." The tall actress looked at me over Katsumi's shoulder and I replied quietly, "I liked the play but not the American sailors."

Katsumi reported this and Hana-ogi blushed and said something which Katsumi was reluctant to translate. "Go ahead!" Joe insisted.

"Hana-ogi-san say Americans to be funny. Not bad." She pressed her hands into her stomach and indicated laughter.

"It wasn't funny," I said. Hana-ogi caught my meaning and frowned, so I added quickly, "But Hana-ogi-san's dancing was wonderful." I imitated her fight with the villains and she smiled.

Hana-ogi's other fans now pressed in upon us and I said awkwardly, "Why don't we four have dinner?" But when Katsumi translated this, Hana-ogi grew very angry, said something harsh and passed abruptly down the flower walk.

I now entered upon a week of dream sequences. The Korean fighting must have exhausted me more than I knew, for my sudden relaxation on the make-believe job at Itami permitted my nerves to find their own level. It wasn't high and I felt as I had once at the Point when we were about to play Navy and I was certain I would louse up the works. At other times I imagined I was back in St. Leonard's totally confused about whether or not I wanted to attend the Point.

Sometimes at night I would wake with a start and believe myself to be in a falling jet fighter up at the Yalu River, and I would struggle to regain control both of the plane and of myself. Then, as I lay in the dark Japanese night I would see hurrying across my midnight wall that lone, exquisitely lovely Takarazuka girl I had seen on the Bitchi-bashi that first day and I would try to hurry after her and find her name.

But in all these imaginings I was kidding myself and I knew it. For inevitably I would think of Hana-ogi-san and I would see her dancing and I would follow the sub-

tle curves of her adorable body and I would see her oval
face smiling at me, ever so small a Japanese smile, and
I would wonder how a man could be so tossed about by
the mere idea of a girl. I had not really spoken to her. I
knew nothing of her character or her personality, but
almost willingly I was hypnotizing myself over this
strange girl. Much later I would recognize that I was
creating for myself the image of love and that without
this image a man could well live an entire and empty life.

So each evening I fed my delirium by standing at the
Bitchi-bashi to watch Hana-ogi pass by and if, during the
preceding hours, I had by chance begun to question
whether she really was as lovely as I imagined, one sight
of her dispelled that heresy. She was even more desirable.
On Friday I returned to see *Swing Butterfly* and at the
final promenade I applauded so loudly that Hana-ogi had
to look at me, but she betrayed nothing and looked quickly away. Saturday night I was really jittery and Mike
Bailey dragged me along on another secret date he had
with Fumiko-san and I spent most of the evening questioning her about the Takarazuka girls, hoping that she
would speak of Hana-ogi.

Fumiko-san said, "My father famous man but he kill
himself when Japanese surrender. No money no hope for
me. I read in paper Takarazuka seek new girls. I brush
my hair each night, study dance, shout with my voice.
I chosen and one year I work ten hours each day and
think this my one chance. Supervisor like me and I go
Moon Troupe with Hana-ogi-san. She kind to me and I
act parts good. I live dormitory with other girls but best
time when Moon Troupe go Tokyo."

I said, "You in love with someone in Tokyo?"

"Love? How I love someone?"

"Aren't you going to get married?"

She looked at me quizzically. "I Takarazuka girl. What
else could I want be?"

Her answer so amazed me that I did an impulsive thing
which astonished me as much as it did Fumiko-san. I took
her hands in mine and said quietly, "Tonight, when you

go back to the dormitory you must speak with Hana-ogi-san. Tell her that I am in love with her and must see her."

Fumiko-san withdrew her hands and said in dismay, "Never hoppen! Hana-ogi-san never speak men. And with American! Never hoppen!"

"You tell her," I repeated, for I was convinced that no one could dance as passionately as Hana-ogi without knowing the outlines and purpose of love. I knew that she could not refuse to see me.

The next afternoon Joe Kelly drove out to Itami and said abruptly, "Wife says you're to be at our house for supper at seven."

"I can't make . . ."

"Be there, Ace," the sawed-off squirt said ominously.

"I've already . . ."

"Be there, Bub. Hana-ogi's comin'."

I cannot remember how, exactly, I got to Joe Kelly's
house that night, but when I finally turned up the alley
from the canal, when at last I saw the little wooden building and the sliding paper doors my heart was hammering
like thunder. I slammed the doors aside and rushed in
expecting to see Hana-ogi standing there. Instead Joe
and Katsumi were horsing around and cooking food.
They told me to sit on the floor and from that position I
watched this couple in love and it occurred to me that I
myself had never lived in a house where love was. My
parents loved each other in the required way and I am
quite sure that General and Mrs. Webster loved each
other, but it was always love for some ultimate purpose:
army advancement, social position in Lancaster, children.
Here I was visiting the house of love itself.

"Joe," I asked as we waited for Hana-ogi, "what was it
you told me in Korea? American husbands talk about
country clubs and getting junior's teeth fixed?"

"Yeah, but if they're married to Japanese girls they
talk about love."

"Suppose you went back to the front now . . ."

"God fabbid."

"What would you talk about?"

Joe held Katsumi off at arm's length and said, "Topic
for tonight. Ace, I fought to get this baby and I'm satisfied with what I got." Then he spoke to her in Japanese
and she burst into an uncontrolled giggle. She started to
jam her hand into her mouth but Joe gave it a terrific
belt and said, "Honest to God, Ace, it's easier to train
a dog."

As he said this the door opened and Hana-ogi entered.
Softly and with infinite grace she slid the doors closed

88

behind her and slipped out of her zori. She was dressed
in a gray-blue kimono and her hair was rumpled. She
stood so silently that Joe and Katzumi did not realize
she was there; so while their backs were still turned I
stumbled awkwardly to my knees and started toward
her, finally gaining my feet. She laughed at my discom-
fort and the sound of her voice was so gentle that I was
compelled to reach down and take her hands to my lips
and try to kiss them, but as I did so she instinctively
pulled them away and I noticed with indescribable emotion that they were a decided ivory. I stood aside to let
her pass and said, "I am so glad you came." She did not
understand my words but even so she nodded in ac-
knowledgment and I thought that she was less irritated
than she had been when I tried to kiss her hand—and
for my part I knew that she was twice as beautiful as I
had ever seen her on the stage when she was dressed in
men's clothes.

Katzumi now hurried forward and embraced the actress while Joe greeted her in broken Japanese, at which
she laughed heartily, and I got the distinct impression
that she was not at all the remote glamorous girl I had
stared at on the Bitchi-bashi, for her gentle good humor
was exactly what you would expect from a good, happy
country girl working in the city.

But I had seen only two aspects of Hana-ogi and she
was infinite, for when I asked Katzumi what her last name
was and when Katzumi blushed and said she wouldn't
dare ask that question I insisted, and when Hana-ogi
heard Katzumi translate she grew extremely angry. I
couldn't understand what was happening but Katzumi,
blushing a fiery red which showed through her yellow
cheeks, said, "Takarazuka girl never tell her real name."

"What do you mean, her real name?"

"Her name not Hana-ogi. Only stage name."

"What is her real name?" I insisted.

Katzumi spoke to the actress and the only word I understood was America and Hana-ogi grew very solemn

and spoke harshly, after which Katsumi said, "She will not say her name. Even I don't know that."

Joe interrupted and said, "That's the way with all professional girls in Japan—geishas—whores . . ."

"Wait a minute!" I cried. "This girl . . ." I reached out to take her hand, but she drew away from me and Katsumi said, "More better we eat."

It was a pretty formal meal. I asked a half dozen questions, none of which Hana-ogi really answered and it was not until Katsumi produced an album of Hana-ogi's pictures that there was any real animation. Then the two girls spoke in rapid Japanese, laughed a lot and sang bits of songs from the famous shows Hana-ogi had starred in. Finally the ice thawed a bit and I learned that Hana-ogi came from the north of Japan, where a woman in a near-by village had once seen a Takarazuka show in Tokyo. This woman had suggested that Hana-ogi apply for the examinations. Her father had been killed in the B-29 raids on Tokyo. Her brother had been hung for what he did to American soldiers in a prisoner-of-war camp.

Hana-ogi's willingness to tell of her family encouraged me to speak and I said I had a good start in the Air Force and with my background I surely ought to become a colonel and from there on it was the roll of the dice. I said that if I did become a general I hoped I would be as good a one as my father. She asked his name and when I said Hot Shot Harry Gruver she grew silent and Katsumi said, "All Japanese know Gruver-san—Guadalcanal." The evening grew formal again.

Hana-ogi rose and indicated that she must go. I was deeply agitated at having seen her, having talked with her—even though it was in translation—and I did not want to have her go. I said, "Katsumi, please ask her to stay."

Hana-ogi replied something sharp which Katsumi refused to translate. When I insisted she stood stubbornly silent, so I appealed to Hana-ogi, who looked at me in a quiet, submissive Japanese way which betrayed no emotion, but which dared me to budge her one inch.

Softly, as if she were a child of seven, she said, "America . . . no!" I could sense in her gentle reply a finality of hatred and steel, but she bowed slightly, smiled with an infuriating complacency, and looked back at me from the sliding doors. "America . . . no!" she repeated softly, but long after she had gone I recalled the graceful way she bent down by the doors to put on her zori, the rare delicacy with which she arranged her kimono, so in spite of persistent apprehension that I was headed for trouble, I determined that no matter what she thought of Americans, no matter what orders Camp Kobe handed down regarding Japanese girls, I was going to see her again.

For the next two nights nothing happened. I posted myself at the Bitchi-bashi to watch the procession of girls and when I saw Hana-ogi, her hair in the wind, step upon the bridge at the opposite end, my heart actually hammered like one of those riveting machines you fix airplane wings with. God, she was like a medieval princess walking out from the palace. She was so straight and proud and sure of herself. And her black eyes shining out like fires from her golden face . . .

"Son, you got it bad!" Mike Bailey warned me on the second night.

"I'm going to see that girl. Tomorrow."

"Son, are you taking this seriously?"

I turned to look at Mike and he seemed to be a complete stranger. "Don't you take Fumiko seriously?" I asked. "Who started this, anyway?"

"Fumi-chan?" he laughed. "Son, a Marine has to be involved with a pretty girl or he isn't a Marine. But who could get serious over a Takarazuka girl? They got sawdust for hearts."

"What is this?" I asked. "A little while ago you were telling me . . ."

Mike scratched his head and said, "I had a cousin once who came to stay with me right before a big high-school basketball game. I looked at the ugly little squirt and said, 'Hell, he can't be gettin' measles.' But he was and I was quarantined. Son, I think you're gettin' measles."

I said, "Tomorrow night I'm going to storm that Bitchi-bashi and I'm going to have a date with that girl."

"Son," Mike said, "you can't have measles but, by God, there are red spots!"

Prudently he stayed away from the bridge on that third night and as the first Takarazuka girls crossed I felt my heart hammering again and soon there was Hana-ogi, accompanied by three other stars, and I stepped right into the middle of them and took Hana-ogi's hand and brought its yellow knuckles right up to my lips and kissed it. Then I said, "I have got to see you," but none of the girls spoke English and Hana-ogi drew her hand away and started to leave, but I no longer gave a damn so I grabbed her by the shoulder and swung her around and kissed her on the lips. We kept our eyes open and I remember that in this crazy moment I could not tell whether her eyes were slanted or not, but they were very black, like the sky at night.

She pushed me away and crossed the bridge and I heard behind me the muttering of Japanese men and I thought, "Oh, damn, a public mess and I'll be court-martialed," but when I turned there was no animosity. The men were laughing and one old fellow with a load of wood pointed at some more Takarazuka girls approaching on the bridge and made motions encouraging me to kiss them too, but I hurried back to the Marine Barracks, where Mike Bailey greeted me with a pair of field glasses and the crack, "It looked good, son. The subtle approach. Grrrrr."

I said, "I promised to see her tonight. I did."

He said, "Ace, don't let this thing get you. If you want to make a play for a pretty actress—O.K. But don't let it get you. Frankly, you looked silly as hell down there on the bridge."

In a few minutes a Japanese boy appeared with a message for Mike and he said, "Fumi-chan wants to see me in the restaurant. She wants you to come along."

When we got there Makino-san, the cook, had already

heard of my behavior and he gave me hell. "Very important in Japan these girls. You do much wrong, Ace-san."

"What did I do?" I demanded. "I kissed a girl."

"A Takarazuka girl," he said with reverence. Before he could argue further Fumiko-san appeared, extremely beautiful and very feminine. She did not cry but she did plead with me and said that something like that could ruin a Takarazuka girl and that if Hana-ogi ever lost her job her mother and her younger sisters . . . "She very poor, Hana-ogi," Fumiko told me.

"What do you mean?" I asked.

"You Americans not know what poor is. Hana-ogi never tasted meat until she came Takarazuka. Never had one nice clothes. Ace-san, you not speak her again—please?"

She told me that Hana-ogi's only chance in life—her one opportunity to escape from terrible poverty—was Takarazuka. "I know this girl," she said solemnly. "Before she come for examination not eat for three days to get . . . How you . . ." She indicated a permanent wave.

She said there was already a likelihood that Hana-ogi might become one of the rare lucky ones—kept on at Takarazuka forever "as teacher of the dancing" when her days as an actress were over. "Here is good life for Hana-ogi-san. There is no other."

I asked Fumiko why she risked seeing Mike Bailey and she laughed. "I not great success. I not poor girl. My family making lots of money again."

Then she pleaded, "Do not come to the bridge again, Ace-san. Please?"

I wanted to see Hana-ogi, I wanted to see her eyes close to mine and her golden face pressed against my lips, but I said, "I promise." To my surprise Fumiko-san kissed me, her beautiful Japanese face leaning across the table, and she said, "American men so good. Even when Hana-ogi-san come home tonight and say, 'American men no good,' I speak her they all right."

But although I kept my promise not to haunt the bridge

it meant nothing, for the very next morning Joe Kelly
wheeled up to Itami Air Field and said with real joy,
"Dinner again tonight, Ace!"

My heart must have bled out through my eyes, for he
laughed and said, "Yep. Hana-ogi came into Osaka late
last night and talked with Katsumi for three hours."

"What did she say?"

"How should I know?" And he rattled off a jumble of
Japanese.

I wish that throughout the rest of my life I could oc-
casionally know the excitement that captured me that
night. I shaved at Itami, polished my shoes and set out
for Osaka. I went nearly crazy in a tiny Japanese taxicab.
The driver was all smiles and said yes, he understood
just where I wanted to go, but we wound up in hell, I
think, and in desperation I had to get a little boy to lead
us back to the main station and I went to Joe's house on
foot. I thrust back the sliding doors and cried, "Hana-ogi,
I . . ." But she was not there. Katsumi was alone, singing
to herself as she prepared dinner. I sat on the floor and
watched her time-christened movements over the charcoal stoves that Japanese women have used for centuries.
For them there were no can openers, no frozen foods.
Each item was laboriously prepared by hand and as Katsumi did this ancient work she hummed old songs and
it seemed to me that she grew lovelier each day—but
how truly lovely I was to learn in a few minutes.

For little Joe Kelly came busting into the house trembling with anger. He threw a package on the floor and
cried, "This son-of-a-bitch of a colonel!"

I had heard Joe sound off against officers before and I
tried to tone him down, but this time he had real cause.
"This bastard, Colonel Calhoun Craford! He rides me.
Every damned day he rides me."

I happened to be watching Katsumi at the brazier. She
never looked up, but I could see a terrible tenseness come
over her entire body. Her ankles, in their white tabi socks,
trembled slightly and I knew she was desperately afraid
for her man.

For I had heard of this Calhoun Craford, a tough guy who hated colored people. Joe said, "Every guy in that outfit who's married to a Japanese girl goes through hell with this bastard Craford."

Katsumi, aware that Joe's trouble had been caused by her, now left the charcoal brazier and came into the middle of the room. She pushed Joe down onto a pillow and took off his shoes. "You not to come on tatami with shoes, Joe," she said softly. She brought him a tiny cup of hot sake wine and when he had drunk this she led him into the other room where there was a Japanese bath and soon I could hear tensed up little Joe Kelly, the dead-end kid, sloshing about in the tub while his patient wife soused him with cold water and rubbed his back. After a while they joined me and Joe scratched himself under the dark blue kimono Katsumi had made him. He said, "To hell with Colonel Craford. Look what I got!" And he produced a bottle of Italian wine which Katsumi took.

Then, as we heard the soft click of zori on the alley stones, we all fell silent and I think Joe and Katsumi were as excited as I, although their hearts couldn't have been pounding as hard. The paper doors slid back and there was Hana-ogi in a green-and-gold kimono, her lips slightly parted in a smile, her brilliant eyes glowing from her night walk and her jet black hair mussed by the wind that blew along the canal. She started to speak but I caught her in my arms and kissed her. This time we closed our eyes, but when we finally drew apart—for she was kissing me too—she passed the back of her hand across her forehead and I think she knew then that for a girl dedicated to Takarazuka and a man dedicated to American military life love could result only in tragedy, and she pushed my hand away from hers and gently removed her zori and sat down on the tatami and spoke quietly to Katsumi, who spoke to Joe in Japanese, and all three of them fumbled around, not knowing how to translate what Hana-ogi had said, so she held out her hand to me and invited me to sit upon the mats beside her, and finally Katsumi said, "She not mad no more."

After dinner Katsumi said, "Joe, we take walk." Hana-ogi did not protest and as soon as the fragile doors slid shut I took her in my arms.

We sat upon the mats unable to say a word. I put my finger on her wonderful face and said, "Nice," but she could not understand. She gave me some instructions in Japanese but all I could do was shrug my shoulders, so she laughed and grabbed my big toe and pulled my cramped legs out straight and patted my knees, indicating that I must be stiff from sitting Japanese style. Then she made a pillow for my head in her lap and in that way we continued our meaningless conversation on the tatamis.

It was apparent to each of us that we would meet many times, but that when she passed me on the Bitchi-bashi she would look straight ahead and it was also apparent that she intended us to be lovers—but not on this first quiet night—and that as the days went by we would postpone one decision after another until finally some external force, say Takarazuka or General Webster, intervened to make the climactic decisions for us, but as she looked down at me with calm eyes, as her wonderful hands held my face and as her slim, graceful legs stretched out at last beside mine on the tatami mats, one question at least was answered. I had often wondered how a self-respecting American could get excited about a Japanese girl. Now I knew.

When it came time to leave, Hana-ogi refused to be seen with me on the street and caught a train back to Takarazuka. Joe drove me over to Itami, where I took the bus to Takarazuka, but something must have delayed Hana-ogi's train, because when I got to my room and looked out at the Bitchi-bashi, there was Hana-ogi crossing it in the April moonlight. I rushed down to speak with her but she passed proudly by, her cream-colored zori going pin-toed along the railroad track to her dormitory.

I didn't sleep much that night because when I got back to my room I found a letter which had been delivered by special messenger. It contained a routine reminder of recent orders issued by Camp Kobe and along the foot in capital letters I read: ANY PUBLIC DISPLAY WHATEVER OF AFFECTION FOR A JAPANESE NATIONAL BY A MEMBER OF THIS COMMAND IS FORBIDDEN. OFFICERS SHOULD NOT EVEN APPEAR ON PUBLIC STREETS ACCOMPANIED BY WOMEN OF THE INDIGENOUS PERSONNEL.

I knew that I was entangled in a ridiculous situation, for I could not walk with Hana-ogi in the city and she could not walk with me in town. If General Webster caught me dating a Japanese girl I would be disciplined and if the Takarazuka people heard of Hana-ogi dating an American she would be fired from the Moon Troupe. It seemed like something borrowed from the play I was in at St. Leonard's. Then I was a prince trying to prevent my niece from marrying a penniless schoolteacher. The kid who played the schoolteacher was a miserable drip in real life and I remember that on-stage I became pretty outraged, but now it was happening to me, and Mrs. Webster riding herd on me and the Takarazuka railroad company protecting their investment in Hana-ogi were going to be a lot tougher than a Ruritanian prince played by seventeen-year-old Lloyd Gruver.

For about two hours that morning as I lay awake—from three to five—I decided the whole affair was too damned silly, but toward dawn I began to see Hana-ogi dancing along the wall of my room and her classical postures, the stamping of her feet and the gestures of her right hand allured me so that I could think only of her tight and disciplined body. My thoughts were filled with the grace of her movement and as the sun rose I fell asleep knowing that somewhere within the triangle of the three cities we would meet.

It came unexpectedly. On a warm day in May I waited for Hana-ogi at the Bitchi-bashi but she did not appear and disconsolately I wandered down to the railroad station to purchase a ticket back to Itami, but as I approached the cage I saw Hana-ogi standing off to one side, holding a ticket in her hand and impulsively, even though we were in the heart of Takarazuka, she came to me and we went to the ticket cage together and we bought two tickets for a small town at the end of the line, and on this lovely day we walked for the first time through the ancient Japanese countryside.

Hana-ogi, unable to speak a phrase of English, and I quite as dumb in Japanese, walked along the rice fields and across the little ridges that ran like miniature footpaths beside the irrigation ditches. We nodded to old women working the fields, laughed at children, and watched the white birds flying. Hana-ogi wore her green and white kimono and her cream zori and she was a bird herself, the May wind catching at her loose garments and the branches of trees tousling her delicate hair.

Wherever we went the land was crowded. Where in Texas there would be one farmer here there were forty. Where the footpaths in New Hampshire might be crowded with three people, here it was overwhelmed with fifty. There were no vacant fields, no woodlots, no mossy banks beside the wandering streams. On every foot of land were people and no matter how far we walked into the countryside there were always more people. More than any day I ever lived in my life I treasure this day because I discovered not only Hana-ogi's enormous love but I also discovered her land, the tragic, doomed

98

land of Japan, and from it I learned the fundamental secret of her country: too many people.

In Korea we used to joke about enlisted men who bought Japanese girls of sixteen or seventeen—a man could buy a young girl anywhere in Japan—and we thought it a horrible reflection on Japan, but today I saw that it would always be possible to find some Japanese farmer who would be eager to sell his daughter to a kind man, for if she stayed at home and had to fight for her share of the skimpy rice in the family bowl she could never do as well as if she went off with a man who could buy rice for her. All the problems we used to laugh about as being so strange—so unlike America—I saw explained this afternoon. The Japanese were no different from us. Their farmers loved their daughters exactly as Iowa farmers love theirs. But there was not enough land. There was never enough food.

I thank God for that May evening walking among the rice fields while the crickets droned at us, for if I had not seen this one particular old man tending his field I am sure that when I finally learned the terrifying truth about Hana-ogi I could no longer have loved her; but having seen this old man and his particles of soil I loved her the more.

He stood where a trail turned off from the main road, leaving in the joint a thin sliver of useless land that in America would have been allowed to grow up in burdock. In Japan this tragic triangle was a man's field, the sustenance of one man's large family. On this May night he was bent over the field, digging it to a depth of fourteen inches. The dug soil he placed reverently to one side until his tiny field was excavated. Then, as we watched, he took each handful of soil and gently pulverized it, allowing it to return to its bed. Pebbles he tossed aside and sticks and foreign things, and in the two days that followed this man would finger each item of his soil. Not for him a plow or a harrow, but the gnarled fingers and the bending back.

It is difficult for me to report these things, for I cannot

explain how Hana-ogi explained them to me. By pointing, by gesturing, by little pantomimes with the old man she explained that he was like her father except that her father's field—before the American bombs killed him—was slightly bigger. But her father had nine children.

It was breathlessly apparent to us as the sun sank below the distant hills that in terribly crowded Japan Hana-ogi and I were seeking a place in which to make love. There was now no thought of Japanese or American. We were timeless human beings without nation or speech or different color. I now understood the answer to the second question that had perplexed me in Korea: "How can an American who fought the Japs actually go to bed with a Jap girl?" The answer was so simple. Nearly a half million of our men had found the simple answer. You find a girl as lovely as Hana-ogi—and she is not Japanese and you are not American.

As we walked into the twilight we drew closer together. She took my hand and also took my heart and as dusk fell over us we searched more urgently from side to side. We were no more looking at the white birds or the old men bending over their fields. We were looking for a refuge—any kind of refuge—for we were desperately in love.

I remember that once I thought I saw a grove of trees, but they were houses, for random trees were not allowed to grow in Japan. Again Hana-ogi pointed to a barn, but it was occupied. In Japan there was not even spare land for love.

But at last we came to a structure that was familiar to me, two inclined massive poles with two more set across them at the top like an enormous capital A, flat at the point. It was the timeless symbol of a Shinto shrine and here there were trees, but as always there were people too. We watched them come through the towering A, stand silently before the shrine, clap their hands three times, bow and depart, the torn white paper and the rice ropes of their religion fluttering quietly in the wind above them.

Hana-ogi took my hand and led me past the shrine until we came to a grassy bank partially protected by four trees. Villagers passed ten feet from us and dogs barked nearby. Across the mound we could see the dim lights of houses, for there was no empty countryside as I had known it in America. There was no place where there were not people. But at last we had to ignore them and it seemed to me as I sank beside Hana-ogi in the May twilight that we were being watched by the million eyes of Japan.

I remember vividly two things that happened. I had no conception of a kimono and thought it a kind of wrap-around dress but when we embraced and it was clear that Hana-ogi intended that we love completely, I tried to undo this gossamer dress, but it led to another and then another and to still more and although we could not speak we fell to laughing at my astonishment. Then suddenly we laughed no more, for I was faced with the second vast occurrence of the day, for when in the fading light I at last saw Hana-ogi's exquisite body I realized with shock—even though I was prepared to accept it—that I was with a girl of Asia. I was with a girl whose complete body was golden and not white and there was a terrible moment of fear and I think Hana-ogi shared this fear, for she caught my white arm and held it across her golden breasts and studied it and looked away and then as quickly caught me to her whole heart and accepted the white man from America.

We returned at last to Takarazuka and as we approached that lovely place we went into separate cars and I waited long till Hana-ogi had disappeared across the Bitchi-bashi before I appeared on the streets, heading for the Marine Barracks. Mike Bailey was in the shower and when he heard me go by he yelled and brought me back to military life with a fearful bang.

He said, "Mrs. Webster saw me in Kobe today and asked me a lot of questions."

"About you and Fumi-chan?" I asked, nonchalantly.

"Don't play coy, son. About you and Eileen."

"What'd'j tell her?"

"It isn't so much what I told her as what she asked."
He waited for me to press the point, but I called downstairs for some cold beer and he said, "She asked me if
you were going with a Japanese girl."

I sort of gulped on my beer and Mike said promptly,
"Of course I said no. You aren't, are you?"

I took another drink of beer and pondered a long time
what I ought to say. Then the pressing desire to talk
with someone overcame me and I said, "I've been walking
with Hana-ogi. We must have walked for five miles and
I'm so deep in love . . ."

Mike was a fine character to talk with at a time like
this. He laughed and said, "I feel like a traitor, Ace,
getting you into this. Hell, I'm the one who's supposed
to be in love."

I said, "It hit me like a propeller zinging around when
you aren't looking. Jesus, Mike, I tell you the truth, I'm
desperate."

Mike laughed again and said, "No need for a guy to
be desperate in Japan. If you can't cuddle up to Hana-ogi
because she's an actress, there's always the Tiger of Takarazuka. Better men than you . . ."

I started to say boldly, "But we . . ." My voice trailed
off and I ended lamely, "The stars came right down and
knocked me out."

Mike looked at me quizzically, then said without
joking, "Look, Ace, I know better than most men around
here how sweet a Japanese girl can be. But don't get involved. For the love of God, Ace, don't get involved."

"I am involved."

"Mrs. Webster said the M.P.'s have instructions to pick
up officers seen holding hands with indigenous personnel.
That's a lovely phrase, isn't it?"

"I just don't give a damn, Mike. To hell with the M.P.'s
and to hell with Mrs. Webster."

"I agree with you, Ace. But while I was talking with
the general's main tank division her daughter came up

and I got a good look. For Christ sake, Ace, that girl's a ravin' beauty. Why do you have to mess around with a Japanese actress if this Eileen is on tap?"

I put the beer down and stared at the floor. That was the question I had not wanted Mike to ask. I saw Eileen as I had known her at Vassar, bright, eager, a wonderful sport. I saw her that winter in Texas when her father was a colonel at San Antonio and I was at Randolph Field. Why hadn't I married her then? Why had she turned down the other young officers and insisted upon waiting for me? I felt like the announcer who asks the burning questions at the end of each radio program about breaking hearts, but I knew that you could turn my radio on the next day and still not get the answers.

I looked up at Mike and said, "I don't know."

He asked me directly, "Are you afraid of American women?"

I said, "I hadn't thought of it."

He said, "I've been over here a long time, what with one thing and another. I've watched lots of our men go for these Japanese girls . . . Hell, I won't be superior about it. I do myself. Frankly and all kidding aside, Ace, I'd a damned sight rather marry Fumiko-san than Eileen. But I just wondered why you felt that way?"

"I don't feel that way. At least if I do I don't know about it. But why do you?"

"With me it's very clear. One thing explains it all. You ever had your back scrubbed by a Japanese girl? Not a bath attendant mind you. That's simple. But a girl who really loved you?"

"What's back scrubbing got to do with it?"

"Ace, either you understand or you don't."

"What are you driving at?"

"I'm trying to say there are hundreds of ways for men and women to get along together. Some of the ways work in Turkey, some work in China. In America we've constructed our own ways. What I'm saying is that of them all I prefer the Japanese way." He laughed and saw that I didn't entirely understand, so he banged his beer down and shouted, "All right! One easy question! Can you imagine Eileen Webster scrubbing your back?"

It was a crazy question, a truly hellish shot in the dark, but I could immediately visualize fat little Katsumi Kelly the other night, taking her sore and defeated husband into the bath and knocking the back of his neck and getting him his kimono and quietly reassuring him that her love was more important than whatever Lt.Col. Calhoun Craford had done to him, and I saw runty, sawed-off Joe Kelly coming back to life as a complete man and I had great fear—like Mike Bailey—that Eileen Webster would not be able or willing to do that for her man. Oh, she would be glad to storm in and fight it out with Lt.Col. Craford, or she would take a job and help me earn enough so that I could tell Lt.Col. Craford to go to hell, or she could do a million other capable things; but I did not think she could take a wounded man and make him whole, for my mother in thirty years of married life had never once, so far as I knew, done for my father the simple healing act that Katsumi Kelly had done for her man the other night.

Mike said it for me. He laughed and said, "There are all kinds of things wrong with Japan. But Japanese women aren't one of them and their view of love suits me fine." Then he added, "But I hate to see you be the one to take it all seriously. Because the Air Force would never let you marry a Japanese girl . . ."

"What would the Air Force have to do about it?"

"You'd see. You're one of their bright young men and they'd bring all sorts of pressures to bear . . ."

"Who's talking about marriage?"

Mike sighed. "That's better. They way you started, you were talking about marriage."

"I said I was confused."

"I'd be confused too if I was involved with two women like Eileen and Hana-ogi." He grew thoughtful and added, "It's very strange. I'd never have picked Hana-ogi.

She's always so mannish. Come to think of it, I've never seen her in girl's clothes. Have you?"

I thought of her rare charm and started to speak reverently but this scared Mike and he said, "Ace, I know damn well you're thinking about marriage and it's going to be tough. Son, it's going to be tough."

I insisted that I didn't know what I was thinking about, but my problem was solved for me in an unforeseen manner. Katsumi and Joe dropped by the air base the next afternoon and Katsumi took care of everything. Haltingly she said, "We have find house for you, Ace."

"A house!" I drew her toward a wall where no one could listen.

"Yes, one small house."

"What do I want with a house?"

"Where else you and Hana-ogi-san stay?"

"Wait a . . ."

"You not love Hana-ogi?"

"Sure I love her, but . . ." I appealed to Joe, who grinned and said, "When a Japanese girl loves you, Ace, it's solid. How you suppose I got my house?"

I said to them, "Hana-ogi could get into trouble . . ."

Katsumi looked at me incredulously and said, "When Hana-ogi come our house to see you it mean she love you. When she walk to Shinto shrine it mean same thing. Where you two make love? Here at Itami? I don't think so. (She pronounced it, "I don' sink so.") Officers Club Kobe? I don't think so. Takarazuka? No!"

I was about to call the whole affair off when Katsumi handed me a map showing that the house was not far from hers. Then she said, gravely, "Today Hana-ogi-san number one girl at Takarazuka. She work very hard for this. You be good man not tell anyone you love Hana-ogi. She make very dangerous come Osaka for you."

"If it's so dangerous . . ."

"But she tell me all time she work hard she think some day she meet . . ." Katsumi blushed and could not continue, so I waited until she gained courage, whereupon she whispered, "Hana-ogi tall girl. Not little fat girl same me. Long time she dream she meet tall man—same you."

I must have shown my disappointment at being chosen because I was six-feet-two, so Katsumi said, "She meet many tall men but no one brave like you—no one brave to stand at bridge many times to see her." That was Katsumi's speech and as she left she said, "Hana-ogi come your new house tonight seven o'clock."

I was now overboard in the slipstream where things happen so fast you never get your parachute open. I was tumbling about and all thought of General Webster's orders, my promotion in service and my early ideas about the Japanese enemy were swirling in confusion. But of one thing I was determined. I would go to that house in Osaka early in the afternoon and I would clean it and I would stock the shelves with food and I would make it a home.

But at three-thirty I was called into an urgent meeting and it was nearly seven when I reached Osaka. I hurried up the main street to where my canal ran off to the right and I passed along the narrow footpath until I came to a little store, where I bought an armful of things to eat. Then I took a deep breath and walked out into the May twilight.

As I approached my house I saw that the sliding doors were open and from them came a bright light and a sight I shall never forget: a tiny cloud of dust followed by the merest flick of a broom. Hana-ogi had hurried to the new house to clean it for my arrival.

I dashed into the room, threw the food on the floor and took her in my arms. I kissed her wildly and pressed her golden cheek next to mine, but instead of the flood of kisses I anticipated she pushed me away, pointed to my shoes and cried, "Oh, Rroyd-san!" For a moment I was bewildered and then she knelt down and started to untie my offending shoes. Quickly I prevented her from doing this, so she picked up the food I had dropped and when she placed it on the shelf I saw that with her own money she had already stocked the kitchen.

There was a pot cooking over the brazier and I looked in, then turned quickly to find Hana-ogi cleaning my shoes and placing them in the corner. I took three steps, lifted her away from my shoes and carried her into the middle of the room, where I stood looking about me help-lessly till Hana-ogi laughed and with her expressive head indicated a closet which I kicked open, releasing the bed roll. I spread it as well as I could with my feet and gently placed Hana-ogi upon it. She closed her slanted eyes for a moment, then looked up and smiled, pulling me down beside her.

In the days that followed I often recalled the stories I
had read about American and English sailors who had
fallen in love with island girls and of how idyllic it was.
But these damnable stories invariably ended with the big
kiss and it had not occurred to me that after the big kiss
these island lovers must have had things they wanted to
talk about. But how did they talk without any language?
How in hell did they talk?

I do not think that those who have always stayed at
home can understand how terrible a thing language is,
how dependent we are upon it. During the tremendous
weeks that followed when May flowers bloomed along
our canal there were times when I almost tore at my
throat trying to find some way to express an emotion to
Hana-ogi. It's all right to gesture at a girl's eyes and indicate that they are lovely but if you feel your heart ex-
pand at the very sound of her quiet approach along the
canal—if you feel the earth tremble at night when she
brings your soft pillow to the bed roll while beside it she
places her canvas pillow filled with rice bran—then you
feel that you must speak to her or perish.

I knew exactly four Japanese phrases. *Ichi ban* meant
number one and I used this interminably. When I first
saw Hana-ogi undressed I gasped at her amazing beauty
and cried, "Ichi ban!" When she cooked a good meal it
was "Ichi ban." When she saw President Truman's picture in the paper I said, "America ichi ban." And once
when she suggested that her breasts were too small I
protested, "Ichi ban! Ichi ban!"

I also knew *Domo arigato gozaimasu,* which meant
thank you. I used it all the time and it was curious how
this phrase of courtesy came to mean so much to us. We

108

were deeply indebted to each other, for we had undertaken unusual risks, so there was an extra tenderness about all we did. When I spread the bed roll I would say, "Dom' arigato" but more often I used the full phrase. I was in a land of courtesy where great courtesy had been extended me.

Of course I knew the universal Japanese words *takusan* and *sukoshi* for *much* and *little*. Every American in Japan used these words as his final comment upon an infinity of subjects. The words look strange to me as I write them, for in Japanese the letter *u* is not pronounced in connection with *k* and it was taksan this and skoshi that just as it was Ta-ka-raz-ka and skiyaki rather than sukiyaki. I remember once when I was moved to great depths by something Hana-ogi had done and I pointed to my heart, put her golden hand above it and cried, "Takusan, takusan!" And I indicated that it was for her that it had become takusan after having been sukoshi for so many years.

And finally I knew that strangest of Japanese phrases, *Ah, so desu-ka!* It was usually abbreviated *Ah, so!* and meant exactly what it would mean in English. It was also shortened to *Soka, Soda,* and *Deska* and I used it for everything. Often I would hear Hana-ogi and Katsumi talking and one of them would be narrating something and the other would repeat over and over in the most mournful way, "Ah, so desu-ka! Ah, so desu-ka!" We all laughed hilariously when Joe found an American newspaper item in which a famous women journalist from New York said that even the Empress of Japan was becoming Americanized because she spoke a little English. "All the time I talked with the Empress she nodded her head and whenever she agreed with me she said clearly, 'Ah, so!'"

Hana-ogi, on her part, had acquired just about as much English. Like all Japanese girls her favorite phrase was *Never hoppen!* She could say this with the most ravishing wit and effectively kill any high-blown idea I might be trying to make, but once when I said that some day she would see New York she said with great finality, "Never hoppen."

A second phrase she used a great deal was one she picked up from Katsumi and it too was common all over Japan: *I don't think so.* Hana-ogi had trouble with *th* and this phrase of classic doubt usually came out, "I don' sink so."

But if Hana-ogi had difficulty with *th,* her conflict with *l*'s and *v*'s and *f*'s was unending. She had acquired, from her Takarazuka shows, a few American phrases which she loved to use on me at unexpected moments, but they were so mangled because of the limited alphabet of sound in the Japanese tongue that I often had to think twice to detect her meaning. Once, at the end of a long night when we stayed up to clean our tiny house she caught me in her arms and cried, "Oh Rroyd, I rub you berry sweet." I was unprepared both for her emotion and her pronunciation and for one dreadful moment I almost laughed and then I looked down at her dear sweet slanted eyes and saw that they were filled with tears and we sat down on the tatami as morning broke and she told me in signs and kisses and strange half-words that she had never thought that she, Hana-ogi—dedicated to Takara-zuka and knowing nothing else—would ever discover what it was to . . . She stopped and we had no words to finish the thought. Then she jumped up and cried, "I make you cawhee." And she took down the coffee pot.

It was true that not being able to talk made our physical love, there on the tatami mats, more powerful, but when that was past, when you lay there on the dark floor and heard feet along the canal path, you yearned desperately to talk of ordinary things, and once I thought of what Joe had said and I wished to God that I might be able to talk with Hana-ogi about the country club or the braces on junior's teeth or anything trivial at all—like the news that Katsumi-san was going to have a baby. I wanted to talk about that baby, what it would be like, would its eyes be Japanese, would it live well in America, but all I could do was to place my hand on Hama-ogi's hard flat stomach and whisper, "Katsumi-san takusan—takusan." And she kept my hand there and said back, "Maybe some time Hana-ogi takusan" and we looked at each other and I think we both prayed that some day Hana-ogi would be takusan.

The matter of praying gave us some trouble, as it did Joe and Katsumi. Joe, being a good Catholic, was repelled when Katsumi established in their home a Shinto shrine, complete with symbols to be prayed to. There were some heated words and the shrine came down, but I don't think Hana-ogi would have agreed to surrendering her Shinto faith, for one day I came home and found that she had erected in our home three separate shrines: Shinto, Buddhist and Catholic. I tried to explain that I wasn't any of the three, but she said she was willing to be all of them for me. I asked her why she honored both Shinto and Buddhism and she said that many Japanese were both and that some were Christians as well, and she found nothing curious in tending the three shrines faithfully and I noticed that she paid just as fair attention to my one as she did to her two.

It became so imperative that we converse with each other that we looked forward with sheer delight to the visits of Joe and Katsumi and I was glad whenever Katsumi sneaked away from Joe's surveillance and came to our house to pray to her Shinto gods for her baby to be a boy and strong. Whenever she appeared Hana-ogi and I would unleash an accumulation of questions about the most trivial things. I would say, "Tell Hana-ogi I like more salt in all my vegetables." Imagine, I had been unable to convey that simple idea accurately. And Katsumi would reply, "Hana-ogi want know, you ever eat octopus?" and I would cry, "Is that what she was trying to ask?" and I would repeat the word *octopus* and Hana-ogi would tell me what it was in Japanese and thus we would possess one more word to share.

But the hoard of meanings grew so slowly that I used to look with envy upon the G.I.'s I saw who had mastered the language. Once buying groceries I met a tough Texas boy with his Japanese girl and they were having an argument over some apples. Finally he asked in disgust, "Hey, whatsamatta you?"

The little Japanese girl caught her breath, grew trembling mad and slapped the Texas G.I. right across the face. Then, hands on hips, she demanded, "Whatsamatta you, you whatsamatta me? I whatsamatta you first!"

The G.I. laughed and picked up a box of candy, saying with a bow, "You my gal friendo ichi ban. I presento you." The little girl put her arm in his, cocked her head on one side and asked him if he thought her pretty: "Steky-ne?" He kissed her and cried, "You're steky-goddamned-ne, baby."

I envied the couple, for they had created a language of their own and it permitted them to convey their affection accurately. Like young children who refuse to be bothered by language, they ignored both Japanese and English and inhabited a delightful world of their own.

I returned with my purchases and asked, "Hana-ogi, what *steky-ne?*" She thought for a moment then put my finger on an especially attractive design on her kimono and said, "Steky-ne." I thought she was referring to the needlework and I pointed to another part of the kimono and asked, "Steky-ne?" but she shook her head.

I was perplexed, so she thought and took my finger and outlined her wonderful oval face, leaving my hand at her chin, asking, "You think—steky-ne?" And then I realized what the word meant and I kissed her warmly and whispered, "Steky-takusan-takusan-ne."

But as the days passed and as we fell more hopelessly in love we discovered that it was impossible to exist as passionately as we insisted without better communication of ideas, so I started to learn a little Japanese and Hana-ogi—who despised Americans and what they had done to Japan—reluctantly joined an English class. She bought a little conversation book which she studied each day on the train back and forth to Takarazuka and one night she volunteered her first complete sentence in English. Screwing up her courage like a schoolgirl reciting Milton, she swallowed, smiled at me and declaimed, "Lo, the postillion has been struck by lightning."

The shock of these words was so great that I burst into uncontrolled laughter and I saw Hana-ogi slowly freeze with hatred. I had laughed at her best intentions. I too was an American.

I rose quickly from the floor to apologize, but when she saw me move toward her she ran away. Grabbing her English book she tore it to pieces and threw them at me. Those pages which fell at her feet she trampled upon and screamed in Japanese as she did so.

Finally I caught her hands and kissed her. I held her head to mine and when she started to sob I could have torn my tongue out. This cruel inability to speak was killing us and we were becoming lost people in a void of ideas . . . We were lovers who could not love and when Hana-ogi had sought to bridge this gap—humiliating herself and surrendering her hatred of the enemy—I had laughed at her.

I realized then that words must no longer be permitted to keep us apart. I lifted Hana-ogi to the bed roll and placing her beautiful legs toward the fire, I held her head close to my heart and burst into my own words, whether she could understand them or not. That night I said, "Hana-ogi, Hana-ogi! I love you with all the heart and mind within me. I've been a barren desert . . . I've been a man flying a lost plane far in the sky and I have never before known a human being. Now I've come to an alien land among people I once hated and I've met you and taken you away from these people and brought you to a tiny house and you have made a shred of heaven here. Hana-ogi, if I've hurt you through my ignorance you ought to lash me through the streets of Osaka, for my heart is in your care and if I were to hurt you I would be destroying myself. Whether you understand or not, these words are for you." And I kissed her.

I believe she comprehended what I said, for with her face now pressed to mine she spoke softly in Japanese and I think she unburdened herself of the accumulated pas-

sions that had been tormenting her word-stricken heart. I
closed my eyes and listened to the wonderful sound of her
voice as she uttered the strange, angular syllables of her
native language. She said one word which sounded like
hoshimashita and I looked up and said it and she laughed
and kissed my lips to keep them still while she completed
her statement. She did not use one word I understood,
but the meaning of her thoughts somehow seeped through
and we knew that we were more deeply in love than ever
before.

From that night on Hana-ogi and I talked with each
other a great deal and we discovered that in love what is
said is far less important to the person spoken to than the
one who speaks. If I wanted to tell her that the days were
growing longer and that I first noticed this during the
year when I was a young boy on an Army base in Mon-
tana, I said just that, and it was marvelous for me, for
then I remembered how I felt as a boy—the great clean-
ness of life and the bigness—and I had a larger heart with
which to love. And Hana-ogi spoke to me of her childhood
and of how she dreamed of going to Tokyo and of how,
when she got there, it seemed so much smaller than she
had imagined. I understood only a little of what she intended, but one thing I understood with amazing clarity:
when she had talked of these things for a long time she
was lovelier than I had ever imagined a woman could be.
In those long nights of talking, there in the bed roll on the
tatami mats, I think we came closer to sharing with complete finality two human lives than will ever be possible
for me again. Forbidden the use of words, we drove our
hearts to understanding, and we understood.

In the morning after Hana-ogi tore up the English book
I gathered the mutilated pages to burn them, but in doing
so I noticed that her book had been published in 1879 by
a brilliant Japanese scholar who had apparently been
bowled over by English during those first wonderful days
when Japan was opening her gates to Western learning.
This gentleman's first sentence "for young ladies to use
when starting a conversation in public" was Hana-ogi's

epic "Lo, the postillion has been struck by lightning," and although I am sure the ancient scholar never intended it so, that sentence became the gag line of an American-Japanese home. Whenever trouble appeared in any form Hana-ogi would declaim, "Lo, the postillion!"

I became intrigued by the book and smoothed out some of the other pages which yielded gems like "The portmanteau of my father is in the room of my mother." Hana-ogi asked me what this meant and I tried to explain, but the more I endeavored the sillier it all became until we were convulsed with laughter and I remember thinking, while Hana-ogi tickled me in the ribs, of the G.I. booklet on Japan which said: "The Japanese have no sense of humor."

But the phrase that quite captivated me was the very first one for use at a formal tea "where the participants are not well acquainted." The professor advised loosing this bombshell: "The camel is often called the ship of the desert." It seemed to me that this sentence was the essence of Japan: few Japanese had ever seen a camel and no one could care less what a camel was like than young ladies at tea, but the stubborn fact remained that the camel had sometimes been called the ship of the desert, so the sentence was judged to be just as good an opening salvo as any other. I tried to explain to Hana-ogi how ridiculous the whole thing was but she went to great pains to explain, with gestures, how the camel strides over the sand and seems to be a rolling ship and how the beast can go for many days without water and how there are two kinds of camels, one with one hump and the other with two. I tried to stop this flood of information, but she grabbed me by the hand and ran me down the alley to Katsumi's, where the two girls fairly exploded Japanese and Katsumi brought out her treasure chest and Hana-ogi ran through the magazines till she found one with her picture on the cover and on the inside were a half dozen pictures of her as a noble Arabian bandit in a desert extravaganza called *The Silver Sheik*. Then she commanded Katsumi to translate and Katsumi said, "But the camel really

is called the ship of the desert." I bit my lip and pointed to
a picture of Hana-ogi in flowing robes and said, "Ichi ban,
ichi ban," but Hana-ogi studied it and shook her head no.
She pointed to another and said, "Very nice," ("Berry
nice," she called it) and this one showed her in better
profile.

From time to time during this long spring of the year I used to reconsider Mike Bailey's question: Did I love Hana-ogi because I was afraid of American women? At first the question had seemed ridiculous. True, I was afraid of the incessant domination of a mother-in-law like the general's wife, but I was certainly not afraid of Eileen, except when she imitated her mother, and so far as I knew I had never been afraid of American women in general. In fact, I had always liked them very much and so far as I can remember there was never a dance at the Point or at any of the Air Force bases that I didn't attend—and almost always with my own date. I decided that American women didn't scare me. But then came the problem of the weekies and I was never again so sure.

I had noticed that for some days Katsumi-san had been trying to speak with me alone and I guessed that she was hoping I might know some special way whereby she could get into the United States. Since I could give her no help I tried to avoid discussing the doleful question, but finally she caught me and asked, "Major, you my friendo ichi ban?"

"Yes."

"Then maybe you buy me weekies?"

"What are weekies?"

"You go P.X. Pleeze, Ace, I not able to buy weekies."

"Why not?" I demanded. "All wives get P.X. cards."

I remember that Katsumi held back, as if not wanting to report Joe's troubles, but under my questioning she said, "Colonel Craford not give me pass. Not give any Japanese wife pass. He hate us. He hate Joe for marrying Japanese."

This made me sore, so I started out for the big avenue

117

where the Osaka P.X. was but I stopped short and returned to the alley. "Katsumi," I yelled, "what in hell are
weekies?"

She slid back the paper doors and tried to explain but
she was promptly overcome with embarrassment and said
only, "Pleeze, Gruver-san. I want to be same like American girl. I want to make Joe takusan happy." So I set out.

At the P.X. two tall guards shrugged their shoulders
when I asked what weekies were and I would have given
up the job except that I was disgusted to have a gentle
person like Katsumi pushed around. So I found one of
those super-efficient Japanese officials who sit at desks
and always seem to know everything. When I consulted
him he frowned noticeably and said, "Fifth floor, frame
four." He spoke slowly, wrestling with each difficult letter
so that his reply sounded: "Hihth hroor, hrame hore."

I took the elevator to the fifth floor and found to my un-
easiness that it contained women's wear. On the whole
floor there were only three men, enlisted soldiers buying
things for their girls. But there were nearly a hundred
American wives and when they saw me in this department they were unanimously outraged. I was obviously
another American man shacked up with some cheap
Japanese girl and I had come here to buy her nylons or a
dress or some other gift as part of my purchase price. I
started to blush as stares of disgust followed me and
mumbled to myself, "You're out of your depth, squarehead." But that was before I knew what weekies were.

I stepped up to the stocking counter and a pert
Japanese girl said briskly, "You are not allowed to buy
nylons, Major, unless you have your wife's card." There
were a half dozen officers' wives at the counter and they
smiled indulgently. I said quietly, "I didn't want nylons.
I wondered if you could tell me where the weekies are."

The American women started to laugh outright and I
was grateful when the Japanese clerk said, with exaggerated politeness, "Over there, Major." She pointed to
the frame containing silk underwear while the women
behind me laughed again.

It would have been simpler, I suppose, if I had cut my throat right then. Certainly the stares couldn't have been any tougher or my confusion greater. But I walked as inconspicuously as I could to the lacy counter where, as if by prearrangement, the clerks waited on everybody else first. So as I stood there, trying to look at some indefinite spot on the wall but always hitting brassieres or girdles, I became aware of the conversation around me. It was intended for me to hear.

The first officer's wife said, "I suppose many of our men get trapped by these girls."

The second said, "I never see them fighting very hard to stay free."

The first replied, "I can understand enlisted men and Japanese girls. Probably never knew any decent girls in America." You could tell from the emphasis that unquestionably the speaker was decent.

The second agreed, "But what is impossible to understand is how an officer can degrade his uniform."

Fortunately a clerk appeared and I said, "I'd like some weekies."

The American wives broke into laughter and the clerk said, in the sing-song professional voice used by Japanese girls, "Small, medium or large?"

I gulped and asked, "What are weekies?" This caused a real flurry of laughter in which the Japanese girl joined.

She reached under the counter and produced an open carton containing a bunch of pink nylon panties. Grabbing one she dangled it in the air and asked, "Small, medium or large?"

Now more women gathered about the counter and there was an outburst of uncontrolled hilarity. I figured that nothing else could happen so I said, "I'll take that one."

At this there was hysterical laughter and the Japanese girl popped her hand over her mouth for a moment, then showed me the band of the panty she was holding. "Major, weekies are one for every day of the week." And she showed me the embroidered word Thursday.

Frantically I indicated the entire pile and said, "I'll take them all."

But the clerk said, "These sample only. Small, medium or large?"

In despair I tried to think of how Katsumi looked. My mind was an aching blank and I pointed blindly at another Japanese clerk and said, "Her size, I guess."

Behind me one of the women whispered sweetly, "He doesn't remember how big she is!"

I looked around me at the faces of my countrywomen. They were hard and angular. They were the faces of women driven by outside forces. They looked like my successful and unhappy mother, or like powerful Mrs. Webster, or like the hurried, bereft faces you see on a city street anywhere in America at four-thirty any afternoon. They were efficient faces, faces well made up, faces showing determination, faces filled with a great unhappiness. They were the faces of women whose men had disappointed them. Possibly these harsh faces in the Osaka P.X. bore an unusual burden, for they were surrounded each day with cruel evidence that many American men preferred the softer, more human face of some Japanese girl like Katsumi Kelly.

As I paid the clerk I overheard the first officer's wife say, "All little Jap girls who live with G.I.'s are crazy for anything that will make them seem more American." The second turned to watch me go and added, "Including American men." But as I left these tough, bitter women and walked through their circle of bleak and unforgiving faces I saw near the elevator an American girl who could have been Eileen Webster. She was beautiful and fresh and perfect and I almost cried aloud with pain to think that something had happened in American life to drive men like Mike Bailey and me away from such delectable girls.

BUDDHIST MONK, 1794: "This bell
we received as a gift from the girls
of Yoshiwara."

Since I now knew that the secret of love is communication, I wish I could tell you exactly how Hana-ogi and I learned to talk in those exquisite days of early love, but I cannot recall how it was done. I do remember the evening when I tried to ask Hana-ogi what her name meant. I was barefooted and wearing the cheap blue-and-white kimono so common in Japan. I sat with my back against the fragile wall, my feet awkwardly out upon the tatami. I tried to convey the idea: "What does Hana-ogi mean?" but I did not succeed for the only two words she understood were *what* and her own name and she naturally suspected that I wanted to know what she wanted. So with tiny gestures and much pointing she indicated our small house of great love and said that all she wanted was to be here with me, that she wanted to hear me splashing in the tub, that she wanted to cook our meals over the glowing fire and that when she slid the paper doors shut in the evening she wanted to lock us in and the world out.

Quietly I sat against the wall and tucked my kimono tighter about me, relishing the delicate thoughts she had expressed for both of us. But then I tried again and this time she cried, "Ah, so desu-ka! The other Hana-ogi! Yes, Rroyd-san. I tell."

It is here that I wish I could explain, but I can't. Knowing almost nothing of my language this extraordinary girl nevertheless told me the following story, while I scrunched against the wall, my knees against my chin. Some of the passages she danced, some of them she pantomimed, and some she spoke in such expressive Japanese that I could fairly guess their meaning. And this is the story she told me:

121

Once upon a time in a small village near Tokyo there
was a girl of great beauty. No one knows her name, but
she was to become Hana-ogi, the most renowned prostitute in the entire history of Japan. As a child she lived
with her widowed mother but it soon became apparent
that her only possible future lay in the green houses of
Yoshiwara, the ancient walled quarter by the marshes of
Tokyo, where the unwanted young girls of farmer families were trained to become glowing and cultivated
courtesans.

The old mother sold Hana-ogi when the rare child was
seven, and for eight years this girl, always more beautiful,
waited on the established courtesans of Ogi-ya, the green
house which she would later make the most famous in
all Japan. While she still wore her obi tied behind with its
long ends signifying that she was virgin, the older girls
taught her the skills of their trade and on her fifteenth
birthday Hana-ogi discarded forever her real name, tied
her obi in front, and took her first customer.

He was a young man from Odawara and he fell so desperately in love with Hana-ogi that he used to haunt the
steps of Ogi-ya even when he had not the money to come
inside. In perplexity he watched Hana-ogi become the
most prized woman in Yoshiwara, and there were more
than four thousand there at the time. She became famous
for her poems, exquisite sighings of the heart and delicate
memories of farm life when the early dew was on the
rice fields. Priests in the temples sometimes told the wor-
shippers of this saintly girl who took no thought of buying her own freedom from the green houses but who
sent all her money home to her old mother. On holy days
Hana-ogi went to a Buddhist temple that was known as
the silent temple because it had no bell to record the
great days and one evening Hana-ogi led a procession of
thousands from the Yoshiwara bearing a bronze bell for
this silent temple. It was her gift to the priests who were
poorer than she.

Her fame became so great that visitors from China
came to see this glory of Nihon. (My Hana-ogi rarely

called her country Japan, never Nippon.) Poets wrote
famous songs about her. Men close to the Shogun came
to talk with her, and above all the painters of the passing world, the wood-block artists who lived along the
edge of the Yoshiwara, made many portraits of her.
Today, in the museum at Kyoto, you can see maybe three
dozen famous paintings of Hana-ogi. When I see them,
said my Hana-ogi, I think that this immortal woman is
speaking to me across the years and I take courage.

Now all the time that the great men of the Shogun's
palace and the world-famous painters were with Hana-
ogi, the young lover from Odawara was watching, too,
and one spring as the cherry blossoms were about to
bloom he abducted Hana-ogi from the green houses.
Where they hid themselves, these two happy people, no
one knows. Whether they had children of their love no
one can say. The years passed and bad luck fell on the
house of Ogi-ya. No more did the rich men and the painters come there and no more did the priests of the nearby
temples receive gifts from Hana-ogi. The portraits of this
unforgettable girl were sold in great quantity, for everyone wished some memento of the loveliest woman Japan
had ever produced.

Then one day there was a burst of glory. (Here the real
Hana-ogi, my living grace, assumed a kind of cathedral
beauty as she simulated an incredible procession.) Hana-
ogi had come back to the green houses. She was thirty-
four years old, more beautiful than she had ever been,
more stately. Young girls walked before her, bearing
flowers. A minister of state walked proudly behind her.
Two men held umbrellas over her head, and she was
dressed in an exquisite blue kimono with rich flowing
robes of purple and the geta upon her feet were eleven
inches high. Within five days the greatest artists of Japan
had issued magnificent pictures of her joyous return, and
we can see them still, the stately processions, the rare,
wonderful woman coming back to her strange world.

It was the golden age! In those days there was singing
and long talks and beautiful pictures and fine women and

Nihon was never so joyous. And queen of the golden age
was this country girl, Hana-ogi. She never explained her
absence, she never told what had happened to her lover,
but people guessed that like all Japanese men he had
grown tired of her and had abused her. She lived at the
Ogi-ya for many years and when she was too old to serve
the visitors any longer she disappeared one day and no
one ever again heard of Hana-ogi.

My living Hana-ogi folded her hands and sank upon
the floor.

I was aghast at such an ending to so powerful a story
and I cried, jumping to my feet, "No! No! What happened
to Hana-ogi?"

It took some time for me to explain myself and then
my beautiful Japanese narrator stared up at me in surprise and said, "In Nihon many girls. Every time new
girls in Ogi-ya."

I shouted that I knew that, but what had become of
Hana-ogi? My adorable oval-face on the floor looked
up in confusion and said, "Hana-ogi become old girl."
(She pulled down the lines of her face and indicated that
a tooth was missing.) "She old, she go."

"But where? Where did she go?"

My living Hana-ogi shrugged her shoulders. Then,
sensing my disappointment, she formed the sign of a
Buddhist temple and made believe to ring the bell which
the ancient Hana-ogi had bought with her few coins
and she indicated that no doubt this most glorious woman
of Japanese history had been thrown out of the Ogi-ya
when her teeth were broken and that she had possibly
taken a position near the steps of the temple to beg alms.

There was an overwhelming ache upon my heart and
I knelt upon the floor beside my Hana-ogi, who had fled
her prison for her lover and whose future was as uncertain as her predecessor's. There was an enormous bond of
tenderness between us and that was the definable beginning of my determination never to surrender this rare
woman, this tender and gracious miracle.

The consequences of such a determination I did not

then foresee, but they were explained to me in part by an event which occurred three nights later. Like any husband and wife we ultimately felt even our perfect home confining and we wanted to go to a movie, but this was no easy trick. Hana-ogi knew that I might be arrested if I appeared on the streets with her and I knew that she would get into serious trouble if she were seen with me, so she left our paper doors first and in five minutes I followed and we met inside the darkened theater and held hands like any beginning lovers, congratulating ourselves on having evaded the chaperones. But our luck didn't hold because this movie concerned the French Foreign Legion attacking a desert outpost and across the screen lumbered a long convoy of camels and Hana-ogi whispered, "Ships of the desert!" and I fell to laughing so hard that finally she clapped her hand over my mouth and cried, "Rroyd-san. Somebody see us."

She was right. People did stare and two women recognized Hana-ogi as the great star at Takarazuka, so that when the lights went up these women choked the aisle and begged an autograph and soon Hana-ogi was surrounded by young girls.

We hurried out a side door and she fled alone down a back street and I ambled up the main street and when I got home I found her sitting dumb on the floor, her head bowed. She told me that she had always known that some time we would be found out and that she was not frightened. She would have to leave Takarazuka but she might find a job in pictures. Or there were certain theaters in Tokyo which might offer her work. She said, "I not scare. But Takarazuka I like very very much." (She said, "I rike berry berry much.")

I suggested at once that perhaps she should leave me and return to Takarazuka dormitory and endanger no longer a brilliant career but she kept staring at the floor and said quietly words which meant this: "I always planned to act till I was past forty, for I shall grow old slowly, and when my days as an actress were over I intended to take the place of Teruko-san, who was the greatest dancer Takarazuka ever had and who now teaches us the classical steps. But when I came here, Rroyd-san, I knew the danger I ran and if tomorrow were yesterday I would come here again."

I think that's what she intended to say and I was deeply troubled by the responsibility I had undertaken and by the resolve I had made never to desert her, but when she saw my silent fears she put her soft hand upon my face and said, "This time only time I be in love. I not stop our love one day before . . ." She made a great explosion with her hands as if the world had fallen in. She embraced me and we fell back upon the bed roll and I undressed her and her slim yellow body shone in the moonlight like a strand of gold that had fallen across my pillow, and she started to whimper and said, "I not speak true. Oh, Rroyd-san, I afraid. I not want to leave Takarazuka. I not want to sit by temple—begging—old woman—teeth broken away. But if I go you now, I never find courage to come back. I never love nobody no more. Never, never. (She pronounced it, "I nebber rub nobody, nebber, nebber.") I not want to be alone. I want to sleep here, with you." Beside my head she placed her hard, tiny pillow stuffed with rice bran and we talked no more, for we were finding, as so many people must, that the ways of love are often terrifying when the day is done and one can no longer avoid studying the prospects of the future.

But next day she gave me proof of the courage she said she did not have. We were eating cold fish and rice when our doors slid back and disclosed beautiful Fumiko-san. A curious change came over Hana-ogi and it seemed that she was no longer in our little house but back on the stage at Takarazuka and I appreciated how desperately a part of her that theater was. Fumiko had come, she said, to warn us. An Osaka newspaperman had seen us at the movies and had informed the Supervisor, who had not reprimanded Hana-ogi that afternoon because he hoped she would come to her senses before he was forced to take official action. Fumiko-san implied that he had asked her to speak with the brilliant star who had so much to lose if she persisted in her indiscretion.

Hana-ogi was deeply disturbed by this news and I became aware that these two girls had long ago formed a team of mutual protection and that they had always stood together as a team against the difficulties and defeats of their profession. Earlier Fumiko had found an American who had imperiled her career by kissing her in public and Hana-ogi had protested. Now it was Fumiko's turn to sound the warning. The two exquisite girls talked for a long time in Japanese and I judged they were assessing the various risks in the situation but Fumiko's arguments did not prevail and she left with tears in her eyes. When she had closed the doors Hana-ogi said simply, "I stay."

I discussed with her the possible results of this choice, even at times coming close to arguing on Fumiko's side, so that Hana-ogi stopped short, stood facing me, and demanded, "More better I go?" When I cried no and kissed her, she closed the discussion by saying, "I stay."

There was a firmness about her mouth when she said this and I was surprised, for I had come to look upon her as the radiant symbol of all that was best in the Japanese woman: the patient accepter, the tender companion, the rich lover, but when Hana-ogi displayed her iron will I reflected that throughout the generations of Japanese women there had also been endlessly upon them this necessity to be firm, not to cry, not to show pain. They had to do a man's work, they had to bear cruel privations, yet they remained the most feminine women in the world. Now that I knew them, these strange Japanese women, I saw the contradiction everywhere. Katsumi was having a baby when she hadn't the slightest idea how it would be cared for or under what flag, yet it was she who bolstered up the spirits of her family. Hana-ogi had placed her career in jeopardy for a few months in a tiny house along a canal with a man who could never marry her. The young girls I saw with their American soldiers, the little women bent double carrying bricks and mortar to

the ninth story of a new building, the old women in rags
who pulled plows better than horses, and the young wives
with three children, one at breast, one strapped on the
back, one toddling at her heels. I concluded that no man
could comprehend women until he had known the women
of Japan with their unbelievable combination of unre-
mitting work, endless suffering and boundless warmth—
just as I could never have known even the outlines of love
had I not lived in a little house where I sometimes drew
back the covers of my bed upon the floor to see there the
slim golden body of the perpetual woman. I now understood why ten thousand American soldiers had braved
the fury of their commanders and their country to marry
such women. I understood why there were supposed to be
many thousands of American-Japanese babies in the
islands. I understood why perhaps a half million American men had wandered down the narrow alleys to find the
little houses and the great love.

On this night I could not sleep. I was agitated by Hana-ogi's problem although as events turned out, I should have been concerned about my own. I was aware that I had found that one woman whose mere presence beside me in the dark night made me both complete and courageous. Toward four in the morning I hammered my pillow in confusion and Hana-ogi wakened and felt my forehead and said, "Rroyd-san, you sick!" And she leaped up from our bed and tended me as if I were a child and I hadn't the fortitude to tell her that I was in a trembling fever because her picture of an old woman huddling beside a Buddhist temple had made me nightmarish.

She cooled my head and wrapped dry sheets about us and I went to sleep assured that somehow we would escape from the inevitable consequences of our acts. But when I woke I was shivering again, not from fever but from outrage. For Lt.Col. Calhoun Craford, a paunchy red-faced man who hated every human being in the world except certain Methodists from his corner of a hill county in Georgia, stood over our bed. His round florid face looked like a decaying pumpkin as he stared down at us.

"Well," he drawled infuriatingly. "You doin' mighty fine down there, Major." He kicked at the bed roll and Hana-ogi drew a sheet about her neck. Then Lt.Col. Craford got purple in the face and shouted, "You get to hell up here, Major Gruver. The Giniral's gonna hear about this." He muscled his way about our tiny room, knocking things over, and I leaped from bed, but before I could do anything he threw my pants in my face and grunted, "Fine spectacle you are. A giniral's son, shackin' up with a nigger."

With an almost premonitory sense I recalled Joe Kelly's

129

violent threat one night when he had come home beat:
"Some day I'll kill that fat bastard." I felt that if Lt.Col.
Craford said one more thing in that room I'd beat Kelly to
the job. I think the colonel sensed this, for he looked contemptuously at Hana-ogi huddled beneath the sheet and
stalked through the paper doors. They trembled as he
passed.

When Lt.Col. Craford showed me in to General Webster's office in Kobe the old man minced no words. "What
in hell does this mean, Lloyd!" He was much more profane than I can repeat and he had all the details. "A fine,
clean, upstanding man like you! The son of a general in
the United States Army. Shacking up with some
cheap . . ."

I stood there and took it. He never mentioned Eileen,
but it was obvious that he was bawling me out on her be-
half. She had been held up to public ridicule. His wife
had been made to look silly. And I had outraged the
military decencies.

He shouted, "Did you sign that paper we sent you
acknowledging my order about public displays of affection with indigenous personnel?"

"Yes, sir."

"Then you know what's in the order?"

"Yes, sir."

"But you defied the order?"

"No, sir."

He exploded. "What in hell do you mean, no sir?"

"I've never been guilty of public affection with a Japanese girl."

Lt.Col. Craford stepped forward and said, "One of my
men saw them in the movies the other night. He followed
them along the back streets. They were holding hands,"
he added contemptuously.

"You're a liar!" I shouted.

General Webster rapped on the desk. "You be still,
Gruver. This is serious business. Now Craford, what actually happened?"

The repugnant colonel coughed, pointed at me with disgust and said, "He flagrantly broke the order, Giniral. Made love on the streets with a Jap girl. Set up house-keepin' with her. We've checked her record. A cheap whore."

"You . . ." I sprang from my position at attention and rushed at Craford. General Webster astonished me by reaching out and shoving me back.

"So you say you weren't seen with her?"

"That's what I do say, General Webster," I cried.

He became quite angry and asked in a low voice, "What do you call living together? Don't you call flagrant cohabitation a public display of affection?"

"No, sir," I said. "Not in terms of your order. We were never seen on the streets."

The general lost his composure and said, harshly, "I'm going to court-martial you, young man. You've broken every law of decency. You're under house arrest. Understand what that means?"

"Yes, sir."

"Watch him, Craford. If he does anything, throw him in the stockade."

"I will, sir," Craford wheezed.

"Furthermore," the general said, "I've cabled your father."

I gulped and he saw that that one had hurt, so I recovered by saying, "All right, sir, but I wish you hadn't."

"I wish you hadn't made an ass of yourself. Craford, take him under guard to his quarters."

Lt.Col. Craford enjoyed humiliating me, especially since I was the son of a four-star general, and he made quite a flourish of depositing me in my informal prison. He marched me into the lobby of the Marine Barracks, up the short flight of steps leading to the elevators, and down the hall past all the open doors. "This is it, nigger-lover," he growled.

As soon as he was gone I called the motor pool to see if I could get hold of Joe Kelly. After the fifth call I made contact and he whispered, "Can't talk, Ace, I'll be over." He arrived around noon that morning and slumped into a chair, "Jeez, Ace, the fat's in the fire."

"What happened?"

"Old Blubber-gut sent a bunch of strong-arm boys to search your house. They photographed everything. I hope you didn't have any Air Force papers you shouldn't have. Anyway, they wrecked the joint and boarded it up for good."

"What happened to Hana-ogi?"

"The neighbors say she slipped out right after you were arrested. Katsumi watched Blubber-gut's men tear up the house. Then she hurried out to Takarazuka with the news but Hana-ogi never batted an eye."

"How can people take things so calmly?" I cried.

"You learn," Joe explained. "When you're a Japanese woman or an enlisted man, you learn."

It was that evening that my real torment began, for when the performance of *Swing Butterfly* ended I looked down from my prison and saw graceful Hana-ogi, moving like a goddess down the flower walk and across the Bitchi-bashi and through the vegetable stalls and onto the path that led to the dormitory and long after she had disappeared I could see the image of that slim and graceful girl disappearing into the shadows—and I became more determined than ever that I must not lose her.

On the third evening after my house arrest began, I was sitting before the dismal meal of Marine food brought to my room by the waiter, when Mike Bailey opened my door softly, cased the joint like a detective, then motioned down the hall. In men's clothes, looking like a would-be janitor, Hana-ogi slipped in to see me. Mike made a hasty sign of benediction and tiptoed out.

I cannot describe how joyous it was to see Hana-ogi in my room. Not only had I been tortured by my longing to have her beside me in the bed roll but—as I realized now—I was even more hungry to hear her soft voice chattering of the day's events and I believe my heart actually grew bigger as she told me of the little things: "Fumiko-san say I crazy. When Colonel Craford smash house two kimonos rost."

"What do you mean, *rost*?"

"Men take. I no find."

I became so incensed over the lost kimonos that I realized that I had reached a new meaning of the word *love*. I was engaged in a heavenly contest with Hana-ogi to see which of us could give most to the other and this experience of surrendering my desires to another human being was new to me and frightening in its implications. I was already thinking vaguely about the future and a perplexing problem popped out as a blunt question: "Hana-ogi, how old are you?"

She counted thirty on her fingers and I felt as if a basket of icicles had been dumped over me, for a woman of thirty and a man twenty-eight seemed abnormal. I had known several officers married to women older than they and it always turned out badly. I was suddenly glum till I remembered that a Japanese girl is considered to be one year old at birth so we figured it out that Hana-ogi wa really only twenty-nine and that furthermore during eigh months of each year we would be the same age. It was extraordinary how much more beautiful she seemed at twenty-nine than she had been at thirty.

Toward morning she dressed and left my room, asking, "You have dinner tonight—Makino's?"

I explained what house arrest meant and said that I had pledged my honor as an officer. She said simply, "I have pledge my honor too. I have pledge the honor of my mother and the food of my two sisters." Then she kissed me and left.

So that night I put my honor way down in the bottom drawer among my socks and crept through the alleys to Makino's and as I climbed the stairs to the little room where I had first seen Hana-ogi my heart beat like the throbbing of an airplane engine and I thought, "God, that I should have become so involved," but when I got there Hana-ogi in green skirt and brown blouse was waiting for me. Old Makino made us tempura and to my surprise I found I was getting to enjoy Japanese food. We talked of many things and Hana-ogi said that soon *Swing Butterfly* (she always call it *Butterfry*) would close in Takarazuka. Maybe it would go to Tokyo. The news was terrifying and I hadn't the courage to discuss what it might mean to us but she said, "I no go Tokyo. I stay here and wait for you."

It was incredible to me that she would give up Takarazuka and I said, "Hana-ogi, you can't."

Before she could reply Makino came running in and cried, "M.P.'s!" Ashamed of myself I crowded into a cupboard and heard the heavy tread of Lt.Col. Craford's polished boots and in that moment I understood what an ugly thing fear was and why we had fought the last war against the Germans: we were fighting the tread of heavy boots. And then like the wind on a stormy day I completely changed and felt disgusted with myself, an Air Force officer breaking my word, hiding in a closet with a Japanese girl who should have hated me. It was the low spot of my life and when Lt.Col. Craford stamped down the stairs I stepped out of the closet and said, "Hana-ogi, I've got to go back."

She looked at me closely and asked, "When M.P. come . . ." She pointed at the closet and asked, "You sorry?" She could not find the right word for *ashamed* but she did bring a blush to her cheeks and she did act out my shame.

"Yes," I said. "I gave my word." But as I turned to go a flood of terrible longing overtook me and I grasped her face in my hands and cried, "Don't go to Tokyo, Hana-ogi. Wait here. I cannot let you go."

Her slim, straight body grew limp and she whispered to me in Japanese, something which meant, "Not Takarazuka or my mother could take me away."

I kissed her hands as I had done that first night. There were a hundred things I wanted to say, but I was choked with confusion. I walked boldly down the stairs, marched openly along the street to the Marine Barracks. Hana-ogi, aware of the deep shame I had felt in the closet and sharing it with me, marched just as brazenly beside me in her distinctive Takarazuka costume and kissed me good-bye at the barracks. "Rroyd-san," she said softly, "I love you takusan much."

When I entered the barracks, my father and General Webster were waiting. My father looked down the street at Hana-ogi walking bravely back to the dormitory and said, "Pretty girl. Almost pretty enough to justify an officer's breaking his word."

General Webster started to bluster but Father cut him short. He took us into the manager's office and let me have it.

My father is no puling one-star general ordered about by his wife. He said, "You idiot. You poor, bewildered idiot."

I have never heard my father swear. He chews gum when he's mad and makes the muscles in his jaw stand out and right now he looked as if he could beat me up. I stood at attention and looked straight ahead.

"What are you gonna do?" he asked contemptuously. "Dishonor your uniform, humiliate your friends?" He walked around me then snorted. "Some officer!"

General Webster said, "You've broken your word of honor and you're going to be court-martialed."

Father cut in and asked, "Well, what are you gonna do?"

I said firmly, "As soon as I get out of here I'm finding another house."

General Webster gasped and Father stormed. "That you won't do! There's a night plane to Korea. Get on it. I had some orders cut. Take them and get out."

I said, "All right, and when I come back it'll be to Hana-ogi."

The effect of this strange name on my father was startling. Apparently he was unable to accept the fact that Japanese girls actually had names and that American officers might love those alien names and the curious creatures to whom they belonged. He shouted, "Ruin yourself over some common whore!"

I had taken a lot these last few days and I'd had enough. I hauled back my right fist and let my father have one below the left ear. He staggered back, got his footing and came at me, but General Webster separated us. We were all trembling and furious but Webster spoke first: "By God, you've struck a . . ."

"Get out of here, Webster," my father snapped. "I'll handle this."

Frightened and dismayed, General Webster retreated and while we watched him go, I had a moment to steel myself for the brawl I knew must follow. Four times in my father's career he had dragged colleagues into a boxing ring where in the anonymity of shorts he had massacred them. Before our fight began I thought in a flash of how strange it was that I had belted my father for saying far less than what Lt.Col. Craford had said and I experienced a dizzy sensation that when he turned back to face me I would see my enemy and my friend.

I shook the dizziness away and cocked my fists, but when he turned he was grinning and chomping his gum. "I take it she's not a prostitute," he laughed.

I started to say, "Sir, this girl . . ." but he interrupted me and pulled me into a chair beside him and asked, "Son, what's this all about?"

Again I started to explain but he said, "I flew out here from the Presidio to knock some sense into you. But you're not in the market for sense, are you?"

I said, "I don't want any lectures."

He laughed and chewed his gum and said, "Son, I wouldn't respect you if you hadn't swung on me. She seemed right pretty and you say she isn't a tramp?"

I told him who she was and he said, "By heavens, Mark Webster must have dropped his drawers when he heard about you having a house. He drove me in to see it. Say, they don't build very big houses in Japan, do they? Say, tell me how you promoted a house?"

I started to tell him about Katsumi and Joe but he said, "Lord knows, son, I hoped you would marry Eileen Webster. Good family, staunch military background. Mother's a bit of a bore but in service you can always get away from her. Say, have you heard the news that really galls Webster? His daughter's serious about a real-estate sales-man from Seattle. Major, I think. Webster's furious and is rotating the fellow back to the States."

He sized me up carefully, chewing his gum, and said, "Y'know, son, if you still wanted Eileen you could have her. Wait a minute! Don't underestimate that kind of marriage. Right now you're all boiled up about sex, but a man lives a long life after that fire goes down. Then you appreciate having a woman you can talk to, some one who knows military life. What do you and Madame Butterfly talk about?"

He waited for me to speak but as soon as I started he said, "Let's get back to Eileen. You ever know any officers married to women who disliked the military? Sad lot. Sad business. Your mother and I haven't been what you might call romantic lovers . . ." He slapped his leg and burst into real laughter. "Could you imagine your mother in a shack along a canal! But anyway we've always been able to talk. We want the same things. We want the same things for you, Lloyd."

He paused and I thought I was back in St. Leonard's on another occasion like this. My father was saying, "Your mother and I want the same things for you, Lloyd," but even then I knew for a certainty that Mother had never wanted those things for me and I had the strange feeling that if she were in Japan right now—if she knew the whole story—she would be on my side and not Father's.

He said, "I suppose you've figured what your present course would mean to things like life plans."

"What do you mean, present course?"

"Well, getting married to a Japanese girl."

"Married!"

"Sure, married." He chewed his gum real fast and then

said, "You mean you haven't thought about marriage? You mean you think you're the smartest guy on earth. Can shack up with a girl, have children even, and never think of marriage."

"I wasn't thinking of marriage," I said weakly.

"I know you weren't," he roared. From the other room General Webster stuck his head through the door and asked nervously, "Everything all right?"

"Get out of here," my father commanded, and I thought how rarely men like him could respect men like Webster or men like the one I seemed on the verge of becoming. "Squaw man," the Army would have called me in the old days. He walked up and down the room flexing his head muscles and then turned sharply, speaking in machine-gunlike tones.

"Don't you see what's gonna happen, son? You're gonna work yourself into a box. You'll be unable to find a solution. So suddenly you hit on marriage! You'll marry the girl and that'll make everything just dandy. Good God, son! You're twenty-eight years old. Why didn't you marry Eileen that summer in San Antonio?"

Softly, with the mention of Eileen's name, that first dreamy summer flooded back to me here in Kobe and I said, "I never really understood, Father. I guess it must have been that bachelor party."

"What party?" he asked suspiciously. "What'ja do?"

"Not what you mean. Remember when General Hayward's son was marrying Della Crane?"

"You mean Harry Crane's girl?"

"Yes. Her father had been killed at the Bulge. . . ."

"Damned brave man. We could use a few men like Harry Crane in Korea."

"So Mark Webster's wife was more or less arranging the wedding. Very formal. But the night before a gang of us younger officers took Charley Hayward out and got him so drunk he was fifteen minutes late for the wedding. Everybody thought it was very funny except Mrs. Webster. After the wedding she gave us a terrible tongue-lashing. It wasn't that we'd spoiled Della and Charley's wedding. It was that we'd spoiled her plans. I've always been afraid of Eileen since then."

"Afraid?"

"Well, sort of. After the ceremony the four of us who had gotten Harry drunk drove out to Randolph Field. Nobody said anything and we drove very fast and once when a Ford truck almost socked us one of the men said, 'That would be the second truck that mowed us down today,' and we all laughed and got drunk again and for the rest of that summer I never really seriously thought about marrying Eileen. Then Korea came along."

"But you have thought about marrying Madame Butterfly?"

"No," I said.

"A son doesn't bust his father, Lloyd, unless he's thinking pretty deeply about something. Look, son. Suppose you do marry this yellow girl. I'm on the selection board and your name comes up. I'd pass you by and if I wasn't on the board I'd advise the others to pass you by. We don't want officers with yellow wives. And where would you live in America? None of our friends will want you hanging around with a yellow wife. What about your children? Y'can't send half-Jap boys to the Point."

I thought it was very like my father to assume that all his grandchildren would be boys who would naturally attend the Point. I was going to say something about this, but he kept talking.

"Son, Mark Webster was blustering. I've talked him into forgetting your court-martial. When I was sore I asked him to cut orders sending you back to Korea. Even yet it's a great temptation for me to approve those orders and tell you to get back there and fight this thing out. But you've had Korea. Say, how are those Russian jets?"

I said they were good and he asked, "Y'think that Russian pilots man those planes?"

I said I thought so but we hadn't captured any.

"Those Russian are bastards," he said. "Real bastards."

I said, "We've been able to handle them so far."

He banged the chair and said, "Son, don't take sex too seriously."

I said, "What should you take seriously?"

He said, "A whole life." He chewed his gum furiously and said, "A whole, well-rounded life."

I said, "Promotions and place in society and things like that?"

He looked at me quizzically and said, "You pulling my leg, son?"

I said, "Like the way you married a general's daughter?"

He said very calmly, "I ought to clout you. I just don't understand you sometimes. In ten years you'll be fighting the Japs again."

"Maybe. But I won't be fighting Hana-ogi."

"How can an officer get mixed up with a Japanese girl and take it seriously?"

I said, "Look, Pop. This gag worked once. This man-to-man . . ."

He looked half amused and asked, "What do you mean?"

I said, "Remember St. Leonard's when I thought I wanted to skip the Point and study English or something like that?"

"Long time ago, I'd forgotten."

"No you didn't, Pop. All the way out here from the Presidio you tried to remember what trick it was that convinced me then to do what you wanted me to do."

He blustered a moment and said, "Son, let's not obscure the facts. I'm here because you're my son and I'm very proud of you. Believe it or not I'm even proud that you had the guts to ignore Mark Webster's stupid order and find yourself a house in Osaka. But I don't want to see a decent American kid like you waste his life. Son, I've watched our men marry German girls and French girls and even Russian girls. Invariably, if you know the man, it's a sign of weakness. They're all panty-waists. Strong men have the guts to marry the girls who grew up next door. Such marriages fit into the community. They make

the nation strong. In your case and mine such marriages
fit into military service. Leave it to the poets and painters
and people who turn their back on America because
they're afraid of it to go chasing after foreign girls."

He chomped his gum and said, much more slowly, "I
ever tell you about Charley Scales? Resigned his com-
mission and joined General Motors. Said he'd make a
lot of money and he did. Some years later he came to
proposition me about joining him. Lloyd, that was in
1933 when the Army was the garbage can of democracy
but I didn't even think twice. I've been tempted in my
life but never by Charley Scales. Right now!" He snapped
his fingers and said, "Who'd you rather be, Charley Scales
or me?"

It was a childish trick but it had a great effect on me.
In my mind's eye I could see Charley Scales, a big, happy
man of some distinction in Detroit and the world. But to
compare him with my father was ridiculous.

Father said, "You talk this over with your Madame
Butterfly. You'll find she agrees with me."

I said. "I will."

He said, "By the way, where'd she learn English?"

I said she didn't speak English and he cried, "You mean
you've learned Japanese?"

I said, "No."

He stopped chewing his gum and looked at me. "You
mean—you have no common language? French, maybe?"

I said, "Well, you see . . ."

"You mean you can't talk together?"

"Well, on a really intricate problem she . . ." I was
going to explain that she danced the words for me, but
I felt that Father wouldn't understand. But he surprised
me.

When he realized that we shared no language he became unusually gentle. I cannot recall his ever having
been quite as he was at that moment. He put his arm
about my shoulder and said reassuringly, "Son, you'll
work this thing out."

He called for General Webster and said gruffly, "Mark,

I was wrong. I'm tearing up these orders for Korea. This kid doesn't need Korea. His problem is right here."

General Webster said, "That's what I told him and look how . . ."

"Mark, don't blow your top at this kid."

"Why not? Disobeying an order, breaking his word, striking a superior . . ."

Father laughed and said, "Now you and I know, Mark, that it was completely silly to issue such an order to a bunch of healthy young men surrounded by pretty girls. But that's beside the point. Don't get sore at Lloyd."

"Why not?"

"Because he's going to be your son-in-law."

"He's what?"

"He doesn't know it yet, and Eileen doesn't know it yet but if you want to do something constructive, keep real-estate salesmen away from your daughter. Because sooner or later she's going to be my daughter, too."

The two generals stamped out of the barracks and in three hours my father was on his way back to the Presidio.

If Father thought that the tricks which had defeated me in prep school would still work he was misled, for now I knew my mind. I had met a delectable woman, one whom I could love forever, and I simply wasn't worried about fathers and generals and Air Force rules. Here on this earth I had found Hana-ogi and by the time my father arrived back in California she and I had things worked out. We made a deal with Joe and Katsumi whereby we took one corner of their house and here we established a life as warm and loving as two human beings have ever known.

I would come home from the airfield to find Joe and Katsumi preparing the evening meal. They would tell me what had happened that day and I would exchange military gossip with Joe, but it would be a nervous time, for I would be watching the door and finally we would hear Hana-ogi's soft steps coming up the alley and Katsumi and Joe would slip away for a moment to gather wood or buy things at the store. The door would open and there would be Hana-ogi, a glimmer of perspiration on her soft golden cheeks. Like all Japanese she carried her books and bundles wrapped in a bright silk shawl tied cross cornered, and when I think of her at the sliding door of that little house I see her kick off her saddle shoes, drop the silken bundle, run her hand through her hair and hurry across the tatami to kiss me. At such times I would catch her in my arms, swing her into the air and drop her behind the screen that cut off our portion of the room. There she would swiftly slip off her Western clothes and slowly fold herself into a brocaded kimono. She was lovely; beyond words she was lovely.

144

But I must not imply that the warmth and wonder of that house came solely from Hana-ogi, beautiful and complete as she was, for I think that I have never seen a more satisfactory wife than Katsumi Kelly. She organized her house to perfection and kept it immaculate, even though Hana-ogi and I were apt to be careless. She could cook, she could sew, she could talk on many subjects and as her pregnancy advanced she gave promise of being an even finer mother than she was a wife.

Sometimes I used to watch her and I recalled with embarrassment that once in the consul's office I had almost refused to kiss her because she seemed so clodden and repugnant with her giggling and her big gold tooth. Now she seemed to me one of the most perfect women I had ever known, for she had obviously studied her man and had worked out every item of the day's work so that the end result would be a happy husband and a peaceful home. I asked Joe about this once and he said, "Ten years from now in America there'll be a club. Us fellows who married Japanese girls. Our password will be a suppressed giggle. Because we won't want them other lugs down the street to discover what gold mines we got."

I asked, "Are all Japanese wives as good as Katsumi?"

He said, "I admit I got somethin' special. But you don't hear the other boys kickin'." We wrapped our kimonos around our legs and sat back to enjoy one of the sweetest moments of the day. The girls were preparing supper and we listened to them talking Japanese. Katsumi spoke rapidly—the day's gossip, no doubt—and Hana-ogi, washing our rice, said over and over at least two dozen times, "Hai! Hai!" The phrase shot out of her mouth with such force it seemed to have come from the very bottom of her stomach, a cry of primeval terror. Actually it was merely the Japanese way of saying *yes*. But in addition to this machine-gun *hai* she kept nodding her head and chanting mournfully, "Ah, so desu-ka! Ah, so desu-ka!" To hear the girls in any trivial conversation would convince you that some sublime tragedy had overtaken us all.

Joe finally asked, "What are you sayin'?"

Katsumi looked up startled and explained, "I speak Hanako-san about a fish my father catch one day."

I started to laugh but Joe asked quietly, "Was it a big fish?"

"More big than this one," Katsumi said proudly. "Hanako-san say she never see such a fish." I liked Katsumi's name for Hana-ogi. Japanese girls often take their names from feminine or poetic words to which they generally add -ko or -yo. Thus at Takarazuka most girls had names like "Misty Snow" or "Spring Blossom" or Starry Night." And their names usually ended in -ko. For myself, I preferred the other form, Hanayo, and once Hana-ogi told me, "Hanako more Japanese but Hanayo more sweet."

The longer I lived with Joe Kelly, reared in an orphanage and rejected by his foster parents, the more astonished I was that he could adjust so perfectly to married life. He was a considerate husband, a happy clown around the house and the kind of relaxed and happy family man you see in the advertisements of the *Saturday Evening Post*.

Speaking of the *Post*, it helped me understand a little better what married life is. On May 30th the girls were all whispers and at dinner they sprang the big surprise! It was an American holiday, so they had pumpkin pie. Where they had finagled the pumpkin we never knew, but the pie was something out of this world, for they had used the pumpkin as you would apples or cherries and had baked it just as it came out of the can and it was really dreadful. I took one look at it and started to say, "What . . ." but Joe cut me short and tasted his piece.

"It's good," he said laconically.

The girls bit into their pieces and you could see them sort of look at each other as if to say, "Americans must be crazy. To eat something like this on holidays." We finished the disgusting dessert in silence and four days later Katsumi, leafing through an old copy of the *Post* saw a picture of real pumpkin pie. She waited till I got home and surreptitiously asked me if that was pumpkin pie. I said yes and she asked me how it stayed so thick and so soft and I told her how you made pumpkin custard and she started to cry and when Joe came home she hugged him and kissed him and told him how ashamed she was and since Hana-ogi wasn't home yet I sat glumly in my corner and thought about the time I had laughed at Hana-ogi for her sentence, "Lo, the postillion has been struck by lightning," and I concluded that Joe's way was better and I wondered how a kid from an orphanage could understand a problem like that while I hadn't had the slightest glimmer.

However, I must not imply that all Japanese women are perfect wives. A trip along our alley would convince anyone that Japanese homes contained every problem to be found in American homes; plus some very special ones. In the narrow house next us lived the Shibatas. He was a minor business official who received practically no pay but had an enviable expense account from which he drew on most nights of the week for expensive geisha parties. He siphoned off part of the expense account to support one of the pretty young geishas on the side. It was rumored that he kept her in a second home near the center of Osaka and traditionally his wife should have accepted such an arrangement with philosophical indifference, but Mrs. Shibata was not traditional. She was modern and tried to stab her husband with a knife. At three in the morning when black-coated little Shibata-san came creeping home we could catch a moment of silence as the door to his house opened, followed by an explosion from his wife who used to chase him with a club. She was notoriously shrewish, and Katsumi and Hana-ogi apologized for her. "Japanese wife expected to understand men like geisha," they said.

Nor were most Japanese wives the patient silent creatures I had been told. When Sato-san, a railroad employee, took his wife shopping she trailed a respectful three feet behind him and never spoke a word unless spoken to by her immediate friends. But at home she was a tyrant and rebuked Sato-san contemptuously for not earning more money. As I came to know the wives of Japan I had to conclude that they were exactly like the wives of America: some were gentle mothers, some were curtain dictators and some few were lucky charms who brought their men one good thing after another. I decided that which kind a man found for himself was pretty much a matter of chance, but whenever I looked at Hana-ogi I had an increasingly sure feeling that I had stumbled upon one of the real lucky charms.

Across the alley lived the widow Fukada and her twenty-year-old daughter Masako, who had had a G.I. baby without being married. Sometimes at night we could hear the grandmother screaming at Masako that she was a slut, and other women in the alley agreed. The American baby was not wanted and was not allowed to play with pure Japanese babies, and although everyone in the alley loved Joe Kelly and Katsumi and although they were proud to have a great Takarazuka actress living among them with her American flier, there was deep resentment against Masako Fukada, who had disgraced the blood of Japan.

Down the alley were the hilarious Watanabes. His wife was almost as broad as he was tall. They got along together fine except that Watanabe-san had a mistress even more compelling than a geisha: he was mad-crazy to play pachinko. He spent all his money at pachinko and all his spare hours at the pachinko parlor. When the police closed the parlor each night at eleven he would reluctantly come home and we would hear fat Mrs. Watanabe shouting derisively, "Here comes Pachinko-san! Dead broke!"

The pachinko parlor stood on the corner nearest the canal, an amazing single room lined with upright pinball games. For a few yen Watanabe-san would be handed seven steel balls, which he would shoot up to the top of the pinball machine and watch agonizingly as they fell down to the bottom, almost always missing the holes which paid the big prizes. The pachinko parlor on our alley was filled from morning till night and everyone was bitten by the pachinko bug, including Hana-ogi and me, and it was a curious fact that my friendship with the pachinko players in that crowded parlor would later save my life.

Across the alley from the pachinko room was the flower shop. You would have thought there could not be in that entire alley one rusty yen for flowers, but almost everyone who lived along our narrow gutters stopped into the flower shop for some solitary spray of blooms which was carried reverently home for the alcove where the gods lived. I cannot recall a moment when there were not flowers in our alcove and I—who had never known a violet from a daisy—came to love them.

The next shop is difficult to describe. In fact, it is impossible because in all the rest of the world there are no shops quite like these in Japan. It was a sex shop where husbands and wives could purchase tricky devices with which to overcome nature's mistakes and short changings. To satisfy our curiosity Katsumi-san took Joe and me there one day. The shy owner listened as we laughed at his amazing collection of sex machines. Then he said in Japanese, "Go ahead, laugh. Young Japanese men laugh, too. But when they're married and reach forty they come to me for help." Katsumi translated and then broke into an uncontrolled giggle. I asked her what she had said and she explained, "I tell him Joe no need help." The shy owner smiled nervously and replied, "At twenty nobody needs help."

But the true wonders of our alley were the children. I could neither count them nor forget them. They had round faces, very red cheeks, straight black bangs, fat little legs and boundless joy. I don't think I ever heard a Japanese child cry. Certainly I never saw one struck and I came to believe that the most delectable children I had ever seen were these noisy, hilarious children. Whenever they crowded around me as I came up the alley I loved Hana-ogi more.

Each house in our alley was desperately packed, so that one tiny room often became the equivalent of a full-sized American home and these teeming masses of people lived and worked and had babies and argued politics just like all people across the world. But there was this difference. Not a shred of anything was wasted, not even the human manure which was so patiently gathered each morning and from which sprang the flowers and the food. I recall certain evenings that spring when I entered this narrow alley at close of day and the front of every house would be open and dozens of children would run, black-bobbed, to greet me and from every open room facing the alley and the people of Japan would speak with me and I shared a warmth and goodness that I had never known in Lancaster or the camps where I grew up. I was one of the people—one of the millions of people who cling to whatever shred of hope and property they can grab hold of, and from this alley with the myriad children and the brawling and the flowers and the unwanted American-Japanese baby and the pachinko games and the sake drinking I borrowed a strength I had never had before.

It expressed itself in an unforeseen way. I was in my office at Itami Air Base when a sergeant appeared to tell me that Lt.Col. Calhoun Craford was outside. The florid colonel stepped in and got right down to business. "You think you're smart" (he said it: *Yawll thank yore smaht*) "gettin' a four-star giniral to come out and save your neck. You accustomed to hidin' behind your pappy's back?" Then he let me have it. "My men been trailin' you, Gruver. We know you and that tramp are holed up in enlisted man's quarters. But we can't touch you because of your pappy. So we're doin' something better. We're sendin' Joe Kelly back to the States."

"But what'll happen to Katsumi?"

The fat colonel looked at me with disgust. "Who's Kats-what's-his-name?"

"Kelly's wife."

"The Jap girl. Not up to us to worry what happens to her."

"You're not breaking up this family?"

"Don't call it a family. The girl's a cheap Jap tramp."

I said that Katsumi was a decent girl, that she was studying to become a Catholic, like her husband, but apparently Lt.Col. Craford hated Catholics worse than he hated colored people, for he said, "And when we finish with Kelly we'll figure out some way to handle you. Father or no father."

He left me and I sat for a long time staring at my desk, contemplating the mess I had made of things. I had proved myself a shoddy officer. I had loused up the life of an enlisted man. I had made Eileen look ridiculous and I hadn't done much better with Hana-ogi. Then I began to weigh what I had accomplished in Japan and things looked brighter. I had come to know what a home meant, an unpretentious home where love was. I had found a beautiful girl filled with tenderness and grace and wit. I had learned at last to share my heart with another human being. And most of all I had discovered the tremendous passion of turning down the bed roll at night and seeing the slim, perfect body of Hana-ogi. I jumped up and cried, "Gruver-san, if you lose that girl you're nuts. Marry her, stupid. Marry her."

But as soon as I had said the words I began to sweat and I remembered all the predictions my father had made that night in the Marine Barracks. My career gone, my wings and their promise lost, my place in my American world vanished and I with an Asiatic wife. It was then that my new-found courage asserted itself.

I recognized the trick my father had played on me. He had planted those poisonous seeds so that they could flourish at just such a moment, and I decided that it was against such tricks that I was revolting. I did not want to become a general like my father, with his cold cutoffness from the world. I didn't want to be a second General Webster, ruled by Eileen. And I certainly didn't ever want to become a Lt.Col. Craford. I wanted to be one man, standing by myself, sharing whatever world I could make with the woman who had helped me to discover that world. In my moment of resolution and light I knew that I would never waver from my purpose. I was going to marry Hana-ogi.

I called Joe Kelly and asked him to meet me at a tiny bar we knew in Osaka where M.P.'s never came. It's impossible to describe such Japanese bars to Americans. How can you explain a bar so small that it has space for only four customers and two hostesses?

"Joe," I said in greeting, "can you keep a secret?"

"Sure, Ace."

"I mean two secrets. Big ones?"

"Hanako havin' a baby?"

"Joe, Blubber-gut is laying for you. He's going to ship you home first chance he gets."

"That's no secret. He threatened me openly two days ago. I didn't tell anybody. Didn't want to worry you. But he shouted, 'All you nigger-lovers are goin' home. Soon.' "

"Joe, I want you to promise me you won't do anything stupid."

"Me? I should be stupid like him?"

"Look. One night I heard you tell Katsumi you were going to shoot Blubber-gut."

"Me? I'm no rod man. What's your other secret?"

I ordered another beer and took a big gulp. "Exactly what papers do you have to sign to marry a Japanese girl?"

Joe whistled and said, "Look, Ace. This ain't for you. Suppose Hanako is beggin' you to marry her! It ain't for you."

"Joe, don't jump to conclusions. I haven't told her yet. But so help me God, I'm going to marry that girl. What are the steps? " He repeated his earlier warning and I asked, "You mean you're sorry you married Katsumi?"

A big grin broke on Joe's face and he said, "One night I told you that bein' married to that Buddha-head was livin'. It ain't. It's somethin' much finer than livin'. It's like you was dead and all the stress and strain was over and all that was left was the very best—and it's the best because it's all wrapped up in her. It ain't livin', Ace. I used to live in Chicago. This is way beyond that."

I sat with my hands over my face and didn't look up for a moment. Then I said, "I feel exactly that way about Hanayo."

Joe ignored this and said, "Ace, I don't believe you could take the bad time they give you."

"What do you mean?"

"They wear you down. Enlisted men get used to bein' worn down but you ain't had the experience of diggin' your heels in real stubborn and resistin'."

"How do you mean?"

"They give you so many papers. The chaplain prays over you. And everything they do they do with crazy smiles, like you was off your rocker and only they could save you. And what's worse, they ask the girl so many heart-burnin' questions. Hana-ogi won't tell you but some night when you kiss her she'll break down and cry for an hour. I don't think you could take it."

I said, "Tomorrow morning I'm starting the paper work."

He said, "Ace, you're a big man. It would make them look silly to lose you to a Japanese girl. So they'll hit you with big stuff."

"I'm ready."

"Ace, they'll hit you with generals and admirals and men who knew your father. The only way you can swing it is to get the help of your Congressman. Who is he?"

"I don't know."

"Where do you live?"

"I don't have . . ."

"Well, where do you vote?"

"I've never voted." For the first time I realized that I was completely a military man. The Air Force was my home. I cast my vote with the talking end of an F-86.

Joe studied this and said, "Don't worry. Practically any Congressman would love to fight your battle. You want me to take it up with Shimmark? He loves to get his name in the paper."

I thanked Joe and said I'd work it out somehow, but that very night they started to throw the big reasons at me, even before I had told Hana-ogi that I was going to give up the Air Force and marry her. It happened a long way off, in Texas, for that night I heard a radio program explaining why the Democrats of Texas were going to support Dwight Eisenhower for President. I had known the general at several different bases and had played with his son. Suddenly, there in the dark streets of Osaka, Eisenhower became the symbol of what a major in the Air Force might become: a man ready for many different kinds of action if his country needed him. For one hellish hour I walked the streets weighing what I was doing and then I found myself at the entrance to my alley, and skinny Watanabe-san had struck it rich at pachinko and ran out in the street to offer me a beer and I got a rosy glow on, and about eleven Hana-ogi came down to take me home, but I did not tell her then of the great decision I had made.

In the morning I sneaked into Kobe, for I did not want either General Webster or Lt.Col. Craford to see me, and I went to the American consulate. Luck was with me, for Mr. Carstairs, the fuddy consul, was not yet in and I could talk privately with his secretary, the horse-faced girl who had married a G.I.

She recognized me at once and said, "You made my kid brother the hero of his whole block."

"How do you mean?"

"Your autograph. The kids take Korea seriously, even if grownups don't."

Although she said this with a smile I noticed that she was eyeing me suspiciously and after I had made a few awkward starts at conversation she put her two hands firmly on her desk and said, "Major Gruver, did you come here to find out about marrying a Japanese girl?"

I gulped and must have blushed, for she added immediately, "I can spot you guys a mile off. What are you ashamed of?"

I asked her what she meant by that and she laughed. "You all think there's some tricky way to get around the red tape. And you're all ashamed to speak to your superior officers." She looked up at me with such infectious amusement that I had to laugh, whereupon she said, "But you, Ace Gruver. I never thought you'd tumble for a Buddha-head."

I fumbled a bit and asked, "Just what are the paper requirements?"

"I can't tell you a thing, Major."

"You work here."

"Forbidden. You military heroes have to clear everything through your chain of command."

"You mean it's as tough as that?"

"It's tougher, Major. We don't want men like you

marrying Japanese girls. We make it extra tough for men like you."

"I was only asking," I said.

"Sure! There hasn't ever been a soldier in here who really intended to get married. They were all only asking!"

"Then you won't help?"

The big girl looked out the door to see if Mr. Carstairs had arrived yet. Satisfying herself on that point she said, "Old Droopy Drawers lives by the book. He'd fire me if he saw me talking with you about legal matters. But I figure if a man can shoot down seven MIG's he's entitled to some help."

She showed me a completed file on a sailor who had married a Japanese girl. I had heard of the paper work. I had even seen some of it during Joe Kelly's marriage. But I had not comprehended how repetitious and degrading it was. I began to understand what Joe meant when he said that only an enlisted man, conditioned to standing in line and taking guff, could see a Japanese wedding through.

I said, "Isn't this a pretty tough obstacle course?"

The girl laughed and said, "If I had my way, we'd make it tougher. Men like you oughtn't to grab Jap girls just because they're available."

"I don't want a lecture," I protested.

"Look, Major. I'm your big sister. Remember? We just made a study of which Americans were marrying Japanese girls. The findings aren't pleasant." She riffled some papers and read off the dismal case histories: "Wyskanski, Noel. Orphaned. No education. Had a fist fight with the Catholic priest. Reform school." "Merchant, Nicholas. Ran away from home. Been in guard house regularly since being drafted. Two court-martials. Threatened the Japanese social worker who proved that the first girl he wanted to marry was a notorious prostitute." "Kelly, Joe. Your friend. Worst record in the Air Force in Korea. Constant discipline problem. Accused of murdering a drunk in Chicago but case thrown out of court on technicality.

Always on the verge of criminal prosecution. Recommended twice for dismissal from the Air Force." She tossed Kelly's paper aside and asked bluntly, "How'd you get mixed up with a dead-end mutt like him?"

"He was in my unit."

"Did you meet your Japanese girl through Kelly?" I hesitated a moment trying to frame an answer but the smart girl understood. She put aside the file and said patiently, "Major Gruver, you're simply not the type. These men—these perpetual failures . . ." She hammered the file and turned away to blow her nose. At that moment the front door opened and in came prim Mr. Carstairs. In one instantaneous glance he saw me and the marriage file and his secretary wiping her eyes. He stepped precisely into the middle of the doorway and said, "My goodness, Major Gruver isn't thinking of getting married to a Japanese girl, is he?"

The secretary looked up and sniffed. "Yes, damn it all, he is. And I've been telling him he's a complete fool."

"You are," Mr. Carstairs said. He passed through our room and said sharply as he left, "But there's nothing to worry about. The Air Force wouldn't let such a stupid thing happen."

When he was gone the secretary asked, "Has your Jap girl started her part of the paper work?"

I said, "Well . . . I haven't . . ."

With great relief the big girl started to laugh. "I understand! You haven't asked her, have you? Thank God!"

I blushed and said, "Look, we're getting married."

She ignored this and said, "I feel so much better. Ace, dozens of you men come in here to ask about getting married. But most of you haven't proposed yet. Then I breathe easy because everything is all right."

"You have some special way of stopping it?"

"No," she said surprised. "It's just that first-class Japanese girls won't marry American men. They prefer Japan. Ace, believe me, it's ten-to-one that the girl you deserve won't marry you, and the kind you can get, you wouldn't want."

I looked at the shabby office and at the pile of marriage reports. Grimly I said, "You can start a new file. 'Gruver, Lloyd. Well educated. Never in trouble. Best man the Air Force had in Korea. Clean-cut American type. Married a Japanese girl because he loved her.' Show it to your Mr. Carstairs every day."

In real anger I went over to the village of Takarazuka, where I waited in a vegetable stall near the Bitchi-bashi and toward noon I saw the first Takarazuka girls go by in their swaying green skirts. Then Fumiko-san passed me and I hid in the back of the store until she had disappeared. Finally I saw Hana-ogi approaching and I had that rare experience that a man sometimes knows when he sees the girl he loves picking her way along a crowded lane unaware that he is watching, and at such times— when the girls are not on their good behavior, you might say—they are extraordinarily lovely and ratify doubly all thoughts and decisions of preceding days. Hana-ogi was like that. She wore a gray kimono flecked with silver and gold, and it encased her lovingly, and her feet in light gray zori threaded an intricate pattern through the crowds of noonday shoppers, and as she drew near my vegetable stall I was fluttering like a broken propeller but at last I knew what I wanted. I reached out, grabbed her arm, and drew her in beside me. The man who ran the stall smiled and moved out onto the pavement as if accustomed to having his shop invaded in that manner every day.

"Hanayo!" I cried with a passion I had never before experienced. "I've made up my mind, and I've started the paper work. We're going to be married."

Apparently she didn't understand for she said, "What do you say?"

"I'm going to marry you. Take you back to America."

I remember that the shop was filled along one wall with enormous white Japanese radishes, four feet long and thick as a man. Hana-ogi drew back against them and held her hand to her cheek, where in the Japanese style

short hair grew down in sideburns. She looked at me for a
moment and tears came into her dark eyes.

"We no speak of marriage, Rroyd-san. No. No."

"I know it's a surprise," I said. "But I've thought it all
out and I'm willing to give up the Air Force and find some
other job."

"But Rroyd, I no go America."

"We'll work that out, too," I said. "Some time they'll
change this crazy law so a man can take his wife home."

"You no understand, Rroyd-san. I no want to go."

I stepped away from the giant radishes and stared at
Hana-ogi. It was incomprehensible to me that any Japanese girl, living in that cramped little land with no con-
veniences and no future, would refuse America. What
was it the officer's wife in the Osaka P.X. had said: "The
damned little Jap girls lay in wait at street corners with
lassos and rope the American soldiers in." I said, "I'll explain it all to you tonight."

But she replied most strangely, "Some day you leave
Japan, Rroyd-san. Before you go I like you see pictures of
real Hana-ogi. In Kyoto."

"I don't want to see any pictures!" I cried. "Damn it, I
came here to tell you we're getting married."

"You get auto tomorrow morning—early." She moved
quickly toward the door of the shop, then turned to kiss
me passionately on the lips. "When you go back America,"
she said, "I want you remember great beauty of Hana-
ogi."

Early next morning we left Osaka in Lt. Bailey's Chevvy and drove along the side of a river which for untold centuries had carried water to the rice fields of this region. It lay far below the level of the road, hemmed in by strong dikes built many generations ago and upon all the land there was the mark of much toil and the footprints of many people. Wherever we looked women were at work hauling and lifting.

Our entrance to Kyoto was memorable, for we saw in the distance the soaring towers of great Buddhist temples, their tiers built with corners upswept in the Chinese style. And along one street we caught a glimpse of the famed Heian Shinto shrine, a glorious vermilion thing with enormour blood-red torii guarding it.

But today we were not interested in shrines or temples. We went along a side street burdened with age-old pines, where underneath a canopy of evergreen we stopped to enter a museum. It was built like a temple, with nearly a hundred statues of stone and wood, as if the old heroes of Japan had gathered to greet us, frozen forever in their stiff ceremonial attitudes. The curator hurried up to us and when he learned that I could speak no Japanese he summoned a striking young man. He was in his thirties, I judged, and wore heavy glasses. He had excellent teeth, a frank smile and a rare command of English.

"I studied at Oxford," he explained, "and served for some years in our store on Fifth Avenue and for two years in our store in Boston. What did you wish to see?" It was clear that he did not know Hana-ogi and that he supposed her to be merely some attractive street girl I had picked up for the day. He was therefore somewhat distressed when she spoke to him in Japanese, so I interrupted and said, "I understand you have an unusual collection of prints of Hana-ogi, of Ogi-ya."

Immediately he withdrew deep inside himself and studied me carefully. Then he looked at Hana-ogi and bowed very low. "You are Hana-ogi-san of Takarazuka," he said in precise English. "You are very beautiful. And you, Major, are Lloyd Gruver. Yes, yes. Even in Kyoto we have heard of you." I did not know whether he meant that he had heard of me as a flier or that he had heard of Hana-ogi and me, but he nodded formally and said, "I can truly appreciate your desire to see the famous prints of the other Hana-ogi."

He led us upstairs, past the frowning Japanese heroes, and I felt that I was in hostile land. In this strange building I at last got the feeling of being an invader, surrounded by an alien religion and a strange art many centuries older than my own native land. I experienced the feeling even more deeply when I sat on the floor in front of an easel while the young curator went to a locked cabinet. Hana-ogi must have sensed my uneasy thoughts, for she put her hand in mine and whispered, "Now you see greatest beauty."

I was totally unprepared for what I saw. I had developed a mental impression of the ancient Hana-ogi. She must have looked, I thought, something like my Hana-ogi: extraordinarily beautiful, yet with a distinctive oriental cast. I believed the pictures of her would look something like Botticellis.

I shall never forget the extreme shock of that first print. The young curator held it from me for a moment and said in reverence, "The first one is of Hana-ogi as a young girl, just come to Ogi-ya. It is by one of our finest artists, Shuncho." Then, bursting with pride and affection, he displayed the picture.

It was disgusting. The girl's face was pasty and flat. Her hair was a mass of yellow combs. She was swathed in seven kimonos that gaped at the neck. But worst of all, her eyes were caricatures, mere slants, and her teeth were

a horrid black. In this portrait of dead beauty I could
not find one shred of loveliness.

I must have betrayed my disappointment for both
Hana-ogi and the curator tried to explain that the design
was controlled by Japanese artistic tradition, the way a
portrait of a woman by Picasso does not appear really
beautiful. I remember trying real hard to remember who
Picasso was, but before I could get it they took away the
first picture and brought in another by an artist whose
name I didn't catch, but my dismay was greater than before. The famous courtesan had the same pasty face, slit
eyes and funereal teeth, but this time her head was
twisted into such an angle that I remember thinking, "If
she doesn't straighten up she'll strangle." In her left hand
she held one of the endless combs which she was jabbing
into her mass of oily hair, and in her right she grasped a
black ebony fan which made the whole picture look
stupid. Even the half dozen kimonos were poorly painted
and in odd colors.

It was the third picture which caused the argument. I
took down the name of the artist, Masayoshi, for he
showed Hana-ogi returning to the House of Ogi-ya after
her elopement. She was dressed in many kimonos covered
by a purple robe and followed by two barefoot servants
carrying an umbrella and a massive bouquet of flowers. I
studied the picture with dismay, for I recognized it immediately as one that Hana-ogi had described for me that
night when she danced the story of her predecessor, but
what she had not told me was that this picture of Hana-
ogi showed a remarkably ugly woman with a big nose,
dirt smears over her eyebrows and paunchy cheeks. "Why
she's ugly!" I cried. I felt defrauded.

My Hana-ogi withdrew as if she had been struck and
the young man pulled the print away. "I am afraid," he
said in clipped syllables, "that you have no appreciation
of our art."

"I was told that this Hana-ogi was the most beautiful
woman in Japanese history."

"She was," the young man insisted.

"But these pictures . . ."

"It's our style of art," he explained.

"But look at Hana-ogi-san here. This one. She's really beautiful."

The young man did not look at Hana-ogi-san. Instead he took the portrait of the ancient Hana-ogi back to the cabinet and returned with another. Quietly he said, "I am afraid you are blind to the problem, Major. But would you like me to explain in a few words?"

"Indeed I would," I said.

"You'll forgive me if they're very simple words?"

"I will. I've heard so much of this Hana-ogi I don't want to go home disappointed."

"If you have a free mind," he assured me, "you will go home elated. The picture I'm about to show you is by one of Japan's supreme artists, Utamaro. Have you heard of him?"

"No."

"No bother, but will you believe me when I say his work is prized all over the world? Good. You are going to see one of his loveliest creations. When you look at it don't think of Hana-ogi. Think only of this heavenly yellow."

He flashed the picture before me and the yellow was indeed like a fine sunlight. He continued his narration, pointing out the perfect proportions of the design, the exquisite line, the subdued color harmonies and the suggested textures. I followed him carefully and agreed with what he said. Then brusquely he said, "As for the face of Hana-ogi, we Japanese think it was sent down from heaven."

The intensity of his comment caught me unaware and from some distant corner of my brain came the affirmation, "The men who knew this woman thought she was beautiful." And immediately there came another terrible memory—of a time when some of us young officers were attending a wedding and we saw the bride and there was a moment of awful silence and somebody behind me whispered, "Well, every man thinks the girl he's marrying is pretty." And I could see myself back in America, about

to introduce my Hana-ogi to strangers who had never
known her and I could feel them cringing away from my
Japanese girl—unlovely to them—as I now cringed away
from the long-dead Hana-ogi. I looked again at the
treasured face, at the curious slanted eyes and the black
teeth and from my own humility and the vanished green
houses of the Yoshiwara came the assurance that she was
beautiful. I said, "I think I understand."

The young man started to take the Utamaro away but
I said, "Let me study it some more." I pointed to the colorful printing in the upper corner and asked what it was.
During the remarkable discussion that followed the
young curator stood crisply at attention with his left hand
upon the easel. I have only to close my eyes to see him
standing there with his faded echo of the great Hana-ogi.

"It's impossible to say what this printing means, Major.
It's a poem, written by some unimportant man who
visited Hana-ogi. These symbols are his name: The man
from the other side of Yanagiwara. That's all we know
about him, a stranger who came from a distant village
and saw the great woman once. But his poem will live
among us forever."

"What did he write?"

"I'm sorry but I cannot tell you the meaning."

"You can't translate the symbols?"

"Oh, yes!" he assured me proudly. "I was translator to
our Foreign Office during the peace treaty at San Francisco. But the Japanese language like Japanese beauty
and Japanese life can never be truly translated. For example, the name Hana-ogi means *flower* and *fan*, and its
symbols are woven into the poem, but what they are intended to mean in this particular poem no one can say.
The stranger from Yanagiwara himself did not know."

"What do you mean, he didn't know?"

"In Japan a man sees a beautiful woman and he ex-
presses words, but they have no specific meaning."

"How can words have no specific meaning? There's the
symbol. Right there. Why can't you read it?"

"Ah, but I can, Major. Trouble is, I can read it in so

many ways. According to one way the stranger from Yanagiwara is saying, 'Even a mere glimpse in autumn of that night-blooming flower, Hana-ogi, floods my soul with summer.'"

"That's clear enough," I said.

"But it isn't clear, because I'm only guessing that that's what the stranger meant, for the words can also be read, 'Hana-ogi is more beautiful than that evening flower I once laid on a fan for a love of old days and brings no chill of autumn to my heart.'"

I was confused. "You mean those same symbols can mean such different things?"

"They can also mean many other things, Major. Our life in Japan is one of implied meanings, hidden significances. For example, they say that you have fallen in love with Hana-ogi-san. Which Hana-ogi?"

At the mention of her name Hanayo-chan put her hand around mine and I said, "Which one? This one. The living one."

"But which of the living ones?"

"This one. Here!"

The young man, who must have hated Americans for taking his art galleries in Boston and London and New York, stood bitterly erect by the easel and said softly, "But there are many Hana-ogi-sans with us today. She is famous in Japan, this girl, and deeply loved. There is the peasant girl who is good to her mother and her six sisters. There is the young courtesan who was in training to be a geisha. Didn't you know that her father had sold her to a green house? There is the famous beauty who was rescued by one of the rich Matsudaira men. The one who committed suicide. His daughter, Fumiko-san, is at Takarazuka now. Or the gracious actress Hana-ogi who always used to be seen with Fumiko-san. Or the ascetic young woman who aspired to be Japan's greatest dancer. Or the reckless girl who ran away with an American flier. You see, we are a very subtle people. Our words mean many things."

I think that Hana-ogi had some intimation of what the

young man was saying, for she kept her hand close about
mine and when he was finished she rose and pulled me to
my feet. Staring purposefully at the young man she said
quietly, "I never tie my obi so," and she pointed to the
picture of long-dead Hana-ogi, the rare, the wonderful
courtesan whose memory still burned and she indicated
Hana-ogi's obi, tied in front the way professional prostitutes did to advertise.

I wanted to maul the young curator for having told me
these things but suddenly he smiled at me and said, "I
must show you one more portrait, Major. In some ways it
is the loveliest of all." He brought us a delicate thing, all
gold and yellow and faded blue. From it a young Hana-
ogi looked back across her shoulder at us, sweet and
beautiful as I had wanted her to be. She seemed to tanta-
lize the mind and in a lower corner of the picture appeared one of her youthful attendants, a child of nine
playing with battledore and shuttlecock. Lovingly the
curator indicated the child and said, "This was Tatsuta.
Even the names of the children who attended our immortal Hana-ogi are recorded." Then quite unexpectedly
he placed his hand tenderly on my Hana-ogi's head and
rumpled her hair. "This one was a Tatsuta, too. See, the
obi tied in back."

I thought for a moment that he had told me of my
Hana-ogi's history because he was in love with her and
jealous of me; but as we left the treasure room I turned
and saw him jealously storing the forty-one portraits of
the famous girl who long ago had graced the green houses
of Yoshiwara and I realized that he was indeed in love
with Hana-ogi, but not with my Hana-ogi.

On the drive home we were silent until we came to a
part of the river bank where three women were tilling a
rice field. Then suddenly Hana-ogi took my hand and
kissed it and whispered, "We very poor. My father no
want to sell to geisha house. Japanese fathers love their
daughters. Same like in America. But . . ." We never said
another word about it, not about the Matsudaira man
who had bought her nor about his daughter Fumiko-san

for whom Hana-ogi now felt responsible. For a few minutes after leaving the museum I had feared that knowing my Hana-ogi's history might make it impossible for me to marry her, but one mention of her father ended such doubts, for I recalled the old Japanese farmer we had watched on that first night we had slept together. That was poverty, when a man sifted each grain of soil by hand to make it yield a little more rice. I knew that if Hana-ogi's father had sold her it was because he had no human alternative. I said with new dedication, "Now we'll get married," but she merely drew closer to me and I believe that she had taken me to Kyoto so that I might know of her childhood and that if the curator had not told me, she would have done so when we studied the pictures. With my right arm I drew her tousled head to mine and drove the car quite slowly beside the ancient, turbulent river.

I was disturbed, however, that she had not yet actually said that she would come with me to America. I judged that she was hesitating in order to provide me with an escape from my rash promise to leave the Air Force. Then, in a dramatic way, I learned that perhaps she really was determined not to marry me, for an elderly woman showed me Hana-ogi's reasons for staying in Japan.

This gentle mask-faced Japanese woman came to the Marine Barracks in Takarazuka accompanied by a smart young woman who spoke good English and they explained that they wished me to accompany them on a matter of greatest importance. I followed them to the Bitchi-bashi, then through the vegetable stalls and onto the footpath leading to the girls' dormitories.

This was the first time I had been on this path and as I approached the building where Hana-ogi had lived before she met me I grew quite excited but then I saw the dormitory itself and it was forbidding: a plain wooden building covered with bamboo matting and protected by a row of cryptomeria trees planted to make a high hedge. The house was like a fortress and I was pleased at the prospect of invading it.

But my guide didn't stop there. Instead, she led me down a narrow path past the cryptomeria trees and up to a small hill that overlooked the river. There she stopped at a curious gate that looked like the miniature entrance to a temple and after opening this she took me into a beautiful garden which surrounded a superior Japanese house made of highly polished wood. It was guarded by an enormous flat stone upon which sat nine young girls wearing the green skirts of the Takarazuka uniform. The girls jumped to their feet and bowed very low until the elderly woman had passed.

She led me to a room covered with exquisite white tatami and containing at one end a raised platform of matched cypress planks polished of a golden brown. It was obvious that this was the room of a dancing teacher.

The woman introduced herself as Teruko-san, one of the first great Takarazuka stars. She had been, in her day, a legend and now she handed the legend down to the young girls waiting for her on the rock. They came to her five days a week and submitted themselves to the tyranny of her masklike face which now drew close to mine.

Teruko-san sat with me on the floor, arranging her kimono with precision, and I saw that her garments were five shades of gray matched in delicate harmony and accented by a single thin line of blue showing about the neck. Her tabi were white and accentuated the outlines of beautiful and powerful feet. They reminded me of Hana-ogi's superb feet and Teruko-san must have intended this, for she said promptly, "Major Gruver, if you cause Hana-ogi to leave us it is not only the great stage she will lose. It is also this." With a slow motion of her hand, as if she were participating in a dance, she indicated the perfect room, stopping with her finger pointed at a frame containing a massive motto written in strong characters by a great Japanese novelist.

She said, "Our motto: 'Be pure. Be right. Be beautiful.'"

Then she said, "When I die Hana-ogi is to follow me, for she is our finest dancer. I believe she is to be even greater than I, for when I danced I was alone and stood out like Fuji-san. But today there are many good dancers and Hana-ogi dominates them all. And do you know why they are good?"

I bowed deferentially toward her and she said, "Yes, they are excellent because I teach them as a famous old man taught me. In this way we keep alive the art of Japan."

As Teruko-san droned on I could hear Hana-ogi's bright voice with its sometimes-hoarse edge cutting at my heart, I could see the meticulous manner in which she folded the edges of her kimono to outline her wonderfully strong neck, and I could see the classic manner in which she danced. I could believe that these things had come in part from this room. Teruko-san said, "If you persist, Hana-ogi will never return to this room."

Then she pulled a clever trick. She said, "You must sit

here, Major Gruver, for I am to give a lesson," and the interpreter went to fetch the nine young girls. They came in quietly, practiced little steps on the tatami then deftly dropped away their green skirts and climbed onto the low stage in bright dancing tights.

Teruko-san was transformed. Instead of a gracious elderly lady she became a vigorous, stage-stamping dancer much better than even her best pupil. She led them through one single step for a long time and I detected one or two girls who looked as if they might honestly become dancers and I realized that Teruko-san had intended that I see in these struggling children—they were fifteen I judged—the Hana-ogi of some years back and as I looked at these lovely faces now perspiring as Hana-ogi did when she had run through the alleys to our home, I could imagine the days and years she had studied.

When the girls left, Teruko-san said, "I have wanted you to understand exactly what you are doing." She led me to the gate and to my surprise dismissed the interpreter and walked with me back to the dormitory, which was deserted in the late afternoon. She nodded to the guard and took me to a small room, pushed aside the paper door and told me to enter saying, "Hana-ogi."

The room was as beautiful as the girl I loved. Along one wall were the lacquered drawers and trays and chests in which she kept her belongings. The rest of the room was bare and clean and glittering. There were eight creamy white tatami, so it was not a big room, and six bright cushions around a very old brazier of gold and green ceramic in which charcoal rested on a pile of gleaming white sand. A low table and four jet-black bowls for food completed the furniture except for one shelf which held copies of the plays Hana-ogi had acted in. The only ornamentation was a single Japanese print in excellent colors of a bridge suspended in the moonlight over a rocky gorge with a crescent moon low in the sky. I felt that I was growing to understand Japanese prints, and the more I understood them the more I liked them.

But this time Teruko-san had been too clever, for it had been her intention that I see this room and lament that I was taking Hana-ogi from it; but it had quite the opposite effect. The room cried out in the late afternoon shadows that I should go ahead and marry its owner. No woman so vital as Hana-ogi could be destined for so narrow a prison. The wood of the room was beautiful, but Hana-ogi was more so. The tatami were neat, the books were important and the Japanese print no doubt represented one of the peaks of art—but so did Hana-ogi, and in addition she was a glorious woman, one who delighted in hurrying through the dark alleys of Osaka to join the man she loved.

But if her room gave me permission to love her, what I saw next gave me a direct order to do so, for as Teruko-san and I passed down the hall from Hana-ogi's room I happened to look through sliding doors that were ajar and saw the room next to Hana-ogi's.

It was remarkable in that it was also of only eight tatami, but it was crowded with dolls and fluffy brown bears and pillows edged with pink and blue lace streamers and tables with birds out of glass and corners filled with delightful odds and ends. It was the room of a young girl who enjoyed all aspects of life and it abounded in that happy clutter so loved by people who don't have to make up their minds. I looked at Teruko-san and she said, "Fumiko-san." Then she pointed to the table, low and exquisitely carved in the ornate Chinese style, and with no English at her command told me that that was the table Fumiko-san's father used when he committed hara-kiri in the debacle of August, 1945. The room frightened me and I wanted to get out of it.

At the entrance to the dormitory I bowed very low and said, "Domo arigato gozaimasu, Teruko-san." She was pleased that I spoke even that trivial Japanese, so she bowed equally low and said, "Do itashi mashite, dozo," and I hurried to the train that would take me back to Osaka just as fast as possible.

How can I recall the journey of a young man desperately in love as he moves across the picture-book landscape of Japan to a city of canals where he will meet his beloved? My train crossed the Muko River and I could see the Bitchi-bashi, where I had often waited for Hana-ogi and where young girls now passed swirling their green skirts. For a few seconds I followed the footpath that led to the dormitory and here four of the great stars walked arm in arm. At the dormitory itself I saw Fumiko-san entering the dark and towering wall of cryptomerias.

Now I was in the countryside and I could see the rice fields crowding right up to the last inch of railroad tie. Beyond were the trim clean villages with roofs of red tile and temple roofs of golden tile. In the fields were old men pulling harrows and women digging, while along the village streets children laughed and played loud jumping games.

There was a momentary thrill as the train pulled into the junction town of Nishinomiya, for I knew that when I looked across the station platform I would see a gigantic poster for *Swing Butterfly* with a huge picture of Hana-ogi in the middle. I spent my time waiting for the through express, wondering what the people on the platform would think if they could have known that in a few endless minutes I would be with Hana-ogi and she would be slipping into a gray and blue kimono so that she could sit upon the floor with me for a bowl of cold fish and vinegar rice?

The express from Kobe roared in and I avoided the coach where the officers of General Webster's command sat very formally in freshly pressed uniforms. Instead I sought out a back car from which I caught glimpses of the Inland Sea and soon we came to where the river emptied into the sea through great concrete culverts, and promptly we entered Osaka itself, where the train plunged through a canyon of ugly houses hung with laundry and into a tunnel which brought me to the noisy, crowded station. As I approached the canal I was alive with excitement. I was young and I was coming to the end of a journey that I wished I might make each day of my life:

from Takarazuka to Osaka, where Hana-ogi was waiting.

And when I reached home the wonder of my journey was increased, for there was Hana-ogi waiting for me with the news that Joe had driven a colonel to Tokyo and Katsumi would be gone for two days on business of her own. Once more we had a home to ourselves. I slipped into my blue-and-white cotton kimono and shared cold fish and rice with her. When the meal was over I said, "Teruko-san came to see me today. She showed me her dancing school. The one that could be yours some day. Now I know why you want to stay at Takarazuka."

She sighed and said she was glad that I understood why she could not come with me to America, but I added, "And I also saw your little room. With the lovely print." I made my hands fall like the gorge in her solitary picture. At this she blushed and held her hand against the stray-hair sideburns along her cheek. I said, "And when I saw that bare room which holds you like a prisoner—no life—no one to love . . ."

I caught her in my arms and a tremendous surge of love attacked us and later when I lay upon the tatami watching her select her clothes for tomorrow I said, "So we'll be married as soon as possible. You'll love New York. You can see hundreds of shows, some like Takarazuka, but none of the actresses will be beautiful like you."

I was imagining her in New York, so I rose and showed her how she could pull the wanton hair that crept upon her cheeks up into place. She did so and studied herself in a mirror. "Now you look like an American girl," I said. She pulled the hair back down and said, "Japanese way more better." But I convinced her that if she wanted to she could look almost American, so she tucked her hair in and the Japanese sideburns were gone. This sounds strange, but I believe that on a New York street few would recognize that she was from Japan.

PHARMACIST'S MATE: "In Kobe
there's this guy who can straighten
her eyes for eight bucks."

In the morning I begged her to stay with me to the last
minute, but she insisted upon leaving early and asked me
to call a taxi. I recall the language we had finally invented
for ourselves:

Hana-ogi: Rroyd-san, you takushi preeze. (Please get
a taxi.)

I: Daijobu, I takushi, get, ne? (All right, I'll get one.)

Hana-ogi: I rike stay with you. Keredomo I train go,
honto. (But I must catch the train, really.)

I: More sukoshi stay, kudasai. (Stay a little longer,
please.)

Hana-ogi: Dekinai, Rroyd-san. No can stay. (I'm sorry.
I can't stay.)

I: Do shi'te, whatsahurry? (Hey, why hurry?)

Hana-ogi: Anone! Takarazuka, my job-u, ne? I job-u
go, ne? (Listen, I have a job.)

I: Chotto, chotto goddamn matte! Takarazuka ichi-ji
start now. Ima only 10 o'clock, ne? (Wait a minute!)

Hana-ogi: Anone! Rroyd-san, you mess my hair, ne? I
beauty saron go, make nice, desho? (Desho is the sweet
meaningless word which makes the sentences of Japanese
girls musical and tender.)

I: No, no, no. Anone! You takusan steky now. (Listen!
You're plenty pretty now.)

But she left, nevertheless, and my last warning was
that she must have her hair done American style. Toward
evening Joe blew in with some Suntory, the Japanese
whisky we had both come to like so much, and we had a
quiet celebration while we waited for the girls and pretty
soon Hana-ogi arrived in her new hair-do. It was a trans-
formation. "Wow!" I cried. "She could walk down Fifth
Avenue and knock them all dead." She blushed nervously

174

and I believe she would have been pleased with her American look except that Katsumi arrived and ruined everything.

She had bandages over her eyes and peered out through slits. Joe immediately guessed that she had been in an accident but I remember looking with a certain agony at Hana-ogi and muttering to myself, "Oh, damn it to hell! She's gone and had that lousy operation!"

And I was right. Dear, good Katsumi wanted more than anything else to look like an American. Then Joe would be proud when he took her home; so on the first day he had left her alone she had sneaked over to the quack doctor in Kobe. For eight dollars he had slashed her upper lids to make the Mongolian fold fall back into place. He had performed this operation over a thousand times and sometimes his remodeling enabled girls to lose their Japanese look completely.

Proudly Katsumi stood before us and dropped away her bandages. Joe cried, "What have you done?"

Even more proudly the little girl opened her eyes slowly, one by one. "Now I have good eyes," she said.

The result was horrible. I gasped and Hana-ogi looked away. But Joe just stood there. He was about six feet from her when she turned to face him and he could see that what had been a glorious and typical Japanese face was now a conglomeration. I was watching Joe but no one could ever guess what he thought just then. Once he started to speak but stopped. Then he went over and kissed his wife and said, "By damn, Katsumi, you look more like an American than I do."

"I so proud," she said, dropping her new face against his arms.

There was a moment of silent intensity in the room and then Hana-ogi said, "Rroyd-san, we walk take, ne?" Joe looked at me and asked belligerently, "Whatsamatta, anythin' wrong?" and I replied, "Nothing at all. I think Katsumi looks swell."

But as soon as Hana-ogi and I reached the canal she cried, "Why she do that? She not proud to be Japanese?"

Deftly she thrust her two forefingers onto her upper lids
and pulled them up into mere slits, crying, "I like Japanese eye. I like!" Then she started to sob and I tried to
comfort her, but she pushed me away and with strong
fingers clawed down the strands of hair that I had
tucked up and they fell upon her cheeks in the Japanese
style. As she did this her fingernails caught in her flesh
and a thin stream of blood trickled down to her chin. I
tried to wipe it away but she cried, "I proud to be Japanese. I not want to be American. I like Tokyo, not New
York."

I had to stand there in the cool night and watch her
slapping at her face until the blood stopped. Then she
turned to me defiantly and said, "You no like Japanese
girl, eh? You ashamed Japanese face. You want me cut
my eyes, too?"

I put my arm about her and kissed the torn skin. I
said, "When you pulled your eyes far up you looked like
the Utamaro print. You were beautiful. But that day in
Kyoto I wasn't prepared for such beauty."

I was about to say more when she clutched my arm and
whispered, "Ssssh!" pointing to a group of young streetwalkers lounging by the canal. They were the unlucky
ones who had not been able to grab onto a G.I. for the
night. Osaka was a leave city for our troops in Korea and
had accumulated more streetwalkers than any other city
in the world, so that any one girl's chances were slim.
They recognized Hana-ogi and gathered about her.

"Is it true," they asked, "that you are marrying an
American?"

When she said she didn't know they were depressed,
for to them the highest dream they could envisage was to
trap a G.I. who might take them to the States, but they
knew there was little chance, for American chaplains and
Japanese secret police investigated all girls, and prostitutes were weeded out. Unemployed for the night, they
pressed in on Hana-ogi and asked, "Have you a picture?"
She had none, so they produced strips of paper on which
she printed her name in the Chinese characters used for

all names. One of the girls studied her signature and asked, "What's your real name, Hana-ogi?"

At first the actress refused to say, then, feeling deep in the Japanese mood, she said softly, "My name was Kaji." Immediately the girl touched Hana-ogi on the wrist and cried, "You are kaji, kaji!" Then she twisted her hands high into the air.

I asked what this meant and Hana-ogi said, "In Japanese my real name means fire."

One of the girls who knew English struck a lighter some G.I. had given her and cried, "Fire, fire!"

Another girl quickly called, "Cigaretto, Major?" I passed a package around and in the night I could see a ring of little flames, and later Hana-ogi said defiantly, "I am proud to be an actress for such girls—for all the girls in Nihon."

When the streetwalkers had departed I resumed my argument and asked, "What did you mean when you said you didn't know if you were marrying an American?"

She made a sign with her hands, like a flame falling through night air, and said, "The fire goes out."

"No!" I cried. "There are some fires that never go out."

She leaned against a tree growing near the canal and said, "Long ago Teruko-san loved the Supervisor. They were very happy and were going to commit suicide at Kegon Falls. But they didn't and now he's a famous man and she's a famous woman and they meet sometimes and have tea. She speak me today."

"But the flame didn't go out—or she'd have forgotten. Believe me, the flame was still there."

Then she said an astonishing thing. "You'll go home and marry Eileen . . ."

"Eileen?" I cried. "Where did you hear . . ." I had never spoken her name.

"Yes," she said. "You marry Eileen (she pronounced it *Eireen*) your father tell me."

"My father?"

"Yes. General Hot Shot Harry. He come see me late one night."

Bitterly I kicked the earth, for I could feel my father ordering things again. "Did he talk you into this?" I demanded.

"No! He say if I want to marry you O.K., but he know I never do it."

"What did he tell you?"

"He very nice, very kind man. He speak you marry Eileen. I think so too."

I pleaded, "Don't believe what he said. Years ago he dragged me into a life . . . I've done all right but it was never my decision."

She touched the insignia on my blouse and asked, "You no happy? Air Force?"

I cried, "It's been one life . . . I've liked it . . . But there could be others."

She grasped my hand tightly and said, "Sometimes I have been afraid of you because you are in uniform. My brother was in uniform and he became cruel. Your army hang him. I am afraid of uniforms." Then she put her head on my shoulder and said, "But you—your father— good men."

I was deeply agitated and struggled desperately to get down—for once in my life—to the hard bed rock of living. I said, "Hanayo, you are the hope of my life. If you leave me all the things . . ."

She said in Japanese, "I know, Rroyd. For me you are also the key. With you I could become a woman and a mother and we could travel in London. I could love you and help you . . ."

She became exquisitely tender and I knew then that with her as my wife I could find the solid basis for existence that had so far escaped me; and I was aware that for her, too, I was the only escape she could ever know. If she rejected me now she could become only the glorious outline of a woman, imprisoned in little rooms or on mammoth stages—loved only by other women.

I lifted her in the air and cried, "Then we'll be married?"

She stared at me and said "No."

I dropped her gently to the bank and kissed her impassive, golden face, thinking bitterly of the stories I had read about white men in strange lands. Always the yellow girl tried to seduce these clean-cut men away from their decent white sweethearts, for everyone knew that yellow girls plotted evil ways to lure white men. And if the yellow girls succeeded the white men sank lower and lower toward barbarism. "Damn it," I cried, "this story's all loused up!" When Hana-ogi looked up in surprise I said, "I'm a West Point honor man. In the story you're supposed to beg me to marry you. Hanayo-chan, please beg me."

She started to laugh at my comic plea, but then I think she glimpsed the empty years that faced her, for she took my hands and held them to her face, confessing in a tone of Japanese doom, "I don't want to become the lonely old woman who teaches dancing." (I recall her words: "I not grad be woman old in house dance teach no man come.")

Her lament burned my heart and I cried, "Then marry me."

This time she answered in a lower voice, still freighted with that inevitable sense of tragedy that seems to haunt the Japanese, "I never intended marrying you, Rroyd-san. Japanese-American marriages are no good. We read about Japanese girls in America—what happened in Cedar Rapids."

"When why did you come to live with me?" I demanded in anguish.

She pressed her lovely head against mine and said softly in Japanese, "I know it was wrong. But for me it was my only chance in life to love a man. No Japanese man would marry me—what the man in museum told you. Oh, maybe a fish-catch boy or a rice-plant boy, maybe such a man would have me. But Japanese men are very cruel to wives like me. Rroyd-san, in all the world you were the only man I dare love."

She started to cry, the bitter lament for a section of her life coming to an end at age twenty-nine. It was hellish to be there with her, to hear her committing herself to the inverted world of the Takarazuka girls and the green, flowing skirts and me to airplanes and the management of war. I grasped her hands and cried, "Hanayo-chan! Please! It's our lives you're speaking of. Marry me!"

Limply and in despair she drew her hands away. Then, raising her arms as if to embrace the entire sleeping city of Osaka she said with tragic finality, "I Japanese. I always Japanese. I never be happy nowhere." (As she said it: "I nebber be grad.") Then the misery of her heart overcame her and she started to cry again. Looking down, to keep her tears from me, she saw one of the crumpled Kodak envelopes used by the P.X.'s in Japan. One of the prostitutes, photographed by some soldier lover, had discarded it. Delicately Hana-ogi stooped for the orange paper and pressed it out. Then with an achingly beautiful hand she pointed to the trademark used by Kodak in Japan: that tremendous and sacred statue of Buddha at Kamakura, the ancient capital. Its vast, impassive face was enshrined as a symbol of the Japanese nation and slowly Hana-ogi's hand left it and indicated her own symbolic face with its beautiful Japanese eyes and classic mouth. "One poet say my face same like this face of Kamakura. I very proud." Then in a tender, forgiving gesture she pointed to our dark alley and asked sadly, "Katsumi-san marry American boy, ne? What happen to her, desho?"

The answer to that one arrived next day in the form of a special Fourth of July present for Joe Kelly, our overseas hero. We had celebrated the holiday by sneaking out into the country with a couple of picnic baskets. In the distance we had heard fireworks going off in some village near Kyoto and Katsumi had said, "Japanese love to celebrate. Even American holidays we enjoy." But when we got back to Osaka, Joe found the fateful letter tucked under the door. We had all known it must arrive soon but even so we were unprepared. Joe's hands trembled as he read the bad news.

"They sending you home?" I asked.

"Yep," he said weakly.

He showed me the sheet of paper which I at once recognized as one not intended for enlisted men to see, and my West Point training welled up. "How'd you get hold of this?"

"A friend of a friend," he said.

I read the impersonal phrases which two months before would have meant nothing to me. "American military personnel married to Japanese wives will be rotated home immediately lest their allegiance to the United States be eroded." Farther down it said, "This applies especially to personnel whose marriages have occurred since April 1, 1952." Then there was the usual baloney passage about commanders providing every assistance to men who must make unusual arrangements for wives forced to remain in Japan.

Joe asked bitterly, "What do they mean by unusual arrangements? Getting her a job in a good whore house?"

"Joe, take it easy!"

"It ain't easy to take."

"Joe, I've seen hundreds of orders like this. They all peter out."

"I think they mean it this time, Ace. Should I write to my Congressman?"

In spite of my original feelings on this point I now said, "Take it clear to the President, Joe." I turned and kissed blackened-eyes Katsumi on the cheek and said, "I wish we had a million gals like you back home."

Joe said, "This is important to you, Ace, because one of these days you may be tryin' to bring Hanayo into the States."

"I'm already trying," I said. Then desperately I added, "Hanayo can't make up her mind but I started the paper work this morning. Just in case." I noticed that Hana-ogi gasped at this and was about to protest, but Joe interrupted by pointing to the corners of the wood-and-paper house.

"I had it good here," he said grimly. "Wonderful wife, baby comin', friends, a home. Well, that's the way the ball bounces." As he surveyed the impending ruin he took refuge in the phrase which our men across Korea had adopted as their reaction to the dismal tricks of war: "That's the way the ball bounces."

For Joe the ball took an evil twist. An implementing letter arrived next day with a cold, hard list of the men who were to be sent home and under the K's Joe found his name. He took the list immediately to Lt.Col. Craford, who said, "I told you you were goin' home. I got four men on that list. Everyone of 'em's been in to cry the blues."

"But my wife is havin' a baby."

"All wives have babies. That's what wives are for."

"Can I be transferred back to Korea?"

The colonel grunted, "You're the fourth guy who would rather go back to war in Korea than go home to the States. You really prefer Korea?"

Joe saw a chance to remain in the area and cried eagerly, "Yes!"

Lt.Col. Craford turned away in disgust and said, "It's disgraceful when a man prefers Japan to America, but when he'd rather go back to Korea it's insanity."

"Then I can go?" Joe begged.

"No!" Craford shouted. "You get to hell home. All of you Jap-lovers, get home where you belong." He looked at Joe's papers and asked, "Where is your home?"

Joe said, "Osaka."

Craford flushed and said, "I mean your real home."

"Osaka," Joe repeated doggedly.

Craford banged the desk and shouted, "You get out of here. I oughta court-martial you."

Without thinking Joe caught him up on it. "Would that mean I could say in Japan?"

Craford became apoplectic and sputtered, "All right, wise guy. All right. When the shipping list comes out you won't have to look. Because your name is gonna be first."

When Joe reported all this I got sore. I've watched my father deal with hundreds of human problems and although he's as tough a general as they come, he always puts men first. In France there was a saying in his outfit: "If your wife is dying, don't bother with the colonel. He'll say no. See General Gruver. He'll say yes." So I told Joe, "You hate the military, kid, but this isn't standard. I'll fight this all the way to General Webster."

I caught the train to Kobe and when we stopped at Nishinomiya there was the poster of Hana-ogi smiling down at me.

General Webster didn't smile. For the first three minutes he never gave me a chance to get a word in. "Who in hell do you think was just in here?" he concluded. "The Supervisor of the Keihanshin Kyuko Railroad!" He waited for this to take effect, but I didn't comprehend, so he said in disgust, "The railroad that runs the theater where you've distinguished yourself—beyond the call of duty."

I waited for the explosion but there was none. General Webster smiled pleasantly and said, "It's all been settled. The Japanese-American scandal has been solved by the Webster-Ishikawa negotiations." He bowed and said, "His name was Ishikawa."

Mimicking a diplomat he continued, "The terms of the Webster-Ishikawa treaty are these." He handed me a sheaf of stapled papers and said, "You fly back to Randolph Field. The actress girl goes to Tokyo."

"When?" I cried.

"Both of you exit these parts on July 10—five days."

Then, to my amazement, he insisted that I have lunch with him, and when we got to the Officers Club Mrs. Webster and Eileen were waiting. We conducted ourselves with the punctilious indifference you give a man who has returned from a leprosarium, but Mrs. Webster was too old a veteran of the social battlefields to play such a game for long. Her opening salvo was, "Have you seen this month's show at Takarazuka? The girl who plays the lead is lovely."

I was still sore about the way Joe Kelly was being treated, so I said to myself, "If all bets are off, here goes," and I said aloud, "I know the girl and she's very talented, but I came to Kobe to try to argue your husband into letting Private Kelly remain in Japan."

"Who's Private Kelly?" Mrs. Webster asked.

"His Japanese wife is having a baby and he's being sent home—without her."

The general grew red in the face and tried to change the subject but Eileen jumped in on my side, "Rotten trick, I'd say."

Her father said, "Don't scowl at me. It's an area order."

"What happens to the baby?" Eileen asked.

The general laid down his napkin and said, "I argued with Kelly for half an hour, warning him not to marry a Japanese girl."

This did not satisfy Eileen who asked, "Does the Army force them to desert their wives? Aren't they legally married?"

"Yes, they're legally married," snapped the general. "We have to allow them to get married and then we have to leave the wife stranded."

"This is serious," Eileen protested. "Doesn't anyone try to prevent such inhuman foolishness?"

General Webster addressed Eileen directly, "I argued with this boy. Lloyd argued with him. Where'd it get us?"

But Eileen said, "I'm not talking about what has happened. I'm talking about the injustice of what's going to happen."

Mrs. Webster interrupted and asked, "How are you involved in this, Lloyd?"

I took a deep breath and said, "Kelly's from my outfit in Korea." (From the corner of my eye I saw the general sigh with relief that I had not embarrassed him by mentioning Hana-ogi, but I had no intention of avoiding the issue.) "And it also happens that I'm planning to marry a Japanese girl myself."

I had dropped my napalm. The general gulped. Mrs. Webster blushed an absolute scarlet and Eileen put her hand on mine and said, "I always knew you had guts."

I said, "Thanks, I guess I'd better go now."

Mrs. Webster asked weakly, "The actress?"

"Yes."

The general said, "Lloyd's not marrying any actress. He's being sent home on Thursday."

I started to leave but Eileen insisted upon walking to the door with me, as if I were the girl and she the escort. "I'm proud of you, Lloyd," she said. "I wish you all the luck in the world." We shook hands and I thought of a dozen things to say but none of them made much sense, so I said, "I'm sorry we got things loused up," and she said, "It was mostly my fault," and then as I was leaving she laughed and said, "Remember the time I asked you if you ever felt like just grabbing me and hauling me off to some shack?"

We both smiled awkwardly at this and she said, "That's just about what you did, wasn't it? But with somebody else." She kissed me on the cheek and said good-naturedly, "Well, I'm glad you turned out to be a man and not a mouse."

When I got back home I found Joe and Katsumi alone in a kind of dull panic. "I been all over it with everybody," he said. "Even went to see the consul, but everyone flashes the marriage papers at you and says, 'You signed 'em. You knew you couldn't take her to America.' As if that made everything just dandy."

Since I already knew that his name was at the head of the list I hadn't the courage to ask him what the latest hot dope was, but he came out with it, "I'm first on the first draft."

Katsumi, saying nothing, prepared the meal while I watched the door for Hana-ogi. She arrived about seven and I could tell that she had already been ordered to Tokyo. She had a nervousness about her that I had not seen before and I wondered if she was aware that I was being flown home. We looked at each other for a moment as she kicked off her zori and then neither of us could continue the duplicity. She ran weeping across the tatami and cried, "Rroyd, Rroyd! I Tokyo go five days!"

I caught her in my arms and hugged her as if I intended to crush her then so that she could never escape. "I fly back to Texas right away."

She pushed me away and cried, "You leave Japan?" I nodded and she burst into sobs, calling to Katsumi in Japanese. The two girls stood in the middle of the room and looked at Joe and me and for the four of us the world slowly fell apart.

There is one Japanese custom I had grown to love and Hana-ogi fled to this as relief from the tension of our crumbling home. She went to the bath corner and started a charcoal fire raging under the huge square wooden tub. When the water was hot she called, "Come on, Rroyd-san. I scrub your back."

I went into the little room where steam enveloped me and washed down with soap, rinsing myself off before I climbed into the tub. The water was almost scalding and Hana-ogi took a kind of soft bark and scrubbed my back for twenty minutes while we talked of that day's decisions.

When my heartache had been soaked away she soaped herself down, rinsed off and took my place while I scrubbed her back. As soon as we exited Joe and Katsumi took over and at nine we were all sitting cross-legged about the sukiyaki bowl while Katsumi served us an excellent meal. Hana-ogi said, "We never forget this time," and the warmth of the bath, the vigor of the scrubbing and the good friendship of our home made us ignore for a while the penalties that hung over our heads. I think we all knew that never again in our lifetimes would we know quite the same intense friendship and love that we shared that night and Joe said glumly, "I hate to think of livin' in some Chicago roomin' house—waitin'."

Toward midnight the inescapable gloom of our position settled firmly upon our little house so that Hana-ogi and I felt we had to break free and walk in the cool night air. The stars over Osaka were the same that had shone upon America seven hours earlier: Vega and Arcturus and Altair. They recognized no national barriers and I found myself—an officer sworn to protect the United States— thinking that some day we might catch up with the stars.

But as so often is the case, no sooner had I entertained this fleeting thought than I willingly became more of an American than I had ever been before. For at the head of our alley appeared a large gang of toughs screaming, "Americans go home! America go to hell! Go home!"

They swarmed down the alley in frenzy. When they reached the house of Masako Fukada, the girl with the G.I. baby, they knocked the door in and dragged her into the street, screaming, "Kill the American bastard."

Before I could do anything, Hana-ogi dashed toward the center of the infuriated mob. Although she was risking her life at Takarazuka, and more besides, she dived for Masako, who was being kicked in the stomach, and threw herself across the girl's body.

This enraged the hoodlums, who waved their torches and shouted in high-pitched voices that Hana-ogi should be killed for going with an American. I started for them but Hana-ogi cried a warning to stay away. This caused the mob to turn toward me and in the lurid light of their flickering torches these fanatical faces looked exactly like the cartoons of the Japanese barbarians we had kept posted in our ready rooms during the war years. I remember one horrible face rushing at me. It was distorted, evil, brutal and inhuman.

"You're for me, you Japanese bastard!" I cried and launched a dive at his belly. Another Japanese swung a club upward at the same moment and I thought my head had been knocked away, but my momentum carried me on and I crashed into the ring leader and felt the wonderful impact of my body against his and the thudding fall onto the ground with him uttering a shaken grunt. I started to smash at his distorted and hateful face. At the same time I had sense enough to shout, "Hey, Joe!"

The little tough burst right through his own paper doors brandishing a rifle butt. He flailed a path to me and we tried to defend ourselves, but I was bleeding from the face and started to faint.

"For Christ sake," the little gangster cried. "Not now! We got 'em runnin'."

The next second he collapsed under three Japanese clubs and I fainted. Later I learned that the anti-American mob would have killed us except for the pachinko players. They were at the canal end of the alley, sitting gloomily in the dark after the closing of the pinball parlor and one of them to whom I used to speak in English when I played pachinko heard Joe shout my name. They realized we were in trouble and they knew we were their friends.

Little Watanabe-san and the man who was keeping two geishas and the man whose wife beat him and the man who beat his wife and the man who had been in the penitentiary rushed up the alley. I am told there was a violent battle, but I knew nothing of it. The last thing I saw was a Japanese face—not one of the evil masks, but Hana-ogi's oval and yellow beauty as she lay fearful and with her eyes closed across the body of unconscious Masako Fukada.

When they brought me to I heard little Joe repeating quietly, "No, no! Don't send for an Army doctor. Get a Jap doctor." He was explaining to one of the pachinko players, "I learned it in Chicago. Never call a cop. Cops never help anybody." When I awakened, with a touchy streak of bruised face, I saw Hana-ogi again. She said, "I not hurt." Immediately I felt better and as the night progressed I began to feel absolutely good, for our little house was crowded with alley people. They stood about in kimonos or sat cross-legged on the floor, sucking in their breath and sipping the green tea that Katsumi-san served them. They said, all of them and with repeated emphasis, "The hoodlums who attacked you—they were not Japanese. They were Korean communists. We are Japanese. We are your friends." I remember one young man, a tough, capable laborer who still wore the peaked cap of the Japanese army. I had played pachinko with him and had given his four children presents. He spoke in mumbled tones and knew no English but he said, "They weren't all Koreans. Many Japanese hate you Americans. But I fought against you in Guadalcanal." (I thought: "In those days you'd have beheaded me.") "And you have behaved much better in Japan than I expected. Now I am your friend. Those in the street, they were communists."

All the same, next day Masako-san and her American baby left our alley and we never heard of them again. Masako's mother stood in the roadway cursing the girl for having caused the riot and the other women of the alley looked away.

That was Sunday. On Monday the Air Force officially notified Joe that he would be flown back to America on Wednesday. To Joe it was the sentence of torture. I found him sitting cross-legged on the floor studying the notice with dull resignation. He looked up grimly and asked, "Why should I be punished? Why should I have to go back to the States?"

Automatically I replied, "The way the ball bounces."

"No!" he shouted. "What's there for me in America?"

I assured him, "You'll get out of the Air Force and find a job and pretty soon Katsumi'll follow you."

He looked at me sadly and said, "I wish it was goin' to be so simple."

I recall every incident of that powerful and uneventful day. I drifted out to Itami to wind up my paper work and have lunch with Mike Bailey who told me, "My affair with Fumiko-san is washed up cleaner than a sergeant's shirt on inspection. She said she was afraid something bad would happen. Suicide, broken life, unwanted baby. She said such things occurred in her family beause they were aristocrats and took life awful hard. She said Hana-ogi was the kind of girl to be. Strong and brave."

I went over to Takarazuka for my mail and found a letter from my father which said, "I follow the war news more intelligently since my talk with you. No doubt your attractive little Butterfly has told you I called on her that night. You're lucky to have known such a fine girl. I have hopes Mother and I shall see you in Lancaster one day soon. Until then, I am profoundly proud of a son who can bag seven enemy planes. Harry."

In mid-afternoon I caught the train into Osaka and once more experienced an overpowering sense of identification with this strange land. The fields I saw could have been fields that Hana-ogi and I were working. The old people were her parents and the fat young babies were ours. The endless struggle for life was our struggle.

Once when Joe Kelly had cried, "I don't want to go back to America," I was on the point of knocking him down as an unpatriotic moron. Now, on the Takarazuka train, I knew that a man can have many homes and one of them must be that place on earth, however foreign, where he first perceives that he and some woman could happily become part of the immortal passage of human beings over the face of the earth: the childbearers, the field tillers, the builders, the fighters and eventually the ones who die and go back to the earth.

I had discovered this passionate emotion in Hana-ogi's country and for me—a United States officer bred in patriotism—the crowded fields between Takarazuka and Osaka, the insignificant canals, the tiny house, the tatami mats and the bed roll unfurled at night would be forever one of my homes.

This haunting sensation stayed with me as I walked through Osaka that sunny afternoon for on passing a print shop I saw in the window an old wood-block portrait of some classic beauty of Japan. She had a mountain of black hair with big yellow combs stuck through, and she reminded me of that day in the Kyoto museum. Instinctively, I stepped inside the tiny shop and bowed to the proprietor. "Do you happen to have a wood-block print of Hana-ogi?" I asked. I wanted to take her with me when I left Japan. The proprietor grew quite mournful and indicated that he had no English, but in a whisk he was out in the street shouting and soon the inevitable girl who had learned the language from sleeping with American soldiers appeared.

"What you want, Major?" she asked.

"I'd like a picture of Hana-ogi."

"Ah, so desu-ka!" The man hurried back to a case and

soon appeared with six of the glossy photographs sold at
Takarazuka. They showed my Hana-ogi as a sheik, a
Venetian gondolier, a Chinese prince and as three other
handsome young men. I bowed very low and said, "I
did not mean that Hana-ogi. I meant . . ." and I pointed
to the picture in the window.

"Soda!" cried the man.

"Ah, soka, soka!" cried the girl, and they indicated by
their manner that if I were interested in such a picture I
was one of them. Two hangers-or in the store joined us
as the man shuffled through a stack of prints. Finally he
produced one, a brilliant thing with iridescent black
background showing Hana-ogi upon the day of her return
to the green cages of Yoshiwara: glorious with amber
needles through her hair and many kimonos. Her eyes
were notably slanted and tinged with blue, her teeth were
jet black and the hair around her ear came down in sideburns. She was timeless and she was Japan.

The little street girl said, "This picture not real. Only
copy. But very old. Maybe one hunner years." The men
watching sucked in their breath and complimented me
as I carried away the living memory of Hana-ogi.

It seems strange, but I can remember each of the trivial things that filled this lovely Japanese day. When I entered our alley I passed the pachinko parlor and stuck my head in to thank the men who had helped me in my brawl with the communists, but most of them were so engrossed in their pinball games that they scarcely looked up. I then crossed the alley to the flower shop and indicated that I wanted a bouquet for our house. The little man—I keep using that word because these men were really so very small—started a cascade of Japanese, then went to the street and shouted till a boy came. Always, in Japan, there is someone who knows English. This boy explained that since I must soon go back to America, the flower man wanted to give me three most special flowers. When the shopkeeper handed them to me they looked like the ordinary flowers that American girls wear to football games. I had often bought them for Eileen Webster but now the boy said, sucking in his breath in astonishment, "Very unusual, chrysanthemum blooming in July." He added that this was the national flower of Japan and looked with absolute covetousness as I took them from the flower man.

Thinking little of the gift I carried the flowers to our house, but as soon as the girls saw them they sucked in their breath just as the boy had done, and Katsumi ran into the street to announce that we had chrysanthemums in July. Soon our little room was filled with neighbors who sat upon their ankles staring at the three wonderful blooms. From time to time new men would arrive, bow to Hana-ogi, sit upon the floor and contemplate this miraculous accomplishment. Even Watanabe-san left his pachinko to see. The boy who had been my translator

193

joined us and explained this strange thing: "On the road to Kobe a florist has a big glass house in which he grows these flowers. In one section there are cloth blinds to keep out the sun. With an almanac to guide him, this clever man causes the sun to set earlier each day so that within the space of three weeks it seems to run the course of four months. The flowers are fooled. They think that autumn is upon them and they bloom." The men sucked in their breath in admiration.

Now Katsumi suddenly felt the first life in her womb and fell slightly forward. Hana-ogi washed her forehead in cold water and Joe, faced by the necessity of leaving his pregnant wife behind in Japan said loudly, "I hope just one thing. I hope Colonel Craford goes home and buys himself a new Buick, light blue, and I hope he's drivin' it down the avenue when I'm comin' up the other way with a Mack truck."

I was about to caution Joe against taking a pass at Craford when I looked up to see Hana-ogi arranging her kimono. It was blue and white, very soft for summer wear. With it she wore two undergarments of thinnest cloth: pink silk and white cotton. I thought I had never seen her so lovely. Unmindful of me she experimented with the sheer lines of her garments until she brought them into a pattern which made her more beautiful than the picture I had bought. I was about to share this with her when she raised both hands and combed down the hair about her face so that it rested in the Japanese style. Studying herself in the mirror, she nodded approval. Then she heard me laugh and quickly knelt beside me. "Rroyd-san," she said. "I got to be this way. I Japanese." I think she expected me to be hurt, but I unrolled the print and as soon as she saw the bold characters in the upper corner she cried, "Hana-ogi! Rroyd-san, you buy?" When we had studied the picture for a moment she went to Katsumi's trunk and returned with a drawing brush and an ink stone. Using the firm Chinese characters long ago adopted for Japanese writing, she added a fresh column of print at the picture's side: "Hana-ogi of Taka-

razuka-za loved an American." I caught her in my arms
and kissed her but in so doing I destroyed the arrangement of color and cloth at her throat so she stood and
fixed the kimonos once more.

For women in love there could be no garment more
entrancing than the kimono. As I watched Hana-ogi I
knew that in the future, when even the memory of our
occupation has grown dim, a quarter of a million American men will love all women more for having tenderly
watched some golden-skinned girl fold herself into the
shimmering beauty of a kimono. In memory of her feminine grace all women will forever seem more feminine.

When Hana-ogi was finally dressed, she and Katsumi
sprang their surprise! They were taking Joe and me to see
the puppets of Osaka. Boldly, for we no longer cared who
saw us upon the streets, we walked through the lovely
summer's dusk to an ancient theater, small and off to
one side, where for many generations the famous puppets
of Japan had been exhibited. The girls, resplendent in
their kimonos, bought our tickets for a few yen and
ushered us proudly into cramped seats, where we witnessed a remarkable performance.

The stage was small and peopled with many men
dressed in black. In their hands they carried four-foot
puppets of strangely human quality who acted out one of
Japan's classical tragedies. At first it was impossible for
me to accept the illusion, for it took three grown men to
operate each puppet and the men were constantly and
completely visible. If the heroine were to walk across
the stage, one of the towering black men openly manip-
ulated the puppet's kimono to simulate walking, another
worked her left arm and kept her clothing arranged,
while a distinguished old man, dressed in a shimmering
kimono and formal winglike jacket operated the puppet's
head and right arm. It seemed ridiculous to have six
human arms so busy in vitalizing one doll, but before I
was aware of the change, I had completely accepted the
convention. Curiously, the towering black men did indeed become invisible, like spirits from another world

organizing human life, and I became truly engrossed in
the tragedy of these dolls.

We were watching one of the many classical plays in
which two lovers commit suicide. In this one a married
man fell in love with a beautiful Yoshiwara girl, whom
Hana-ogi identified for me in the dark as "just like old-
time Hana-ogi." I don't imagine any American has ever
really understood the ins and outs of a Japanese tragedy
but I did get the impression of two people caught in an
increasingly unbearable set of pressures. Just what these
pressures were I never grasped but Hana-ogi and Katsumi wept softly and when I asked what about they said,
"It's so sad. People talking about this man."

But what I did understand was the musicians. For the
mysterious men in black never spoke. The dialogue was
sung by an amazing man accompanied by four musicians
playing samisens. Maybe *sung* isn't the right word, for
I have never heard more eerie sounds. The singer was
a fat, bald-headed man in his late sixties who sat on his
haunches, and as tragedy on the puppet stage deepened
he would lean forward and scream in unbelievable fury
until his round face became purple and the veins stood
out in his neck. During love passages he would narrate
the scene in a quivering feminine wail and as the remorse-
less pressure of society bore down on the lovers he would
make his voice rough and horrible like a broken saw
against a rusted nail. To hear this man was a terrifying
experience for I had not known the human voice to be
capable of such overpowering emotion. I would defy
anyone not to be unnerved by that stupefying voice.

Now, as the hounded lovers approached the historic
scene at Amijima where they would commit suicide together, the mysterious black figures on the stage whirled
about in what seemed like a confusion of fates, the
wooden dolls marched stiffly to their doom and the inspired story-teller shrieked in positive terror while the
muted samisens played doleful music. There was another
sound in this remarkable tragedy, but this I wasn't aware
of until the curtain had closed: all the women near me

were weeping and as I looked away from the epileptic singer, his face at last relaxed as if he had gone suddenly dead, I saw lovely Hana-ogi sitting with her hands folded in her kimono, sobbing desperately. She was so bereft that tears might have come to my eyes, too, but when I turned her face toward mine I saw that she was in no way unhappy. A look of ecstasy had captured her wonderful face and her eyes glowed. I was astonished and whispered, "What's the matter, Hanayo-chan?"

"It was so beautiful," she said.

"What? The singing?"

"No," she replied softly, taking my hand. "The double suicide. It was so tender."

"What do you mean?" I asked.

The women around me were rising now and on each face I saw this same look of ecstatic satisfaction. Apparently the double suicide had inspired them even more than it had Hana-ogi. I was not surprised, therefore, when she made no attempt to explain this mystery, but when I looked at Katsumi and saw on her tear-stained face the same look of rapture I had to acknowledge that for the Japanese audience this double suicide had provided a vitally satisfying experience.

"What's it all about?" I asked Katsumi, indicating the weeping women.

"The lovers," she said quietly, pointing to the now barren stage. "At last they found happiness."

"They're dead," Joe said.

As we walked through the broad, clean streets of Osaka back to our canal I became hurtingly aware that there would always be many parts of Japan that Joe Kelly and I could never penetrate. "What happened back there?" I asked Joe. "All I saw was a bunch of dolls and a man shouting."

The little guy laughed as if he hadn't anything to worry about and said, "Every three weeks Katsumi-san breaks down into sobbin' fits. You'd think her heart had broken. Used to scare me sick. Then I found out what was cookin'. First time it was an ex-army general who shot himself because he was charged with stealin' government money. Katsumi said it was so beautiful she had to cry. Next time it was a geisha from Kyoto. Cut her throat. That was especially lovely."

Hana-ogi heard me laugh and turned sharply. I expected her to upbraid me but instead she took my hand and sniffled. "You not understand," she said. "To have courage. To have honor. Is very beautiful."

As we entered the pathway leading to our canal, conversation was broken by a substantial commotion. We heard voices crying and hurried to our own alley in time to see the launching of a magnificent display of fireworks. "Ah!" Hana-ogi whispered. "I forget. Tanabata!" And long after the fireworks had ceased the people of our alley stood staring up at the stars. In Japanese Hana-ogi explained: "Vega, the princess star, fell in love with Altair, the herdboy star. Unlike American fairy stories, the herdboy married the princess without any trouble; then like our stories, he loved his wife so much that he allowed his sheep to stray so that the king threw him onto the other side of the Milky Way river. Once each year in July he swims the river and makes love with his princess. For the people of Japan this Tanabata is the night of love."

But Hana-ogi and I as we spread our bed roll reasoned that we had two more nights to spend together, so we left the love-making to the princess and her shepherd while we lay side by side listening to the exquisite sounds of the Japanese night. The old blind man who massaged sore muscles and burned moxa powder on nerves to make them well passed along our alley, sounding his melancholy flute and tapping with his gnarled cane. For a while there was silence. Then we could hear Watanabe-san coming home from his pachinko game with his wife snapping at his heels. Hana-ogi snuggled close to me and said, "All time we never fight," but I touched the trivial scar beneath her sideburns and asked, "What about the time I wanted you to become American?" Then she grew somber and said, "Because I know you, now I

better Japanese. You better American." Then I almost
broke down. I wanted to lose myself in her love and con-
fess, "I can't live without you, Hanayo-chan. God, I cannot face the lonely world without your tenderness." But
I knew that we had two more nights to spend together
and I was afraid that if I allowed myself full sorrow now
the next nights might be unbearable. I choked once and
buried my face against hers, feeling her Japanese eyes
against my lips, her black Japanese hair against my face.
"Oh, darling," I whispered, "why can't you marry me?"
She clasped her arms about me as she had done that first
night in the woods by the Shinto shrine and said, "Some
people never love anyone." (She said it: "Rots peopre
nebber rub nobody.") "Oh, Rroyd-san, I love you till my
feet are old for dancing—till my teeth break off same like
Hana-ogi's."

I thought I could not bear this but then came the
sweetest night sound I have ever heard, the soft passage
of the noodle vendor, pushing his belled cart while he
played a rhythmic melody upon his flute. All through the
night the noodle men passed through the streets of Osaka
sounding their lovely melody. Some used five running
notes ending in a faint call. Others played a minor tune.
Some played random notes and a few, whom you came
to remember and cherish, played songs that might have
been termed love songs, for they seemed always to come
by when you were sleeping with the girl who shared your
bed roll on the tatami.

For the rest of this night, as I recall, Hana-ogi didn't
even place her arm across my body and although it seems
ridiculous this is what we said. I asked, "Don't you think
we ought to take Joe and Katsumi to dinner tomorrow?"

She replied, "No, I think we should."

"Damn it, Hanayo, will you explain once more why
you say, 'No, we should,' and 'Yes, we shouldn't.' "

Patiently she went over it again. "In Japanese polite
to say that way. If you speak no to me, I say no to agree
with you."

"I still don't get it."

"Ask me a question."

"Don't you want to marry me?"

"Yes, I not marry you."

"But what I asked was, 'Don't you want to?'"

The game stopped for she whispered, "No, no, Rroyd-san. I do want to."

I grumbled, "I can't understand either your grammar or your heart."

She placed my hand upon her heart and the delicate golden warmth of her slim body swept over me and she said, "My heart for you takusan, takusan. Remember when you say me that?"

I remembered, and as the sweet song of the noodle vendor echoed down our alley we fell asleep.

If Monday was peaceful, Tuesday was not. Hana-ogi and I woke about eight-thirty to find that Joe had left for one last appeal to Lt.Col. Craford. Katsumi, sensing that we would want to be alone, went out to lament with friends, so I started a fire and Hana-ogi, wrapped in a sheet, tried to get breakfast, but I kept pulling the sheet away until she finally surrendered it altogether, whereupon we propped a chair against the sliding doors and let the fire go out.

At eleven Hana-ogi dressed for Takarazuka. I tied her obi for her and she insisted that I leave the ends dangling almost to the floor. Taking a few mincing steps she cried, "I maiko girl!" Then deftly she swept the ends together in a bow, symbol of older girls, and said, "I virgin no more. I married woman." So far as I can remember those were the last words she said that morning. I watched her go down the alley and all the women in the open-front stores and houses called out to her on that summer morning.

She was gone only a few minutes when Joe came back. He was licked. He threw his cap on the floor and asked in final despair, "Ace, what can I do?"

"Take a deep breath," I said. "Stick it out. They'll have to change the law."

"In Washington they got fifty senators like Craford. You think they're gonna change the law?" He looked wild-eyed.

"Joe! Ease up."

"How can I? Ace, I'm a no-good punk. If I go home without Katsumi it's pool halls and hamburger joints. I I couldn't take it."

"For a while you have to."

201

He sat down cross-legged on the tatami and said grimly, "In Chicago I killed a man. A mixed-up affair— not all my fault. They couldn't pin anything on me. I'm not apologizin', because it could just as well have been my fault. Because I was no damn good. And if I lose Katsumi I'll be no damn good again."

I knew there was something I ought to say, some standard word of courage, but I couldn't think of any. Joe said, "A guy like you, from a good home—you wouldn't understand. For the first time in my life I'm livin'. At night when I hear Katsumi come up the alley shufflin' her wooden shoes—later when she puts that crazy hard, little pillow next to mine—when I see the plain goddamn goodness in that girl . . ." He looked down at the tatami and I guessed that he had tears in his throat. I wanted to say that I knew but I was tied up.

"Joe, promise me you won't get into trouble with Col. Craford."

He looked up at me as if Craford were already dead. "Him?" he sniffed. "The only time I believe in God is when I think of that fat slob. God must be keepin' score on bastards like that. Otherwise nothin' makes sense."

I said, "Remember, Joe. You promised you'd make no trouble with that . . ." I searched for a name and suddenly the total misery of Joe's problem rose in my mouth like bile. I grew purple and cursed Craford for several minutes. I cursed my father and General Webster and Mrs. Webster and every convention that made it impossible for Hana-ogi and me to marry. Then I stopped, but I was still quivering with accumulated fury.

Joe looked up at me and said, "Thanks, Major. I thought you felt that way."

I was still shaking. I said, "Even so I believe things'll work out."

He said, "I don't."

There was nothing to add. He knew how I felt. He knew I was with him. Maybe I had steered him away from some hot-brained mistake. That's the best I could hope, so I went over to Itami to clear out my desk and borrow Mike Bailey's car, but as I left the air base for the theater, where I was to see the last performance of *Swing Butterfly*, I had a disgusting experience which even at the time seemed to me a premonition of tragedy. Outside the main gate of the air base at Itami a broad road stretched for more than half a mile. It was filled with cheap dance halls, beer joints, razzle-dazzle dives and plain whore houses. In front of each establishment lounged gangs of young girls and the stretch was known as "The 1,000 Yard Dash." It was claimed that any American in uniform who could negotiate this honky-tonk strip and keep his pants on would receive a prize of $1,000 for heroism beyond the call of duty.

As I drove out of the air base for the last time I saw the frowsy halls: "Village Bar," "Club Little Man," "The Flying Bull," and "Air Force Heaven." Then, to my disgust, my car stalled and three girls promptly surrounded it. One climbed in and said, "O.K. General. Where we off to?" Immediately an M.P. appeared and hauled the girl back onto the strip and gave me some brotherly warning, "Watch out for her, Major. She's no good." He saluted and pointed to a saloon up the stretch, "If you want something real nice, Major, you can trust the girls at the 'Silver Dollar.'"

When I got my car started I saw with dismay that from the other direction had come a Packard from Tone-yama Heights, the nearby residential district where the big brass lived, and in it were two colonels' wives who knew me. They watched with disgust as the three persistent little street girls started to climb back into my car as soon as the M.P. had left. As I chucked them out I thought that some day in the future I would recall Hana-ogi and I would have to speak her name to someone and if he had been at Itami he would remember "The 1,000 Yard Dash" and the brassy prostitutes and he would wink at me and say, "Boy, do I know those Jap girls?" But he wouldn't know, and nothing I could ever tell anyone who had seen Itami would explain Hana-ogi. I shivered at the wheel of my car and mumbled, "All this should have happened fifty years from now. Then maybe there would have been a chance. In my day there was no chance for such a marriage." I saw myself in years to come. Junior officers would boast, "You can say that General Gruver looks tough and formal but did you know that when he served in Japan he ran off with a geisha girl? Yep, took her right out of a house." But they would never know.

However, the distaste of this experience along the strip was expelled by Hana-ogi's exquisite performance. When I had first seen her I had been insulted by her burlesque of Americans and I had been unable to appreciate her ability. Now my reaction was different, for I discovered that even against my will I had to laugh at her lampoon of Americans. The reason was simple. She had studied with intimate care my mannerisms and now reproduced them in burlesque form. When she lit a cigarette she mimicked me, when she propositioned Madame Butterfly it was me trying to kiss her on the Bitchi-bashi. This time I, more than anyone else in the audience, enjoyed her burlesque of Americans.

As her big dance number approached I became apprehensive, for I suspected that her aping of Americanisms would dull her Japanese touch, but I was wrong, for in her samurai there was now a freedom and swagger that no maiko girl, as Hana-ogi termed the virgin dancers, could have created. Hana-ogi was the artist. Even more than mistress or wife, she was an artist, and if her American jitterbugging was more hilarious for having studied an American at close hand, her Japanese classical dance was stronger for having known that American not as a subject for study but as a lover—as one who cried eagerly to marry her. I understood what she had said the night before. She was now a better Japanese.

When intermission came I wanted to rush backstage and embrace her and tell her that no matter if she lived a million years cooped up at Takarazuka, I would be with her every time she danced—but I was not to see her, for I could not get into the dressing-rooms.

CPL. SHARKEY: "You damned
Buddha-heads, you gotta stand back
from the door."

So the rapture was lost. The great deep rapture I felt
when watching Hana-ogi perform was never reported to
her, for as I took my seat at the beginning of Act II an
M.P. came up to me an asked, "Major Gruver?"

"Yes."

"You'll have to come with us."

The curtain had not yet risen, so Hana-ogi did not see
me leave and I was grateful for that, for I was trembling.
I thought that Lt.Col. Craford was shipping me home
early, but when I got outside and I saw two other M.P.'s
with guns I asked, "What's up?"

"Airman Kelly," they said.

"Joe?"

"Yep. Deserted."

"Impossible. I saw him this morning."

"We know. We thought you might tell us . . ."

Another M.P. broke in and said, "He was called special
at 1300. He was scheduled to fly out tomorrow but a
special plane came through and Col. Craford said, 'Get
him on it.'"

The first M.P. said, "I checked him in at the airport
at 1250 but before the plane took off he beat it."

"We figured you might know where he is."

"No! Last time I saw Kelly . . ."

"When was the last time?"

"About 0815. No! It was 1120."

"You know where he lives?"

"Sure."

I had a dry ugly taste in my mouth as the siren wailed
into Osaka. At Itami I asked, "Did the plane take off?"

"Yep. It's desertion."

I began to sweat. Now Joe Kelly was really done for.

Insubordination and desertion would be the charge and he might never get Katsumi into the States, so I asked, "Jesus, are you sure he deserted?"

"I checked him in. Sharkey saw him leave."

We stopped at the canal and I led the way to the alley, where two M.P.'s tried the door. It seemed to be barred, so they were going to break the freshly mended paper, but at that moment it seemed like my house and I didn't want the paper broken, so I said, "Maybe a chair's against it. I'll use the window."

One M.P. came with me to the back of the house while I forced open a window and started to crawl in. While my leg was still suspended I saw Joe. He was on the floor with his head blown apart by a .45. Across him, obviously having died later, lay Katsumi with a kitchen knife plunged completely through her neck.

For a moment I didn't call out or anything. All I could do was look at the floor—at the two lovers who had needed each other so much. The M.P. came up and looked over my shoulder. Then he called loudly, "You better break the door down, Sharkey."

I watched the frail doors bend and break. I heard the clatter of wood and the tearing of paper and the doors through which Hana-ogi had so often come at dusk, dropping her silken packages on the floor, were gone. Sharkey took one look and said, "Get the camera. You wanna catch this just as it happened."

Sharkey barked to the man at my shoulder, "Eddie, you inform the Jap police." Then he saw me and said, "We'll need you here, Major."

I got down out of the window and walked around to the front of the house where a crowd had gathered and where children were screaming the tragedy across the canal to other children. An old man pried his way in through the broken doors and came out to report accurately upon the double suicide.

I was numb with helpless anger. Of all the people in the world, Joe and Katsumi Kelly should have been protected and kept alive. I thought of them laughing and helping each other and I got all sick inside, but then I thought of Hana-ogi, who would be coming home soon and I grew panicky for her because the photographers had arrived and were taking pictures like mad.

And then I saw, on the outskirts of the crowd, two of the little prostitutes Hana-ogi and I had met the other night. They were already working the main streets and had stopped by to witness the tragedy. I said to them, "You remember Hana-ogi?"

"Sure, Major."

"You watch up there. Tell her to go back. Please."

"Sure, Major. You got cigaretto?"

The other girl pointed to the house and jabbed herself in the stomach as if with a knife. "They kill?"

I nodded and they stared at the house with grim fascination. "Japanese girl and G.I.?"

I said yes and the little girls moved toward the head of the canal where they could intercept Hana-ogi while the reporters swarmed at me. They were bright young men, most of whom spoke English, and I had enough sense to keep my mouth shut, for if I had said anything at all I would have blurted out, "They wanted to ship him back to America but he insisted upon staying in Japan." Finally I composed myself and said, "He was with my outfit in Korea. This is a complete shock."

The reporters saw somebody else and swarmed away but one stayed and asked, "Aren't you Ace Gruver?"

I nodded.

"You the one living with Hana-ogi?"

I wanted to shoot him dead but everything had collapsed now, so I nodded grimly and he pointed up the canal.

There at last she was, Hana-ogi. Late afternoon sun played upon her tousled black hair and illuminated the fall of her kimono. With eager pin-toed steps she hurried along the canal, coming so close that I could see the slant of her adorable eyes and that sweet mouth always ready with a teasing smile.

The two prostitutes stopped her, informed her of the

suicides and tried to prevent her from joining the crowd.
She ignored them and started coming toward me down
the canal bank but the newspaperman who was standing
with me broke away, ran toward her and spoke rapidly.
She peered across the crowd searching for me, and when
she failed to find me she broke away from the guardian
prostitutes and the warning newspaperman to fight her
way resolutely toward the very spot where the police
waited.

In that moment I could see the reckless collapse of
her world and instinctively a shout rose to my lips.
I called in panic, "Lo, the postillion!"

She stopped. The smile that had crept upon the edge
of her lips vanished and her lovely face once more became an impersonal mask. Standing on tiptoe, she peered
across the crowd, still seeking me, but I hid myself so
that she would have to go back. After a moment she
turned away from the crowds that shoved toward the
suicide house and I last saw her moving with extraordinary grace back to the main street. The summer breeze,
drifting down the canal, tugged at her kimono and twilight rested on her hair. I can still see the folds of cloth
meticulous about her neck. Then she moved behind a
pillar and I never saw her again.

For just as I started to run after her, Lt.Col. Craford
waddled up and he seemed almost to relish the tragedy.
It proved he was right and that guys like Kelly were no
damned good. He saw me and lurched over to repeat
his warning that he was shipping me . . .

"You bastard!" I cried. "You stinking bastard!"

He jumped back as if I had kicked him and began to
bluster but I couldn't take any more. "You swine! Kelly
told me what you said to him, you bastard! You killed
this kid!"

He was astonished at my outbursts and suddenly became aware that if I was really outraged I might carry
the fight to my father, so he tried to pacify me, but I
said, "Don't be afraid of me, you dirty bastard. I'm not
going to squeal on you—but you murdered this kid."

He withdrew and a Japanese police official said, "You come with me," and for three hours while I ached to seek out Hana-ogi I had to answer questions and fill out reports as to the death of Katsumi-san. It was after ten o'clock when I was released and I caught a cab whose driver gasped when I said Takarazuka, but he drove me there and at eleven that Sunday night I hurried past the cryptomerias and into the dormitory where Hana-ogi lived.

Apparently I was expected, for old Teruko-san and her grim-faced interpreter were waiting for me. "Hana-ogi-san is not here," they said firmly.

"I know she's here!" I cried.

"Hana-ogi-san is on her way to Tokyo."

"She can't be! I saw her!"

"Please, Major Gruver. Hana-ogi-san is not here."

Unthinkingly, I forced my way past the two women and along the corridor on which Hana-ogi lived. The Takarazuka girls peered at me as I stormed past, then sighed when I reached Hana-ogi's empty room. It was so empty. The little things that made it hers were gone.

From the next room Fumiko-san appeared and said, weeping, "Hana-ogi-san really go, Major."

I turned around like a madman. It couldn't end this way—across a canal, over the heads of a hundred people at the scene of a suicide and Hana-ogi departs forever. "She's here!" I insisted.

I stood helpless and then saw in one corner of her room a zori that she had forgotten. I stepped across the tatami on tip-toe as if she were still there, reproving me for not having removed my shoes, and I lifted the zori and it seemed as if her powerful, inspired foot were there in my hand, with the big toe clinging to the zori strap and the Japanese music beginning and the samurai dance about to start and Hana-ogi . . . oh, Hana-ogi . . .

"Hanayo-chan!" I shouted. "Hanayo-chan! Where are you?" From their doors the beautiful Takarazuka girls stared at me impassively. The world seemed to grow dark and I screamed, "Hana-ogi, don't leave me." Then

I felt Fumiko-san put her hand on my shoulder. "You go now, Rroyd-san. Is no more." And she led me to the roadway.

GENERAL WEBSTER: "Whatever
makes you a better man makes you
a better husband."

General Webster called me in to Kobe next day and said,
"That was a dreadful affair last night in Osaka." He asked
me if I had heard any rumors that Lt.Col Craford had
handled the affair badly. I wanted to put a blast on the
fat blubber-gut who had murdered Kelly, but something
old and powerful inside me argued, "Why start a military
mess?" and I kept my mouth shut. Then I shrugged my
shoulders and said, "I guess Craford handled it O.K."

But immediately I knew that I was reverting to the
man I had been when I first argued with Kelly against
marrying a Japanese girl. I was defending the Army
against the man and I felt ashamed of myself. I must
have shivered, for General Webster said gruffly, "Lloyd,
don't take this so bitterly. Kelly's dead. Nobody can do
anything about it. You told me yourself he was a dead-
end punk—beyond saving."

I looked at the general. A man under his command
had committed suicide rather than return to the United
States and he was shrugging it off. I asked, "What about
that colonel in Tokyo who shot himself rather than leave
his Japanese girl? Or the major in Yokohama? Were they
punks?"

"Yes! They were second-class men. I've seen reports on
seven such suicides and they were all shoddy material.
First-class men sometimes fall in love with native girls,
of course they do. But they get over it. They forget the
girls and they go home. They go back to work."

"Damn it!" I shouted. "Why do men like you and my
father call them native girls? Can't you believe . . ."

General Webster was remarkably patient. He stopped
me by thrusting a yellow paper into my hand. "I suppose a young man's no good if he doesn't have the guts

211

to fight for what he thinks is right," he said. "You've had the courage to fight for Joe Kelly and his native girl. It was gallant, Lloyd, but it wasn't necessary. Read it."

The yellow paper was from Washington and it said a law was being passed to permit men like Joe Kelly to bring their Japanese wives into the States. "Now they do it!" I cried.

"They were doing it all along," Webster said. "Everyone knew the old law was bad."

I thought of Joe and Katsumi lying in blood and I felt sick. I had to see Hana-ogi. In all the world she was the only person who could help me now. My heart and my mind cried out for her. "Sir," I blurted, "I've got to get to Tokyo."

"It's forbidden, Lloyd. You're flying home."

"I don't care what happens. I've got to see Hana-ogi."

The general winced as I used the strange name, then said calmly, "If you disobey another order . . ."

"All right, I'll leave the Air Force. I'll get a . . ."

I expected General Webster to hit the roof, but when he's away from his wife he isn't so bad. He said, "Sit down, Lloyd. I'm not going to throw my weight at you. You're being a stupid idiot and we both know it, but you come by it naturally."

"What do you mean?"

"This seems like 1924."

"I don't understand," I said dully.

"Your father was mixed up with a girl—the one I told you about. There was one member of our class you've never met. Chap named Charley Scales. He had a chance in '24 to drop out of service and take a good job with General Motors. So your father decided to marry the girl and chuck the Army and go along with Charley, but some of us saner fellows talked him out of it. Must run in your family."

"My father was going to leave the Army?"

"Yep. He was all broken up." General Webster laughed and scratched his chin. "I remember that we were quite sorry for him. We thought he was pretty weak to be broken up like that over a waitress. Look at him now."

I said, "I think he made a mistake in 1924."

General Webster breathed a sigh of relief and said, "So do I, but I guess any man has a right to get mixed up with a waitress once . . ."

"I don't mean that. I mean he probably should have married the waitress."

"Lloyd! Your father a Chevrolet salesman!"

"I mean he should never have married my mother. They've never been happy."

"Happy? What's happy? He's a great general."

"I think he's made a mess of his life."

General Webster got mad. "You think! Who in hell are you to think? Only a few men in any generation can be great generals. Don't you forget it!"

I said, "I still want to marry this girl."

"Son," General Webster said, "the Supervisor of Taka-razuka and I stayed up late last night figuring how to keep his outfit and mine free of bad publicity over the suicides. We protected ourselves and we can't let you ruin things."

"At least give me a chance to say good-bye to her!"

"No, she herself wanted it this way."

"She didn't!"

"I saw her. She said to send you back to America."

I said, "I don't believe that." So he handed me a letter which had been written two days before. I knew because Hana-ogi had written it on my stationery and as I read it I could hear her gentle voice groping its way through my language:

Darring,

Pretty soon (That was a phrase I used a lot . . .) our rast night. I Tokyo go. You America go. (A passage was scratched out, then . . .) I not think fire die. Frame not go out. I think you many times. (Then she added a passage from her phrase book . . .)

Ever your devoted and humble servant,

and the letter was signed with the Chinese characters representing her name. How strange they were, those characters, how beautiful, how deeply hidden from me behind the wall of Asia!

I wanted to fling myself upon the floor and weep as Hana-ogi might have wept had we been at home, but instead there came to me that sad and final Japanese word which she had refused to teach me: "Sayonara, Hana-ogi. Sayonara, you beautiful dancer. You've chosen the tough way. I hope your gods give you the courage to follow it. Sayonara, Katsumi, little mother. Forgive me that I once thought you too ugly to kiss. You can't know it now but I fought my way through four M.P.'s to kiss you good-bye and fat Col. Craford shuddered. Oh, Katsumi, sayonara. And Goddamn it, Sukoshi Joe, you died too soon. They're passing a law right now to let guys like you bring your wives home. It was a good fight that night until I fainted. Sayonara, Sukoshi Joe. You did it too soon. To the alley and the canal and the little houses and the pachinko parlor and to the flutes at night—sayonara. And you, Japan, you crowded islands, you tragic land—sayonara, you enemy, you friend."

But even as I said these words I knew that I had to put them out of mind, for I was forced to acknowledge that I lived in an age when the only honorable profession was soldiering, when the only acceptable attitude toward strange lands and people of another color must be not love but fear.

Like the voice of my own conscience I heard, as from a great distance, General Webster saying, "Pull yourself together, son. Whatever makes you a better man makes you a better officer."

I looked up and said, "What?"

"I oughtn't to tell you this, Lloyd, because it isn't official yet. But as soon as you get back to Randolph Field they're making you a lieutenant-colonel."

Instinctively I saluted.

The general said, "We'd better move along. Eileen wants to drive us to the airport."

WILLIAM STYRON
SOPHIE'S CHOICE

'The most haunting and powerful novel I've read this year'
Daily Express

William Styron's narrative of artfully sustained suspense takes
us back to pre-war Poland, to Auschwitz, through a past strewn
with death that Sophie alone survived — until, at the core of
this electrifying story, we reach the essence of Sophie's terrible
secret — the choice she had to make.

'A novel of stunning audacity and imaginative range'
New Statesman

'SOPHIE'S CHOICE is one of those rare, important novels
that widen the experience. At the end of it all, it may have posed
more questions than it has answered, but it has also powerfully
and hauntingly changed our perceptions, and that is the book's
quiet and mesmeric strength' *Woman's Journal*

'Sophie will haunt me for many a day' *Sunday Telegraph*

0 552 11610 6   £2.95

CORGI BOOKS

MICHENER
SPACE

The enthralling sage of America's exploration of space
. . . the incredible successes of the Gemini and Apollo
manned flights, the Viking landings on Mars, the breath-
taking performances of the Columbia – these and other
awesome achievements of the space programme form the
background to James A. Michener's monumental new
novel – one in which he blends fact, fiction and future
possibilities, and which will delight and enthral his
millions of readers.

THE NUMBER ONE INTERNATIONAL
BESTSELLER!

0 552 12283 1   £2.95

CORGI BOOKS

STEPHEN VIZINCZEY

AN INNOCENT MILLIONAIRE

The fabulous new bestseller from the author of *In Praise of Older Women*.

Born in New York but raised in Rome, Paris, London, Madrid, worried about starving even while living in luxury, Mark Niven sets his heart on recovering the treasure ship *Flora*, which sank in 1820 somewhere between Barbados and Florida. Searching for the wreck, he falls in love with the neglected wife of a jealous husband, and his love as well as his dreams of riches turn into nightmare experiences . . .

An Innocent Millionaire is a superb story of innocence, adventure and corruption, from a writer at the height of his powers.

"A truly noble performance, a fairy-tale of our times on the grand scale"
David Hughes, The Mail on Sunday

"A marvellous story, written by a master"
Terry Coleman, The Guardian

0 552 12401 X   £2.95

CORGI BOOKS

A SELECTED LIST OF FINE TITLES
FROM CORGI BOOKS

WHILE EVERY EFFORT IS MADE TO KEEP PRICES LOW, IT IS SOMETIMES NECESSARY TO INCREASE PRICES AT SHORT NOTICE. CORGI BOOKS RESERVE THE RIGHT TO SHOW NEW RETAIL PRICES ON COVERS WHICH MAY DIFFER FROM THOSE PREVIOUSLY ADVERTISED IN THE TEXT OR ELSEWHERE.

THE PRICES SHOWN BELOW WERE CORRECT AT THE TIME OF GOING TO PRESS (JANUARY '86).

All these books are available at your book shop or newsagent, or can be ordered direct from the publisher. Just tick the titles you want and fill in the form below.

CORGI BOOKS, Cash Sales Department, P.O. Box 11, Falmouth, Cornwall.

Please send cheque or postal order, no currency.

Please allow cost of book(s) plus the following for postage and packing:

U.K. Customers—Allow 55p for the first book, 22p for the second book and 14p for each additional book ordered, to a maximum charge of £1.75.

B.F.P.O. and Eire—Allow 55p for the first book, 22p for the second book plus 14p per copy for the next seven books, thereafter 8p per book.

Overseas Customers—Allow £1.00 for the first book and 25p per copy for each additional book.

NAME (Block Letters) ....

ADDRESS ....

....